THE RESISTANCE GIRLS

ALICE G. MAY

Boldwood

First published in Great Britain in 2025 by Boldwood Books Ltd.

Copyright © Alice G. May, 2025

Cover Design by Colin Thomas

Cover Images: Colin Thomas and Shutterstock

The moral right of Alice G. May to be identified as the author of this work has been asserted in accordance with the Copyright, Designs and Patents Act 1988.

All rights reserved. No part of this book may be reproduced in any form or by any electronic or mechanical means, including information storage and retrieval systems, without written permission from the author, except for the use of brief quotations in a book review. This book is a work of fiction and, except in the case of historical fact, any resemblance to actual persons, living or dead, is purely coincidental.

Every effort has been made to obtain the necessary permissions with reference to copyright material, both illustrative and quoted. We apologise for any omissions in this respect and will be pleased to make the appropriate acknowledgements in any future edition.

A CIP catalogue record for this book is available from the British Library.

Paperback ISBN 978-1-83703-503-8

Large Print ISBN 978-1-83703-502-1

Hardback ISBN 978-1-83703-501-4

Ebook ISBN 978-1-83703-504-5

Kindle ISBN 978-1-83703-505-2

Audio CD ISBN 978-1-83703-496-3

MP3 CD ISBN 978-1-83703-497-0

Digital audio download ISBN 978-1-83703-498-7

This book is printed on certified sustainable paper. Boldwood Books is dedicated to putting sustainability at the heart of our business. For more information please visit https://www.boldwoodbooks.com/about-us/sustainability/

Boldwood Books Ltd, 23 Bowerdean Street, London, SW6 3TN

www.boldwoodbooks.com

For all the brave women who put their lives on the line to keep Britain safe in World War Two.
And for Steve, who kept me supplied with cups of tea and plenty of encouragement during the writing process.

1

MARCH 1942

I signed The Official Secrets Act in a cluttered basement that smelt of damp. It was two o'clock on a Friday afternoon. A narrow puddle of sunlight spilled across the desk from an open window set high in the wall. Cheerful birdsong from outside contradicted the gravity of my actions in the otherwise silent room. Pen in hand, I read the document with care. The consequences of breaking this oath, of letting a crucial piece of information fall into enemy hands, were dire: prison, even the hangman's noose. Wartime sentences were brutal, and carried out with swift, merciless precision. Was I sure I wanted to do this?

A small voice of pure steel from deep inside me whispered, *yes*.

My fingers shook as I signed. The ink smudged.

There. It was done.

Father would be furious. About me signing. The smudge wouldn't surprise him. His habitual glowering expression ghosted through my mind. He would never believe that his useless daughter could be hand-picked to serve her country.

Tommy would love it, though. Assuming he wasn't dead, of course. I pushed that awful possibility away.

Major Stapleton whisked the papers from beneath my hands, as if she was afraid I might change my mind.

Not a chance. For the first time in my life, I was utterly resolute. I'd been waiting for this: a chance to escape. *To live a different life.*

A cup of tea replaced the papers. It was pathetically weak, yet very welcome. I took a sip, careful lest the adrenaline racing through me made the cup rattle against the saucer.

The major threw me a brisk smile. 'Jolly good. That's the legal stuff dealt with.'

'Where will you send me?' The question was out before I could stop it.

'I can't say. Not yet. Still, I have no doubt that your unique skill set, combined with our rigorous training program, will make you a very valuable asset. If that proves to be the case, you can expect to be assigned to a key location.'

I rose to my feet, striving for a nonchalance that belied the bubbles of excitement skipping around inside my chest. Was I scared? Of course. I'm not daft. War is dangerous and unpredictable. But it also brings opportunity. And I planned to make the most of it.

* * *

Six weeks previously, January 1942

Platform five at Waterloo station was packed. Steam from the train behind me hissed around my ankles. Green, blue and brown uniforms surged past on either side. I tugged the hem of my olive-green Auxiliary Territorial Service jacket into place. The pride I felt at being in uniform hadn't waned. It warmed my insides, despite the chill of winter. A thrum of excitement rippled through me. London. The capital. I took a deep steadying breath. The air was full of hot metal, smoke and the crackle of bustling importance. A far cry from the sleepy Hampshire village I'd abandoned with glee that morning.

I settled the strap of my gas mask box on my shoulder and scanned the sea of faces. Where was he? There! 'Tommy.'

'Wren. You made it.' Tall and smart in RAF blue, my brother engulfed me in a bear hug.

My smile couldn't get any wider. 'It's good to see you.'

'How are things at home?' he asked, releasing me.

'Oh, you know. Eventful. Farmer Barnes and Maria are turning the lawns at Ashworth into vegetable beds.' I wrinkled my nose. 'Father is torn between righteous indignation and bellowing contradictory instructions.'

'Who's Maria?'

'She's the land girl,' I said. 'She arrived last week. Farmer Barnes needed the extra help now that both of his boys have been drafted.'

'Well, if Ashworth Manor doesn't dig for victory, why should the rest of the village?'

'Exactly. And it has distracted Father from carping on at me all the time, which is most welcome.'

Tommy grimaced. 'He doesn't mean it, Wren. You're just not the sort of lady he understands.'

'I am painfully aware of that,' I said. At only just over five feet in height, and with dark brown hair, I hadn't inherited my mother's tall, blonde movie-star looks, or her grace and deportment. Father's constant criticism during my childhood had sunk into my bones, leaving a permanent sense of failure.

As usual, Tommy fell into the role of peacemaker. 'He was raised in a different time.'

I rolled my eyes. 'When ladies did needlework, played the pianoforte and sat around waiting for a husband.'

'Exactly. Although we both know women do far more than that, even if polite society prefers to pretend they don't.'

'I hate sewing. I'm tone-deaf. And as for finding a husband...' I shuddered at the thought of exchanging the devil I knew for something that could end up being infinitely more suffocating.

'You'll meet the right chap one day. It'll be love at first sight.'

'Don't talk such rot. There's no such thing.'

He laughed. 'I bet there is. You'll go all gooey-eyed and that'll be that.'

'I jolly well won't,' I said with fervour. 'The last thing I need is to hitch myself to some fella who'll want to tell me what to do. No. My freedom is too valuable.'

'So, what will you do?'

'Well, if Silvia Porter can train as an ack-ack girl—' A woman in brown uniform dashed past, forcing me to step aside to give her room.

'Little Silvia, from the village?' asked Tommy, taking my arm to steady me as more troops poured onto the platform, intent on boarding the train. 'The timid blonde?' He angled his body to shield me from the crush as we inched towards the main concourse.

'Not so timid now. She's up here, in London, fighting off enemy bombers.'

'You know the anti-aircraft girls don't actually fire the guns, don't you? They just work out the range and height of incoming planes to calculate the aim for targeting.'

'It's still jolly brave. And important.' I tutted. 'Women are part of this war too. Even the village postmaster's daughter is driving ambulances in Southampton.'

'If *you're* going to learn to drive, the enemy better give up right now. Nothing will be safe.'

I pulled a face. 'Let's not squabble. You're leaving soon.' I brushed a speck of lint off his sleeve. 'Congratulations on your promotion to flying officer. You look very smart. Where are they sending you? Can you say?'

'It's all hush-hush, I'm afraid. I will write, but it'll get censored. It means the world to me that you came to see me off, sis.'

'I'm sorry Father refused to come.' The rafters of Ashworth were still trembling from the intensity of his displeasure.

'It's fine.' His smile didn't quite reach his eyes. 'My train leaves in just over two hours. I thought we could get a cup of tea. Come on. There's someone I'd like you to meet. I bumped into him on the way over.' He grabbed my hand and weaved us through the crowd to the station entrance where he ground to a halt in front of a tall figure dressed in an army greatcoat that had seen better days. The man was leaning against a pillar reading a copy of the *Evening Standard* that declared the bracing headline: *Six-Hour Bombing Raid but London Will NOT be Beaten*. He straightened as we approached, folded his paper and tucked it into the cavernous pocket of his coat.

'Wren,' said Tommy. 'Allow me to introduce Captain Edward Landers. He's a bit bashed up after a clash with the Jerries. But you're on the mend, now, aren't you, Ed?'

Edward was gaunt and pale, his uniform hanging from his frame. I smiled and my breath caught. *Those eyes.* Serious, watchful and... beautiful. Intense green, with golden-brown lines radiating out from the pupils. The rest of the world fell away. The bustle of the vast station concourse faded to nothing.

A prickling sensation spread under my skin, as if every cell in my body was suddenly paying attention and they all had a single focus. Edward Landers.

The whistle of a departing train sliced through the air, making me jump. The spell was broken. I gathered my scattered wits. What on earth was wrong with me?

'I am indeed on the mend,' the man replied. His voice, deep and resonant, warmed my insides like melted chocolate.

Tommy's gaze bounced between Edward and I, a wide grin on his face. I narrowed my eyes at him. He flashed me a mischievous wink before addressing his friend. 'I always promised that I'd introduce you to my twin, didn't I, Ed? Well, here she is; the former Miss Serenity Ashworth – Wren for short – and now *Private Ashworth*, of the Auxiliary Territorial Service.'

Captain Landers pushed away from the pillar. The corner of his mouth twitched, as if he wanted to smile but had forgotten how. He offered me his hand. 'It's a pleasure to make your acquaintance.' His fingers were long and graceful, his grip firm yet at the same time gentle.

I cast around to find my voice. 'I'm delighted to meet you, Captain Landers.' A memory stirred at the name. 'Goodness. Not *the* Edward Landers?' I shot a glance at Tommy. 'From university?'

My brother nodded. 'The very one.'

A gasp of laughter caught me by surprise. 'Then, I am in your debt, Captain. It was your idea for Tommy to send copies of his lecture notes hidden in the pages of Jane Austen novels, wasn't it?' That fact alone endeared him to me.

'Guilty as charged.' He gave a curt nod. 'I thought it a shame you couldn't study at Oxford alongside us, given your interest in mathematics.'

I ducked my head. Being forced to stay behind had outraged

and devastated me in equal measure. 'Father would never have allowed it,' I murmured. 'But reading "silly romances" – as he calls them – is exactly the sort of thing he thinks ladies should do. You cannot begin to appreciate how much I looked forward to receiving those notes.' I shot a grin at Tommy. 'And they helped me not to miss this rascal brother of mine quite so much too.'

Edward placed a hand on his heart. 'Then I am glad.'

'I told you she liked it.' Tommy clapped his friend on the back with hearty exuberance.

The impact caused Edward to stagger. 'Steady on, Tom. I'm not as nimble on my pins as I was.' That was when I saw his cane and the way he favoured his left leg. I tore my eyes away. It wouldn't do for him to catch me staring.

'Sorry, old chap,' said Tommy, not sounding the least bit apologetic. 'Let me make it up to you. Wren and I are going to a tea room around the corner before I catch my train. Why don't you join us?'

Edward paused as if tempted, then shook his head. 'I couldn't intrude.'

Part of me was relieved at his words. My strange reaction to him was disconcerting. I had never experienced anything like it.

Tommy turned pleading eyes towards me. 'He won't be intruding, will he, Wren?'

'Of course not,' I murmured. 'We would be delighted.' I remembered the letter in my pocket. I'd only planned to show it to Tommy. Perhaps this was an opportunity to get two opinions on my dilemma. After all, Tommy would no doubt be biased, whereas Edward had no reason to be. 'Please join us, Captain.'

His eyebrows rose as if I had surprised him with the intensity of my words. 'In which case, how can I refuse?'

2

A short walk from the station took us to a café that smelt of gingerbread. Red and white checked tablecloths decorated tables crammed with service personnel. The buzz of multiple discussions filled the fuggy warmth around us as we worked our way to an empty spot right at the back.

'Where are you posted, Wren?' asked Edward, pulling out a seat for me.

'Sadly, I'm still at Ashworth Manor,' I said. 'Father didn't want me joining up at all. When I did it anyway, I suspect he pulled strings to get me posted back home as soon as my basic training was complete. So, I'm only typing and filing rather than doing something more dashing.'

'Typing and filing are important,' he replied. 'Events need to be recorded and messages need to be sent. Who are you typing for?'

'Colonel Williams.' The colonel's barrel-chested form and his bracing, yet kind, manner sprang to mind as soon as I mentioned his name. 'He's in charge of the engineering corps stationed with us.'

'Father volunteered the family pile for requisition,' said Tommy. 'Mind you, I'm not convinced he fully understood the ins and outs of what that would mean.'

'How so?' asked Edward.

Tommy grimaced. 'Ashworth is not exactly Chatsworth or Blenheim. It's just a small manor house in the New Forest. It was gifted to one of our many times great-grandfathers, James Ashworth, by Charles the Second. A reward for services rendered during the civil war.'

'Actually,' I corrected. 'It was James' wife, Fairchild, that should have been rewarded. Charles was on the run from Oliver Cromwell's roundheads and *she* hid him until he could escape to France. When he became King Charles the Second after the restoration, he acknowledged the debt he owed her. But, back then, married women couldn't own property in their own right, so he gave Ashworth to her husband, instead.'

'Which is exactly the same as giving it to her,' said my brother, a playful light in his eye.

'Don't tease, Tommy,' I said. 'You know how I feel about this. *Fairchild* took all the risks and *James* got all the reward. It's not fair whichever way you look at it.'

'You're right. It isn't,' said Edward.

I felt an immediate rush of warmth at his agreement. 'You see, Tommy? It's not just me who thinks so.'

Tommy laughed. 'Don't get her started on women's rights. We'll be here all day. Anyway, back to Father and Ashworth. He was incensed when the doctors told him his health meant he couldn't rejoin his old unit after war broke out. He still wanted to be involved and thought Ashworth Manor could be critical to the war effort. So, he started the requisition process. Only, it's not exactly turned out the way he hoped. He's not too impressed with those engineers. Is he, Wren?'

I shook my head. 'He finds the lack of control frustrating – as well as the fact that he can't use any of the main rooms apart from his bedroom and the library. Even his office now belongs to the colonel and is out of bounds to him. *I'm* more involved in what's going on than he is, and I'm only a secretary. He resents that and would forbid it, if he could.' I forced the memory of our most recent altercation from my mind.

'I expect he just wants to keep you safe,' said Edward.

'No. He says women are a liability in war,' I said with a tight smile.

Edward frowned. 'That's harsh.'

I shrugged. There was no point telling him how fraught my relationship with Father was. He wouldn't understand. How could he? Even Tommy didn't. Not really. We might be twins, and I love my brother with all my heart, but *I* was the one Father blamed for Mother dying in childbirth, not him. If I'd been a boy, maybe it would have been different, but the fact that I was a girl, and not a very ladylike one at that, was a problem. I tried. I really did. I tried to be dutiful and follow the rules; to be respectful, genteel and decorous, no matter how boring it was. It didn't make any difference. I was a disappointment and always would be.

The one thing I knew in my heart was that if I didn't get away from Ashworth and my father I'd spend my whole life feeling inadequate. The decision to start again somewhere new was something that had been growing steadily for a while as I watched and waited for an opportunity. The war, while it was unbelievably awful with so much loss of life, and suffering and untold hardship, was my chance to escape.

Edward's gorgeous eyes studied me with solemn intent as if he could hear the unspoken narrative in my head. 'If you could do more to help the war effort, what would it be?' he asked.

'I'm not sure yet. Code-breaking maybe, or radio communications.' I grinned. 'Something exciting like that.'

'You'd be brilliant at either of those,' said Tommy.

'I'd do anything, really. Motorcycle messenger, perhaps. Or maybe the munitions factories.' I gave a wry smile. 'I'd make a dreadful nurse. I'm squeamish. But if that's where I get sent, then I'll give it a go. I just want to be useful.' I remembered the letter in my pocket. 'Actually, I was hoping to ask for some advice about—'

The intense rise-and-fall wail of the air-raid siren cut through the busy chatter in the tea room. The door crashed back on its hinges and an air-raid warden called in, 'Enemy aircraft spotted. Get to a shelter.'

Chairs and tables scraped the floor. Customers and tea room staff moved as one for the exit. My heart leapt into my mouth. Living in the forest, I'd had no direct experience of the Blitz, other than to watch from the safety of Ashworth Bay as enemy aircraft pounded the Isle of Wight across the water, or Southampton docks along the coast. For the most part, enemy planes spotted over Ashworth Manor were headed inland with more valuable targets in their sights. However, when the pilots returned, there was a risk they might jettison any unused bombs over the forest in order to lighten the planes for the trip home. I had experienced many an uncomfortable night crammed into our Anderson shelter in the damp darkness, trying to sleep.

This was different. Being part of a large crowd moving through the streets together with such focused determination was both impressive and unnerving.

'Where do we go?' I asked.

'Back to Waterloo.' Edward took my hand in his. A delicious warmth spread from his palm to mine and then up my arm, making it difficult to concentrate on his words. 'It's rare to get raids, these days, especially during the day. Last year, we had them all the time. Don't worry, it'll be safe enough in the underground.' He moved with surprising speed in spite of the cane. 'Stay close and you won't get jostled.'

Several vehicles raced past. Ahead of us, an elderly man stumbled, stepping off the pavement and into the path of a car. It swerved, missing him by a whisker. Now it was on a direct path towards us. Time slowed. I watched the gleaming bonnet approach but couldn't make my legs work.

'Watch out!' Edward's voice was sharp in my ear. A weight hit my side, strong arms shunted me sideways into an alley, and up against a brick wall. There was a crash and the sound of breaking glass. 'Are you hurt?' he said.

Dazed, I shook my head. My bruises were nothing compared to what might have happened. 'I think so.' Alarm shot through me. 'Tommy!' I pushed away from Edward and dashed back to the road.

The car had hit a shopfront, smashing through the window, sending bricks and mortar flying across the road. A figure was slumped over the steering wheel inside. The crowd heading for the underground had slowed, with many people stopping to stare.

I started forward.

Edward seized my arm. 'Wait.'

I jerked free. 'We have to help. Why is everyone just standing there?'

He grabbed me again. 'We need to secure the area first. It's standard procedure.' He pointed up. 'That glass is seconds from falling. It's not safe to approach.'

I followed the direction of his finger. A section of window, the frame twisted and the wood splintered, was hanging by a thread. Reaching the car safely was almost impossible.

'We can't just leave him,' I said.

'And we won't. But, if you go in there now, you risk being the next casualty, which will only make things worse, and delay an effective rescue.'

I should have thought of that. It was obvious now that he had pointed it out. I mentally kicked myself. There was so much I didn't know.

'Look.' He nodded past the shopfront. 'Tommy is already working on it.'

Tommy and another man hefted a length of wood from the pavement and used it to nudge at the dangling glass.

'I'll go and help,' said Edward. 'If we can brace the damage, then we can get to the car.'

'What can I do?'

'Get the rest of this crowd moving. They need to be in the shelter, not here gawping.'

'I...' But he wasn't listening. I gazed at the crowd. There were so many of them. How on earth was I going to get them to listen to me? 'Move along, please,' I said, my voice sounding feeble. 'Please get to safety.' I cleared my throat, ready to try again, louder.

As I opened my mouth another voice bellowed. 'Oi! Come on, you lot, move along. There's nothing to see.'

I turned to see another ATS private waving the crowd away. She was small, even shorter than me, yet she carried herself with supreme confidence, and behaved as if she expected people to listen to her. She shot me a wink and carried on calling out, 'Go on, get off out of here. Get yourselves down that shelter.'

I shuffled alongside her, did my best to mirror her body language and actions, and added my voice to hers. 'Please, move along. Thank you. Get to safety.' Soon the onlookers started to move away. I glanced over at the private and murmured. 'I wish I had your confidence.'

'Just pretend you know what you're doing,' she replied with a laugh. 'My da always said there'd be a use for my sass, one day. Maybe today's that day.'

A huge clatter behind us made me jump. I turned, expecting to see that the remainder of the window had fallen. Instead, the pendulous section of glass and frame had been secured with wooden beams. The driver of the car emerged, looking bashed and dazed, but alive, and was escorted away by a couple of soldiers.

Edward approached, brushing dust off his hands and straightening his uniform. 'All sorted,' he said. 'We'd better get down to the shelter. Tommy said he'll meet us down there.'

3

I fell in by his side. We walked in silence to the underground entrance and down the long staircase to the platform. All around, people made themselves comfortable on the floor, pulling out books and newspapers, preparing for a long wait. It was damp and cold, the air stale and thick with expectation. Edward and I wandered on to find space to settle. My ears strained for the sound of bombs falling on the streets above, potentially cutting off our route back to the surface.

'Will we be able to hear... you know?' I pointed up at the roof.

'Bombs?' Edward shook his head. 'We're too far underground.'

A rat scurried along the metal rails beyond the edge of the platform. I shuddered, my stomach churning. Hearing about air raids on the wireless and reading about them in the newspapers was tame compared to being *in* one. It felt so immediate, real and *dangerous*.

'There's Tommy.' Edward stood up and raised a hand. 'Over here, Tom.'

'That was a bit of excitement, wasn't it?' said Tommy cheerfully, as he settled down with us. 'Luckily no one was seriously injured. Shame about that shop, though.'

Edward nodded. 'Another damaged building to add to London's growing tally.'

'You all knew exactly what to do,' I said. 'It's remarkable.'

'It's just training,' said Tommy. 'Nothing to it.'

Privately, I disagreed. If Edward hadn't stopped me, I'd have dashed into that accident scene and made things worse. The ATS private who had got that crowd moving was everything I wanted to be. Self-assured, practical, good in a crisis. The whole episode underlined how much I *didn't* know.

'What are your plans now, Ed?' asked Tommy, changing the subject.

'I've no idea.' Edward gestured to his damaged leg. 'This is going to be an issue, unfortunately. I have an appointment later today at the War Office. I'll find out what happens to old crocks that are no longer any use at the front.'

My fingers tingled. Looking down, I saw that I had reached a comforting hand out to touch his sleeve. 'You're not an old crock,' I murmured, pulling my hand back. 'You were injured in service to your country. You're a hero.'

'Hardly. I'm just lucky to be alive.' He curled his lip in disgust. 'I expect I'll get a desk job somewhere and spend the rest of the war filling in forms.'

Tommy snorted. 'It's the paper pushers who are really in charge of this thing, my friend. Mark my words, you'll be running the whole damn show before too long.' He turned to me. 'Back in the café, you mentioned you wanted to ask us about something.'

'Oh, yes! This.' I glanced from side to side to check no one was listening and pulled an envelope from my pocket. Stark, official lettering stamped across the top: ON HIS MAJESTY'S SERVICE. 'It's from the War Office. It says confidential. I'm not even sure if I'm allowed to show you. I don't know *what* to do.' I straightened a crumpled corner before handing it over.

Tommy scanned the contents before passing it to Edward. 'Take a look at that, Ed. What do you think?'

Watching Edward's beautiful eyes march across the page, reading words that were seared on my memory, felt strangely intimate.

> Dear Private Ashworth,
> It has come to my attention that you might be interested in volunteering for a more challenging assignment. If this is the case, please present yourself at the public lounge on the fourth floor of Harrods, Knightsbridge, at 2 p.m. on Friday 6th February.
> I look forward to making your acquaintance.
> Yours sincerely,
> Major Belinda Stapleton

He paused for thought, eyes narrowed. 'When did you get this?'

'Ten days ago,' I replied. I didn't know who Major Stapleton was, or how she knew of me. At first, I'd assumed it must be a mistake. Then, I'd kept rereading it and a small kernel of excitement had germinated. Something more challenging was exactly what I wanted, and if that took me away from Ashworth then all the better.

Edward leaned closer. 'Will you go?'

'Yes. I mean, it's today. It makes sense. I'm in London anyway. I can go as soon as I've waved Tommy off.'

Tommy tapped the letter, his face serious. 'I know you said

you wanted some excitement, but have you considered that this could be dangerous?'

'You're the one going off to fight, brother dear,' I scoffed. 'I'm only going to Harrods for a chat and maybe a cup of tea, if I'm lucky.' The lights overhead flickered. I glanced up at the roof of the tube station. 'Or, I will be, if we get out of here in time.'

'I mean it, Wren,' insisted Tommy.

The clatter of hurried footsteps on the stairs to the platform heralded the arrival of a skinny youth. 'False alarm,' he called in a loud, carrying voice just as the single, steady note of the all-clear siren echoed along the tunnel.

'Excellent,' said Tommy, getting to his feet and checking his watch. 'There's still plenty of time to get my train.'

Edward handed me back the letter. We shuffled along the platform, following everyone else. 'It's all a bit too cloak and dagger for my liking, Wren,' he said. 'I think you should probably give that meeting a miss.'

His words were like a hammer blow. He clearly didn't think much of me. Given how useless I had been at the car accident, why would he think anything else? But I was better than that. Deep down I knew I was.

'I hate to say it, sis,' said Tommy. 'I think Edward is right.'

I hid my crushing sense of disappointment behind a rueful smile. 'You're both as bad as Father. You think I'm just some useless woman who can't be trusted to do anything important.'

'No,' said Tommy. 'It's not tha—'

'You can think what you like.' I thrust my chin up, my back ramrod straight, and stalked towards the stairs. 'I know otherwise.'

Edward followed. 'It's not that at all. I'm sure you are incredibly capable and could fill any number of roles.' His limp was more pronounced than it had been earlier, his progress clearly painful. Time spent sat on the cold platform floor must have caused his injury to stiffen up. Normally, I would have slowed in sympathy, but anger and defiance kept me focused on moving forwards, desperate to get to the surface. Edward gave my elbow a gentle tug and a flash of electricity shot up my arm. I paused, keeping my stance rigid, praying my pain didn't show.

'I'm sorry, Wren,' he said. 'I know that wasn't what you wanted to hear. Look. If you genuinely want to do more, then you should. Speak to your senior officer. This Colonel Williams sounds a sensible chap. Make a formal application to move somewhere else. He might even be able to put a good word in for you and get you into radio communication or coding or some such. There will be a way, you know.'

Tommy's cheerful voice came from behind. 'I rather like the idea of you receiving radio messages from all us fellows fighting abroad, sis. Have a chat with your colonel, like Edward says. Give this whole mysteriously more challenging role malarkey a miss.'

They both meant well. I knew that. So why did it feel as if Father was standing there ordering me about? The back of my neck prickled. I shouldn't *have* to rely on a man's recommendation to find my path. Even a nice one like Colonel Williams. I wanted to forge my own future.

I jerked my head, feigning agreement. 'You're right. Of course you are.'

My response appeared to satisfy them both. Back at street level, people peeled off in all directions, hurrying back to their busy lives. A fire engine blasted past, bells all a jangle.

'I've twenty minutes before my train,' Tommy called over the din.

Edward offered Tommy his hand. 'I'm afraid I have to go, my

friend. Good luck with your deployment. Give them hell.' Turning to me, he gave a small bow. 'It was lovely to meet you.'

'Goodbye, Captain,' I murmured and watched him leave, feeling strangely bereft.

What nonsense. I pushed that feeling aside. He was just a man. I didn't have to do what he said. I was going to Harrods. If I didn't, I knew I would spend the rest of my life wondering what might have been. Certainty landed around my shoulders like a heavy cloak. Whoever this Major Belinda Stapleton was, *she* had contacted *me*. She seemed to think I could be of use. That had to mean something.

4

How I managed to keep a cheerful disposition during my parting with Tommy, twenty minutes later, I will never know. He might drive me up the wall with his teasing, but he was my twin; the other half of me. He grounded me and I loved him. We'd spent every waking moment of our early years together. An inseparable pair. Back then, I'd not appreciated how different our lives would be as we grew. Then he was sent to boarding school and on to university, leaving me behind. I had missed him, with all my heart, but I'd always known he would return for the holidays. This time it was different. We both knew he might not come back.

All around us on the platform, hundreds of military personnel were having similar conversations with loved ones. Kitbags were loaded into carriages. Doors slammed with heavy finality. Soldiers leaned through open windows for final kisses from sweethearts, or called out last-minute messages.

'Stay safe, Wren,' he said, sweeping me into a bracing hug. 'Whatever you decide to do about that letter, I need to know that you'll be here when I get back.'

'You stay safe too, Tommy,' I replied, my voice thick.

He gave me an extra squeeze before releasing me, and climbed onto the train.

The guard blew his whistle. 'All aboard.'

Tommy called out, 'I'll be back before you know it.'

'And I'll be here.' I pinned a bright smile to my face with such determination that my jaw ached. Wherever he was sent would be fraught with danger. Yet, he didn't seem afraid. I couldn't help a spark of envy at the excitement that clearly bubbled under his skin. I wanted that sense of purpose; that self-worth. That anticipation of adventures to come.

The train pulled away in a cloud of whistles, steam and straining metal. My world went all wobbly around the edges as I blinked back tears. The chaos died away and the platform cleared, leaving me rooted to the spot. It was decision time. Either I took a train back to the New Forest, or I went to Harrods and met with Major Stapleton. I turned Tommy's and Edward's warnings over in my mind. They were right. Meeting the major was potentially risky, but no more so than Tommy leaving to fight. There were no guarantees of safety anywhere in wartime. And if I didn't go, there was a chance that I would never forgive myself.

Tugging a handkerchief from my pocket, I blotted my eyes and set my jaw. Dangerous or not, I was going. Decision made, I set my feet in the direction of Knightsbridge. I was going to Harrods, come what may.

The streets of London bore all the hallmarks of multiple bombing raids. Entire buildings were missing. Damaged walls stuck up like broken teeth with broken pipes sticking out. Mountains of rubble blocked pavements and spilled across pockmarked roads. Overhead, huge barrage balloons hung in the sky, ominous grey lozenge shapes dangling a web of almost invisible chains designed to force enemy bombers to fly higher, pushing them into the range of anti-aircraft guns.

Harrods itself was untouched. I scurried into the women's restroom to check my appearance in the mirror, keen to make a good impression. Adverts in all the women's magazines insisted that we had *a duty to beauty* because it would lift everyone's spirits. Newspapers reported how much Herr Hitler detested women wearing makeup, and red lipstick in particular, which triggered a sudden surge in perfectly lined and coloured lips on all British women. I loved the fact that, unlike other cosmetics, lipstick wasn't rationed. Our government's way of encouraging every woman in the country to indulge in a colourful display of defiance – a subtle two-fingered salute to the enemy. I slicked a fresh layer of cherry red gloss onto my lips, tucked a few stray dark brown hairs into the twist at the back of my head and pinched my cheeks to add some colour. With a final adjustment to my service cap, I headed for the stairs.

On the fourth floor, the public lounge was empty apart from a petite woman in an ATS uniform with the gold and red crown of a major adorning her shoulders. She had brown hair neatly restrained in pin curls and an expression of polite welcome on her face.

'Private Ashworth?'

I gave a crisp salute. 'Yes, ma'am.'

'At ease. I'm Major Belinda Stapleton. Do sit down. Can I offer you some tea?'

I accepted hoping that Harrods would still be able to produce a decent cup, even in wartime. I wasn't disappointed. A smattering of polite conversation followed: the weather, my journey, the scarcity of certain luxuries. Eventually, Major Stapleton leaned forward and rested both hands on the table as if getting down to business. 'I hear that you enjoy physical exercise, Private Ashworth. That you speak several languages *and* that you like mathematics.'

It sounded like she might know more about me than I did. I frowned into my cup. 'I do enjoy exercise. I run and swim. I used to sail, too. A small dinghy, nothing huge.' Fleeting memories of happy days pottering around on Ashworth Bay with Tommy skipped through my mind. 'That was before the ban on recreational sailing after Dunkirk, of course.'

'Of course.'

'With regard to maths... well.' I lifted one shoulder. 'Numbers often make more sense to me than words.'

'And what about languages?'

'I speak both French and German, but I am not fluent.'

She gave me a searching look. 'Have you thought how you might contribute more to the war effort?'

Was this woman reading my mind? 'I think of little else.'

'Would I be right in thinking that you are open to doing something that might prove quite challenging, should the opportunity arise?'

'Yes, ma'am.'

'Good.' She sat back. 'What do you understand by the term "Blitzkrieg"?'

I frowned. 'An article in *The Guardian* said Blitzkrieg translates as "lightning war", and that's why they call the air raids the *Blitz*.'

'That's part of it, certainly. But it's not just air raids. Blitzkrieg in its full meaning is a most deadly form of warfare. A swift, surprise attack using multiple mobile forces in combination: air, sea and land. It's violent, intimidating and very effective. And it's how countries like Poland and France have been subdued in the enemy's relentless march across Europe.'

I nodded, remembering hearing about such attacks on the

wireless as I sat by the hearth in the relative safety of the library at Ashworth.

'Everything I've heard and read about you, Private Ashworth, tells me that you are a patriot and that you can be trusted.'

I wondered exactly what she had heard and from whom she had heard it. 'I can.'

'Excellent. Please keep what I am about to discuss with you to yourself.'

I nodded. 'Yes, of course. You have my word.'

She lowered her voice. 'We've had numerous confirmed intelligence reports outlining specific details of the enemy's invasion plans for Britain. We don't know when they will strike, but the Führer is manoeuvring his troops into position.'

I blinked several times, my mind racing. 'Where will they land?'

'It could be anywhere along our coastline from Devon to Norfolk.'

A chill crawled up my spine. The thought of enemy soldiers on British soil was abhorrent. 'I'm fully prepared to fight.'

The major's answering smile was grim. 'That's good to know. Hopefully it won't come to that. Right now, our biggest problem is a little smaller and a lot more slippery.'

'I don't understand.'

'Spies,' she said. 'Enemy agents are dropped off on our shores under the cover of darkness with the sole aim of infiltrating local communities and gathering intelligence.'

'That's why they've taken all the signposts down in the New Forest, isn't it?' I asked.

'Yes, that's one of a number of initiatives designed to make life difficult for unwelcome visitors. If the enemy can establish an effective intelligence operation in Britain we are done for. It would be the last piece in the puzzle enabling them to gather what they need to bring a full-scale blitzkrieg to our shores successfully.'

I bit my lip, the leaden weight of horror settling around my shoulders. That couldn't be allowed to happen.

'However,' she continued, 'I believe we have something that could counter the threat of these spies.'

'What?'

'Women.'

'I don't understand,' I said.

She shrugged. 'Every community in the country has intelligent, adaptable, capable women, all going about their business, not drawing attention to themselves or expecting any rewards for their hard work. Women get overlooked and undervalued on every level merely because of their gender.'

Every word the major spoke struck a deep chord with me. It was the story of my life: constantly being ignored or disregarded.

'And yet,' she continued, 'these women see things. They hear things. They *know* things.' She raised both hands palm up. 'And who better to spot a stranger in our midst than those most invested in caring for our communities on a day-to-day basis?'

Of course. Now that she mentioned it, it was obvious. I glanced from side to side before whispering, 'Are you suggesting we need a secret army of women?'

'Am I?' An arch smile spread across the major's face.

A bubble of delighted laughter surprised me. 'Yes, ma'am. I believe you are. And if that's the case, please count me in.'

She checked her watch before getting to her feet. 'Thank you for coming, Private Ashworth. It's been lovely to meet you. I'll be in touch. I am trusting you to keep everything we have discussed most secret.'

'Yes, ma'am.'

She paused, locking eyes with me. 'I will know, if you speak out.'

My mouth went dry. 'I don't doubt it, ma'am.'

I gave a brisk salute and, almost before I knew it, I was pushing my way through the bustle on the streets of London outside.

5

There is a heightened sense of awareness triggered by a discussion about spies. As if every sense in your body switches up a gear and you start spotting suspicious activity everywhere. As a result, my journey home from Waterloo was draining. While the usual noise and jolting associated with train travel was to be expected, I found myself surreptitiously observing everyone around me and wondering if all was as it seemed. Thoughts of the major and that extraordinary meeting tumbled over themselves in my mind. Edward's serious expression as he warned me to be careful added an extra layer to my mental confusion. But it was Tommy's last words to me that echoed the loudest. *Stay safe, Wren. I need to know that you'll be here when I get back.*

By the time I arrived at the station and alighted, I was exhausted. Spotting Maria with the pony and trap picking up supplies for Farmer Barnes at the station entrance, I begged a lift as far as the main gate to the Ashworth estate. The rhythmic clip-clopping of the hooves against the road and the cool breeze on my face soothed my frayed nerves as I listened to her rattling on about the latest letter from her sweetheart. Eventually, she called the pony to a halt. I jumped down from the trap and thanked her for the ride.

The late afternoon air carried with it the clean scent of pine. Gravel scrunched under my shoes as I walked up the long drive towards the house. The sun was about to dive behind a phalanx of trees on the horizon, and the encroaching dusk threw a shadowed cloak over the six high chimneys of Ashworth Manor. My breath started to form little puffy clouds before my face as the evening chill drew in. The plain stone hall originally built in the fifteen-hundreds had subsequently been subsumed within a larger baronial-style remodelling in the mid eighteen-hundreds. The result was a stunning three-storey red-brick structure with carved stone doorways and an ornate entrance porch. The upstairs windows were already dark. Someone inside was busy closing blackout blinds at the huge bay windows on the ground floor.

I shivered, although whether that was from the chill night air or the fact that I could already hear Father's raised voice coming from inside the house, I couldn't be sure. I scurried through the main door into the panelled entrance hall, wondering what had set him off this time. Following a string of loud expletives, I eventually tracked him down in the library. It was a generously proportioned room lined with dark shelving, books and a large stone fireplace. Colonel Williams stood on the silk rug before the empty hearth, being berated as if he were a disobedient child.

Father's moustache quivered with rage. 'If I'd known that a prime property like Ashworth wouldn't be valued by the military, I would never have agreed to this.'

'Indeed, Major Ashworth,' replied the colonel, his tone solemn. 'And yet we have to understand that the War Office knows what it's doing. I have orders instructing my engineering corps to make way for a maternity home and that is what we shall do.'

'It makes no sense.' Veins were standing out on Father's neck.

'Unfortunately, the higher-ups disagree. They have information that you and I are not party to. My engineers can easily be accommodated over at Bransgore, whereas Ashworth Manor is perfect to shelter the large number of expectant mothers to be evacuated from Southampton.' The colonel shook his head. 'The city and the docks are taking quite a pummelling, you know.'

'Oh, my goodness, yes,' I said, from my position by the door, well aware that I would divert Father's wrath from the colonel to myself. 'What an opportunity to show everyone what a hero you are, Father.' I infused my voice with as much bright enthusiasm as I could muster, ignoring the scowl that crossed his face the instant he realised I was there. 'We must offer shelter. Ashworth can set a shining example for the whole community.'

'You're back, are you?' he grunted, skewering me with his eyes. 'Your mother would turn in her grave knowing you were gallivanting about the country on your own.'

Such comments about my mother always found their mark. I ducked my head, swallowing down a sharp response. Defiance never got me anywhere. 'I'm sorry, Father. And you are quite right, of course, but I couldn't not go to see Tommy off. It—' My voice broke, and suddenly I wasn't acting. Tears sprang to my eyes and my voice wobbled. 'It might be the last time I ever see him.'

His bushy eyebrows beetled together but he stayed silent.

I lifted my chin, taking advantage of his discomfort. 'Surely, if there are women and children at risk, Mother would have wanted them to come here, wouldn't she?' I opened my eyes extra wide. 'Especially pregnant women and new-born babies. They must be so scared.'

He chewed his lips, deep in thought.

I pressed on. 'I saw the damage from the air raids with my own eyes, today. The sirens went off, too. It was a false alarm, but it was utterly terrifying.'

'More fool you for going to London,' he growled.

'Please, Father. They must be so frightened. It's the right thing to do.'

He turned back to the colonel. 'Why *are* there still women and children in Southampton? Shouldn't they already have been evacuated?'

'You're right, of course,' said the colonel, shooting me a look full of unspoken gratitude. 'And many were, when the bombing started. But as you know there has been a lull in attacks and many have returned to their homes. Now, with this new offensive ramping up, they need relocating again. It takes time to arrange these things. And Ashworth has the chance to play an important part in that process. The women can have their babies here before being moved further afield.'

Father shuddered. 'Can you imagine the noise? The chaos? No. This house should accommodate the military. Play an active role in defending this country. The women and children can go somewhere else.'

'Unfortunately, neither you nor I can influence that.' A wicked gleam flared in the colonel's eyes before disappearing. If I had not been looking straight at him I would have missed it. 'I do appreciate your position, Major Ashworth,' he said. 'The upheaval will be quite untenable for you. Might I suggest a strategic retreat from the main manor house altogether? Perhaps the gatehouse would suit you better?'

'But... but...' Father spluttered. That he could be evicted from the main house altogether clearly had not occurred to him.

The colonel wasn't finished. 'I understand that it is empty at the moment. In fact, before we leave, my men could help you to make the move. They are engineers after all. Any alterations that might be needed to make you comfortable could be done in a jiffy.'

This had been the colonel's agenda all along. The twinkle in his eye told me Father had played right into his hands. I averted my gaze, my face rigid. 'When do you and your engineers leave, Colonel Williams?'

'In six weeks,' he replied. 'Time enough to make suitable arrangements for everyone. Including sorting out the gatehouse for your father.'

I hurried over to the long velvet drapes and adjusted them to make sure they completely covered the windows. 'It's a good suggestion, Father. You'd have your own space and you won't be bothered by any noise. Mrs Baker can go with you and act as cook-cum-housekeeper.'

Before Father could unleash a tirade of ire in my direction, the colonel jumped in. 'That's an excellent idea. The maternity home will bring their own catering staff. Your cook won't want to share her kitchen with them. She'll be much happier moving to the gatehouse.' As if that settled everything, he turned to me. 'I am glad you're back, Private Ashworth. I have several urgent letters that need typing. Do you have time, now?'

In spite of my exhaustion, I recognised his question for what it was: an opportunity to escape the room and leave Father to process his potential change in circumstance alone. 'Certainly, Colonel. I would be delighted.'

Father huffed and puffed and poured himself what was sure to be the first of several large brandies. I made a mental note to send our one remaining footman in later, to ensure Father made it up to bed to sleep them off, before following the colonel from the room.

* * *

Over the next few days, my administrative tasks kept me busier than usual, which was a blessing as it kept me out of Father's way. It also meant that I had barely a moment to myself. However, it didn't stop thoughts of Major Stapleton and her proposal from dancing through my head. Unfortunately, Edward's intense warning usually followed them until they waltzed together to the rhythm of my every keystroke. The major's invitation was exactly what I wanted, but what if *I* wasn't good enough? The memory of Edward's gorgeous eyes entreating me not to go to Harrods wouldn't leave me alone. And then there was Tommy and the echo, *Stay safe, Wren*. Each time I reached a conclusion, the dance started again and I was back at the beginning.

I had spent the first twenty-two years of my life being told I was useless. I didn't want to believe it, but it's hard not to let that sort of thing take up residence in your head. What if Father was right? And what if Edward had seen that? What if he could tell I wasn't up to whatever it was the major had in mind?

Plans for the engineering corps' withdrawal from Ashworth were relatively simple and progressed at a significant pace. The corresponding paperwork for the incoming maternity home was more complicated. The whole of the main house, all three floors – including the family bedrooms – and the basement were to be repurposed for incoming hospital staff and patients. A team of military specialists arrived to carry out some structural modifications and set about temporarily boarding off areas of the house in the hope of keeping any dust from spreading. The planned changes included Father's study, a room on the ground floor off the main hall. This was to be the new hospital commander's office. More telephone lines were installed.

Not party to any of the details of these changes and powerless to influence them, Father paced the library floor, snarling like a wounded lion at anyone foolish enough to approach. I was an easy target for his frustrations. According to him, I was incapable of getting anything right. Every encounter with him chipped away at my self-confidence.

Before he finally agreed to move to the gatehouse, he insisted on it being extensively remodelled. The colonel authorised the changes with his usual good humour, not baulking at Father's insistence that the military should pay for everything. The work started with all possible speed. Exasperated by Father's behaviour, I avoided contact with him as much as possible. And rather than move out to the gatehouse too, I took the opportunity to stake a claim on an empty room in the new staff block being built at the back of the main house. This was a long, single-storey building that led across one side of the rear yard and joined the house to the stable block behind, creating a three-sided courtyard.

My new room, a snug cubbyhole right at the far end of the corridor, was big enough for a bed and a large trunk in which I could store some of Tommy's precious belongings. A small wardrobe built into the wall was crammed with my own things. This space proved a blessing. It was somewhere I could escape the chaos of the main house from time to time and find a little peace.

Father made strenuous objections when he heard of my decision. He barged into the office where the colonel and I were busy working on transport arrangements for the upcoming move. 'You can't stay in the main house, girl,' he said, all bark and self-important bristles. 'You'll be in the way.'

'On the contrary,' said the colonel, casting me a reassuring glance, 'Private Ashworth will be needed here to offer essential clerical support to the incoming staff.'

Relieved, I closed my ears to Father's ranting, and loaded the typewriter with fresh paper. My gratitude at the colonel's ability to deflect Father's outbursts knew no bounds.

'I appreciate that all this change is unsettling for you, Major Ashworth,' the colonel said. 'Don't forget that you are making a huge sacrifice for your country and it will be noted by those in authority.'

Petulant lines carved grooves either side of Father's mouth. 'I should hope so.'

'Most definitely. Even more so, now that Private Ashworth might be reassigned.'

'What?' Father's eyebrows jumped so high they nearly shot off his face.

The hairs on the back of my neck sprang to attention. *What?* My fingers paused midway through a sentence.

'Where is she going?' demanded Father.

Good question, I thought.

Colonel Williams passed me a sealed envelope. 'Official orders from the War Office arrived, this morning, Private Ashworth. You are to report to Haverhill in West Sussex, next week. Just for the day, I believe, for the moment. However, this might mean a permanent move for you soon.' He gave me a nod and an approving pat to the shoulder. 'Applied for a transfer, did you? Well done. Jolly good luck to you.'

I took the letter with nerveless fingers. 'I didn't... I mean, I'd like to... but... but I haven't...' Panicked haste to set the record straight before Father exploded made coherent speech impossible.

'Really? That's interesting.' Colonel Williams scratched his head then snapped his fingers. 'I've mentioned you in several dispatches. Said what a great help you are. I wouldn't be surprised if they feel you need additional training to be secretary for the maternity home.' He turned to Father. 'Either way, Major Ashworth, you must be very proud of your daughter. Now, come, let me show you where the main maternity ward is going to go and what the builders are proposing to do.' Steering Father from the room, he shot me a wink and closed the door, leaving me to read my letter in peace.

I tore the envelope open with shaking hands and drew out a folded piece of paper.

Dear Private Ashworth,

Subsequent to our meeting on 6th February, I am pleased to invite you to take the train to Haverhill in West Suffolk on 20th February.

Colonel Williams has been instructed to advance you the cost of your ticket.

On arrival, exit the station and cross the road. There is a bench outside the Rose and Crown public house. Please wait here. An army vehicle will arrive shortly thereafter. You will recognise it by the numbers 490 painted in white and red on the front wing. This vehicle will take you to your final destination.

Once you have completed the task you are asked to do, you will be returned to the station to travel home the same day.

Yours sincerely,
Major Belinda Stapleton

A bubble of excitement fizzed in my belly at this second mysterious communication. As the weeks had dripped past since that meeting at Harrods, I had begun to wonder if I would ever hear more from the major. And now I had. It was real. The question was: what was I going to do? Did I give in to Father's criticism and Edward's concerns? Were they right?

All I knew for certain was that I was even more desperate to get away from Ashworth. I smoothed out the letter. I would go. It was only a day, after all. It couldn't hurt to find out a little more about the major's proposal.

6

A painfully early start, added to the inevitable wartime travel delays, multiple changes and overcrowded carriages meant that the journey to Haverhill should have been a draining experience. Fortunately, excitement sang in my veins all the way. Alighting at the pretty village station, I still had a spring in my step even though I was more than two hours later than expected. I followed the instructions to the letter, wondering if the prearranged car had already been and gone without me. There was nothing I could do about it, so I settled myself on the bench and waited. An hour later, my positivity was waning. Just as I contemplated returning to the station with a heavy heart, the car arrived. The driver didn't speak, he merely opened the rear door for me to climb in. Taking my cue from him, I sat in silence for the long, winding drive through country lanes that followed.

I was deposited outside a remote farmhouse. Gusts of wind tugged at my coat as the car disappeared from view in a cloud of dust. The sun dashed behind a bank of ominous purple clouds.

Somewhere nearby a dog howled. I stared around at the deserted farmyard. Icy fingers trailed down my spine. It was getting late. Dusk was closing in. I was alone, in the middle of nowhere, with no idea what was actually happening or what I was supposed to be doing. A very small part of me began to wonder if I should have listened to Edward after all, then I gave myself a shake and told myself not to be silly. I was a strong, independent woman. I could do this.

Throwing my jitters off, I knocked on the solid oak door. Silence. Just as I was about to give up, the door creaked open. An officer peered out, the crest of the Royal Corps of Signals clear on his uniform, a disinterested expression on his face. My heels click-clacked apologetically against worn slate tiles as I followed him along a narrow corridor to a small room with a low ceiling. There was no furniture other than a table dominated by a large radio set, and a single ladderback chair.

Major Stapleton was nowhere to be seen.

The taciturn officer handed me a piece of paper. 'Read that.'

I glanced at it.

'Aloud,' he barked, waving an impatient hand.

Ignoring his lack of manners, I cleared my throat and complied, wondering what on earth was going on. My voice was clear and steady. I was determined not to show any sign of my growing unease. The words I read made no sense. Nevertheless, I persevered. Co-operation seemed the wisest choice under the circumstances.

When I finished, the officer pointed at the radio. 'Now, again. Into the microphone.'

Having complied, I was ushered back outside.

'Wait here,' said the officer. He closed the front door, leaving me alone in the bleak, rain-lashed farmyard. Drawing the collar of my uniform up, I huddled under the porch, and wondered, what now? A short time later, the car with the mute driver returned and took me back to Haverhill station. With none of the excitement that had sustained me earlier in the day left, the train journey back to the forest gave me plenty of time to ponder the wisdom of engaging in Major Stapleton's mysterious game.

7

It was late by the time I arrived back at Ashworth Manor. The house was suspiciously quiet. I found the colonel in the hall. It was as if he had been waiting for me. The absence of his habitual hearty manner told me something was amiss.

'My dear, I am so sorry.' He removed his glasses, polished them furiously and cleared his throat. 'There's been a telegram. You should go to your father. He's in the library.'

Thick fingers of dread squeezed my heart. Without waiting for him to finish, I dashed along the corridor, barely able to breathe. A myriad of dire possibilities dogged my heels. In the gloom of the library, Father stood staring into the empty fireplace, a scrap of paper clenched in one fist. His shoulders hunched, his head bowed. I'd never seen him look so broken.

'Father? What is it?'

Silence stretched between us making me wonder if he would ignore me. Then, he turned. Tears tracked down his face, grief chiselled into every line. He gasped out one word: 'Tommy.'

That single utterance was a punch to the gut. 'No! Please, no,' I said. 'Dear God, please, no.'

'My boy. My poor boy.' Father stretched a hand towards me. He swayed on his feet. I helped him to a chair and eased the telegram from his shaking hand. My eyes scanned the print, afraid of what they would see.

Missing in Action

A peculiar cocktail of relief and despair washed through me, the two contrary emotions fighting for supremacy. Not dead. Thank God, but... missing? Missing how? Missing where? What did this mean? I needed answers that this scrap of paper simply couldn't provide.

After pouring two stiff whiskies, I passed one to Father and threw my head back to swallow the other in one go. The fiery liquid burned a trail past my frozen heart to sit like a puddle of molten lead in my stomach. I sank onto a footstool, and took Father's limp hand in mine.

'We mustn't give up hope,' I said. 'He isn't dead. I know he isn't.' But I didn't know that, did I? How could I? 'We have to believe that he'll come back, Father.'

He turned curious eyes towards me, almost as if he had never seen me before. 'You sounded just like your mother, then.'

'Did I?' I said in surprise. I'd expected him to berate me for being sentimental and holding on to foolish hope.

'Perhaps you're more like her than I realised.' He sighed. 'Let us hope you are right, my girl.'

He'd never called me 'my girl' before. He'd often used the scathing term 'girl'. The addition of that small possessive pronoun changed the way it landed. It was almost – dare I say it? – affectionate.

I dropped my forehead to rest on the arm of his chair and the two of us sat in silence; together, locked in immeasurable sorrow. Eventually the grandfather clock in the corner chimed the hour. Eight o'clock. Father stirred, his chair creaking in protest. He rested a heavy hand atop my head. 'What's done is done. The cards are dealt. We shall have to wait and see how the hand plays out. All we can do is hope that the odds are on Tommy's side.' After struggling to his feet, he left the room.

I stumbled to the window and peered out through a gap in the blackout curtains. I knew that, thanks to Farmer Barnes, the previously pristine lawns were gone but, in the darkness, I couldn't see the new patriotic vegetable beds. Before my eyes were memories. Ghosts of the past. Tommy and I chasing each other as children. I couldn't imagine a world without him. The one person who had always stood up for me. My brother. My twin. My friend.

He couldn't be dead.

I would know. Surely, I would know.

The library door opened. Uneven footsteps and the tap of a cane edged into my grief. That strange bubbling sense of hyper-awareness that I'd experienced only once before started again. I twitched the curtain back into place and blotted my face with my sleeve before turning.

Edward looked in better health. The deathly pallor that had haunted his features, the day we met at Waterloo station, had lifted. He'd also put on weight. Not much, just enough to dispel the impression that he might snap with the lightest of touches.

He stopped a few feet from me and gave a stiff bow. 'I am so sorry to hear the news about Tommy.'

'Thank you,' I mumbled.

'For what it's worth, Missing in Action doesn't necessarily mean—'

'I know what it means.' My tone was sharper than I intended. I snatched a breath and steadied myself. 'It doesn't mean he's dead. And anyway, he isn't. Dead, I mean. He can't be. I won't accept it. But it doesn't exactly mean he's all right either, does it?'

'Tom would want you to have hope.'

I don't know where the anger came from. It was more intense than anything I'd ever experienced and I couldn't stop it. 'I don't need you to tell me what he would want,' I hissed. 'I know him better than anyone.'

'Forgive me.' His voice was warm and soothing, no hint of irritation at my behaviour.

My skin tingled at his proximity, adding to my confusion. I shouldn't be reacting this way, not when Tommy... Yet the urge to throw myself into Edward's arms, seeking comfort, was almost overwhelming. He was Tommy's best friend. Probably the one person in the world who loved Tommy almost as much as Father and I did. I could see the confusion of grief clouding his eyes. Taking a firm hold of myself, I inched away. If I gave in to my pain, it would swallow me whole. I couldn't let that happen. 'Why are you here?' I asked.

'I was nearby when I heard. I couldn't not come.' He pointed to the paper scrunched in my fist. 'I had hoped to beat the telegram. I thought you might need a... well, a friend.'

'That was kind.' Helpless to stop myself, I swayed towards him. He dropped his cane and grasped my upper arms to steady me, his gaze locked with mine. I could have drowned in those eyes of his. Full of compassion. Not pity. Understanding. If anyone could appreciate how lost I felt at the prospect of Tommy being hurt, it was Edward.

We stood together, not speaking, just being. His mere presence, the physical contact between us, was indescribably comforting. My strength began to return. I dropped my eyes to his lips and wondered what it would feel like to kiss him. Even as the thought crossed my mind, a door slammed elsewhere in the house, making me jump. Loud voices echoed in the corridor outside. Edward stepped back, releasing me.

I shook my head to clear it, my heart beating fast, like the wings of a startled hummingbird. What was I thinking? Tommy was missing in action. Edward was Tommy's friend. Under the circumstances, kissing him was not an option. In fact, given his opinion of me, and the fact that I had ignored his advice about meeting with Major Stapleton, kissing Edward wasn't *ever* going to be an option.

'Forgive me,' he muttered, reaching for his cane. 'I should not have intruded.'

I tamped down on the maelstrom of emotions whirling through me. 'You meant well. And, for what it's worth, you were right. I did need a friend.' I scrabbled around for my manners. 'Can we offer you a room for the night?'

He glanced at the grandfather clock. 'No. Thank you. I still have some distance to travel this evening. Unless there is something I can do to help either you or your father.'

I shook my head.

'Then, I will take my leave.'

Alone in the library after he had left, I was a mass of conflicting emotions. The urge to go for a run was uppermost in my mind. Running was something Tommy and I did… had done together. Most people thought it an odd activity, and definitely not ladylike, but for some reason, exercise always helped me to think. I needed to think now, more than ever. I hurried to my room and changed into a loose pair of trousers, a top, and suitable shoes. Keeping my head down, I slipped outside.

It was dark. The half-moon lent sufficient silver light for me to make my way across the garden towards the treeline. As I pounded the ground, one foot after another, my tumbling thoughts soon slowed and a sense of calm returned. Wherever Tommy was, whatever had happened to him, running was one of the few tangible connections with him that I had left.

What on earth would he think of me almost kissing his friend? I increased my pace, trying to outrun the memory.

'Halt. Who goes there?' A tall, gangly shadow moved from the trees to block my path.

I skidded to a stop, my breath coming in rapid bursts. The crisp night air was heavy with the scent of tree sap and damp earth.

Torchlight shone in my eyes for a second before being switched off. The squeaky tones of the postmaster's seventeen-year-old son came out of the darkness. 'Miss Ashworth, what are you doing here?'

'Private Ashworth,' I corrected. 'And I could ask the same question of you, James Tully. This is Ashworth land. You're trespassing.'

'Private Tully,' he said. His tone told me my sharp address had been a mistake. He drew himself up to his full height. 'I'm here on official Home Guard business. It's my duty to patrol the coast, Ashworth land included, to keep watch for enemy activity. Show me your identity papers.'

I cursed under my breath. They were back in my room along with my uniform, ration book and gas mask. 'I don't have them.'

'Then I'm going to have to report you.' I could hear smug satisfaction in his voice.

'Is that really necessary?' I seethed. 'This is my home. It's not like I am out in the village without them.'

'You're supposed to carry them at all times,' he insisted. 'You could be a spy.'

'Don't be ridiculous. I'm not a spy.'

'That's what a spy would say, though. Isn't it?'

'Oh, please?' I said, through gritted teeth. Why was he being so difficult? 'You've known me all your life.' We'd never been friends, admittedly, but we were part of the same community. We couldn't help but know of each other's existence.

'It doesn't matter. You could still be a spy.'

I remembered what Major Stapleton had said about the threat from enemy spies infiltrating coastal areas and the fight went out of me. I should be grateful that he was doing his duty. After all, *I* knew I wasn't doing anything nefarious, but the next person he stopped might not be so innocent. 'You're right, Private Tully. I apologise. But I'm not a spy. I promise.'

His chest swelled with pompous importance. 'And you're also not supposed to be out during blackout, either. This is exactly the sort of suspicious activity I'm here to record.'

'Again. You're right. Forgive me.' I hated grovelling, but he could stir up a lot of trouble for me if he chose to. Hopefully, if I was conciliatory enough he would leave me alone. I let out a deliberately shaky sigh. 'It's just the shock, you see. I... we... I mean, Father received a telegram from the War Office.'

'Did he?'

'It's Tommy.' My voice broke. The reality of my twin's situation hit me afresh. Tears leaked from my eyes unbidden. I had to force words past a lump that appeared in my throat. 'He is missing in action. I, uh... I... I just needed to get out. And I...' I swallowed down a sob.

'Well.' James coughed and scuffed his feet against the earthen path. 'I suppose I can overlook it, this time.'

'Thank you.' Fighting to regain control of my emotions, I poured an extra measure of breathy girlish gratitude into those two words. It had the desired effect.

'As long as you head straight home,' he growled.

'I will.' I crossed my fingers behind my back.

'See that you do.' He stepped back and turned to go. 'And remember your papers next time you leave the house.'

I dashed a hand across my eyes. Frustration at the whole situation made me shake with fury. This was my home, my family's land. Letting some self-important teenage bossy-boots order me about set my teeth on edge. I focused on taking long, slow, deep breaths in and out, and waited for the rhythmic beat of his footsteps to die away before carrying on with my run. More alert to my surroundings, now, I prepared to disappear into the trees should I encounter anyone else. It wasn't long before I arrived at the clifftop path overlooking Ashworth Bay and came to a stop.

Bristling with sharp wooden stakes and rolls of barbed wire, the shoreline bore no resemblance to that of Tommy's and my childhood. I tore my eyes from the anti-invasion measures on the beach and, instead, gazed across the water towards the Isle of Wight. The moon sailed out from behind a cloud, a silvery glow highlighting the incoming tide as it crept up the beach towards me. Two buoys bobbed in the water. The one further out, level with the end of the headland, was where Father's coastal cruiser, *The Lady*, used to be moored. The other buoy, closer in, was for the dinghy. Tommy's dinghy really, but he and I shared everything. Both boats were gone now. Stored in dry dock in compliance with War Office restrictions. The empty moorings screamed of so much more than missing boats.

Missing in action isn't dead.

Tommy was still out there somewhere. I had to believe it. My brave and honourable brother couldn't be gone. He knew the risk he was taking when he chose to serve his country. I prayed he would be back. In the meantime, I was damned if I'd sit at

Ashworth typing and waiting for news. I was frightened for Tommy – of course I was – but I was angry too. Angry in a way that made my bones burn. I needed to do something. I wanted to hit back at the enemy, any way I could. It no longer mattered if I was good enough or not, I was doing it. I would give Major Stapleton two weeks' grace to contact me with details of her mysterious operation, and if that came to nothing, I would ask the colonel for his help to get reassigned to a post where I could make a real difference.

My mind was made up. I was going to fight this damn war on my terms. Come what may.

8

I didn't have long to wait. A third letter from Major Stapleton arrived within days, instructing me to report to a place called Highworth, in Wiltshire, the following Friday. I set off armed with a steely determination to do whatever the major required, no matter how dangerous.

Early spring sunshine bathed the platform at Highworth village station in a warm, uplifting puddle of gold. I climbed down from yet another overcrowded carriage and checked my orders for what felt like the thousandth time before making my way to the General Post Office as instructed. The diminutive woman behind the counter had a grandmotherly demeanour. Her silvered hair was pulled back into a neat twist at the nape of her neck above a delicate lace collar. I smiled tentatively, coughed quietly to clear the dust of travel from my throat and murmured, 'I'm Private Ashworth. I was told to speak to Mrs Margaret Street and ask if she has a message for a Mr Frank Butterworth about Audrey Payne.' I suspected that the latter part of my sentence was some sort of password or code.

'I am Mrs Street.' Peering over the top of small, round

glasses, the woman swept me with the sort of assessing look that always left me feeling inadequate. I straightened my spine and tried to look confident and capable, and reminded myself that I had been asked to come. Therefore, Major Stapleton must see something of worth in me. 'Wait there,' she said and disappeared into a back room. Five minutes later, she returned. 'Mr Butterworth is sending a car for you. Take a seat on the bench outside.'

I did as I was told. Light birdsong rang out from the trees on the village green opposite where early daffodils and primroses pushed up through the grass. I passed the time watching villagers going about their business. Eventually, another army vehicle with the number 490 marked on the wing arrived and transported me on a long, winding trip through the countryside to a minor stately home. Like Ashworth, the house had multiple chimneys, but there the resemblance ended. This property was larger, built from pale stone with carved trims and sported huge bay windows criss-crossed with anti-blast tape.

Major Belinda Stapleton was waiting on the drive. 'Thank you for coming, Private Ashworth. How was your journey?'

I gave her a crisp salute. 'Fine, thank you, ma'am.'

She led me up a flight of stone steps, through the main door of the house into a wide hallway with a black and white tiled floor and cream walls.

'Major Stapleton. Forgive me for asking but I have responded to your invitations on three occasions now, and yet, I am none the wiser as to what is going on. You sent me haring across the country merely to read out loud from a piece of paper, last month. While I am not objecting, I would like to understand.' The words were tumbling from my mouth in my haste to make my position clear. I needed to know that this was going somewhere. 'If you have a role for me, I will accept it gladly. If not, then please tell me so I can apply elsewhere.'

She smiled, not seeming the least put out by my blunt approach. 'I admire your enthusiasm. Last month, I needed to know if you could be clear and concise on the radio and not improvise. The best way to do that was to get you tested.'

'I see.' How intriguing. 'May I ask why?'

She cast an assessing eye over me. 'If I am going to ask someone to put their life on the line for our country, it seems only fair to find out if they have the skills to do what is needed before I raise the question. Don't you agree?'

I nodded. It was a valid point.

'And if they don't already have those skills,' she said, 'then I need to know if they have the ability to learn them.'

'I am happy to learn whatever you need me to,' I assured her, a little spark of delight flaring at the thought of the knowledge I might gain.

'I appreciate that. Before I explain further, you will need to sign some papers.'

'What sort of papers?'

'The Official Secrets Act among other things. Once you have signed, you will not be permitted to speak about this meeting, or any project associated with it, to another living soul. Are you willing to do that?'

My heart leapt at the thought. The Official Secrets Act. Oh, my! Proof that this was important. Finally, I was getting somewhere. 'Yes. Absolutely.'

'This means not talking about what you are doing at all, to anyone. Not even your own family. Not a single word, anywhere; whether you're out and about, at a café or restaurant, on any form of transport whether public or private, in your billet or your home.' She peered closely at me. 'Can you do that?'

I jerked my head in a single emphatic nod. 'Yes.'

'Then, follow me.' The major led me to down a flight of narrow stone steps to a cramped room in the basement where I read a lengthy document, the last line of which declared: *I hereby swear that my words shall not betray the immense trust that has been placed in me.*

I signed.

Twenty minutes later, I was back on the ground floor, perched on an antique sofa in a drawing room that was in a far better state of repair than anything back at Ashworth Manor, listening to the major as she outlined her project.

'You and I spoke before about how the enemy is advancing across Europe relatively unchecked,' she said. 'And that with much of France now occupied, plans for an invasion of Britain have come to light.'

A shiver scampered down my back. The French army was supposed to have been one of the best in the world, and yet it had crumbled before the relentless German advance. 'I thought your idea to use women embedded in local communities as agents was, quite frankly, genius.'

'Thank you. There is a lot more to my secret army than that. I think women have the potential to be a powerful weapon in this war. Unfortunately, not many senior figures agree. Nevertheless, I have received backing from none other than Prime Minister Churchill himself. He has tasked me with setting up an experimental special operations unit. I want you to join the initial training program.'

I could barely contain my excitement. 'I would be honoured to.'

She held up one palm. 'Hear me out, first. We are still working on some of the details and, at this time, specific information relating to what we are calling the Special Duties

Section of the women's auxiliary unit is on a need-to-know basis. There is very little that I can tell you, at this stage.' She leaned a fraction closer, her gaze intent. 'I'm looking for people who can pass relatively unnoticed. I believe that you are tough, intelligent and capable.'

Unused to compliments, I didn't know what to say, but I desperately wanted to be the person she thought I was, so I nodded.

'You hold a junior rank,' she continued. 'Which is good. People will assume you are not important. Basically, I need you to be you, but a more highly trained version. Ready to spring into action should the worst happen.'

Invasion. I swallowed down nausea. 'What sort of action?'

'Well, that depends. On the surface you will be posted somewhere to do a relatively mundane job for the war effort. Something that will not draw the attention of anyone, whether British citizen or enemy invader. At the same time, you will keep your eyes and ears open. As to what other potential duties you might have, we can discuss that *if* you complete the initial stages of training.'

'I see.'

'Don't underestimate the training process though,' she warned. 'It will be hard. You might not pass.'

'I understand,' I said, dismissing the thought of failure. Whatever they threw at me I would give it my all. Nothing was going to get in my way.

She gave a brisk nod. 'In which case, we have our first six-week training program starting in mid-March.'

My foot jigged with excitement. That was only a matter of a few weeks away. 'What areas will the training cover?'

'A range of things, from languages and coding to self-defence, explosives manufacture, weapons handling and general guerrilla warfare tactics.'

'I see.' I dug my nails into my palms to remind myself to stay in my seat and present an outwardly calm appearance. Inside, I was skipping with delight. This was exactly what I'd been looking for. An opportunity to learn and grow; to get involved in things I would never in a million years be allowed near if circumstances were different.

'I'll make arrangements for you to attend. If you pass, there will be a further period of additional training before you are fully briefed and deployed. I won't lie to you, Private Ashworth. It will be tough. You will need to be strong and committed.'

There was no doubt in my mind. 'I am, ma'am. I promise. I'm ready for this.'

'Understand this as well. If all goes to plan, no one will ever know of your contribution to the war, other than as a lowly private in the ATS. There will be no glory attached to this assignment.'

A steely cloak of resolve settled over my shoulders, Tommy's face crystal clear in my mind. 'I don't need glory.'

'What do you need?'

There weren't enough words to explain. Somehow, I doubted the major would understand how restricted my life had been. She was strong and confident and seemed to know exactly who she was. It wasn't appropriate to tell her that I longed to be exactly like her rather than what I currently was: a useless female who was always in the way.

Instead, I settled for simply saying, 'I need to know that I've done my bit.'

9

Exactly a month later I arrived in what used to be the main drawing room of Hannington Hall, a huge country house in Wiltshire five miles to the west of the village of Coleshill, ready for training. I couldn't wait to get started. I clutched a small kitbag of essentials, the only things I had been permitted to bring, and stared around in greedy fascination, drinking everything in. Apart from an intricate baroque ceiling, the only other remnants of the room's previous incarnation as the home of landed gentry were three sets of ornate French doors that marched along the far wall, their glass panes covered with lines of protective tape. Stripped of its former glory, the room was furnished with rows of functional wooden benches. Light sections of the bare floorboards spoke of absent rugs, and a cold draught seeped from the immense, empty fireplace to snatch at my ankles.

The sergeant who greeted me gave me a serious, assessing stare. He pointed to an empty space on a bench. 'Sit. Wait. No talking.'

While I was curious to see who else had been a recipient of

Major Stapleton's mysterious letters, good manners prevented me from openly staring. In one quick glance around the room, I registered an eclectic mix of young women: some slight, some sturdy, some dark, some blonde, some in uniform, some in civvies. All waiting in silence. The air was thick with beeswax polish and anticipation. The muted rhythm of marching feet filtered in from outside. A grandfather clock tick, tick, ticked in the corner. Posters screamed 'Loose Lips Sink Ships' and 'Careless Talk Costs Lives' from the walls. The first slogan was accompanied by a picture of two women in headscarves gossiping. The second showed a hapless male busy spilling a gutful of confidential information to a Mata-Hari type, his eyes glued to her generous bosom. An unlikely scenario, I felt, but never having been in possession of anything resembling a big bust, I couldn't be certain.

Confident heels clip-clopped out in the hall, announcing the arrival of a statuesque woman in a neat blue suit and bright red lipstick. Older than me by at least a decade, she had a mane of dark hair with a silver streak at the temples. Confidence rolled off her in waves. She scanned the room, before taking a seat next to me. The instant she spotted the wall art, she crossed her arms and muttered, 'Typical,' under her breath.

I liked her immediately, and threw her a quick smile, whispering. 'Hi, I'm Wren.'

She grinned, smoothed her silver streak behind one ear. 'I'm Jo.'

Major Stapleton strode in, brisk and business-like. She stopped before us, hands clasped behind her back. 'Welcome, all. You've expressed a desire to serve your country. I applaud you. The next few weeks will be hard. You will learn self-sufficiency, how to defend yourself, and how to do whatever is necessary to survive and hold your position against the enemy.'

She pointed at the posters. 'The top brass think women can't be trusted.' She paused to allow a murmur of disgust to ripple around the room and die out before continuing. 'They think we are weak and foolish and need protection. It's time we prove them wrong. Let's show them that women are just as smart and capable as men and that we can fight to defend our homes.'

Jo uncrossed her arms. 'Hear, hear,' she muttered under her breath.

'Please bear in mind that we have several cohorts of recruits from different projects undergoing multiple training schedules here. Your first task is to ensure that you do not reveal any information about who you are and why you have been recruited. In that vein, whilst here, all recruits are to use first names only to address each other. You will not reveal your surname, your origins, or any nature of your true identity to anyone. Not to those arriving with you today, or to any of those already here. Once your time here is done, you are unlikely to see each other again. You are not here to socialise; you are here to learn, and to work hard.' She paused, meeting the eyes of each person in turn. 'These measures are for your own protection, the protection of everyone else *and* the operation. In short, you cannot divulge that which you do not know.'

The sinister implications of that last statement made my flesh creep.

'You will also keep away from the men's quarters and training areas, which are on the far side of the property,' she added. 'They will assume you are here for the standard basic training, and we want to keep it that way.'

The sergeant passed the major a clipboard. She glanced down at it. 'The following are your hut allocations. As I call out your names, please form a line over here.' She pointed at the first set of French windows and then read out hut numbers and names.

People shifted on seats, glancing around, waiting for their names before shuffling into line.

I got to my feet when it was my turn, delighted to hear Jo's name called immediately afterwards. We were in the same hut. That had to be a good sign. Together, we examined the four other women assigned to live with us. A wiry redhead, Louisa, had a ready smile and dancing eyes. A pocket-sized brunette, Constance, seemed painfully shy and whispered, 'Please call me Connie.' Finally, a studious woman with a kind face and a watchful air called Felicity – who whispered, 'Call me Fliss' – shuffled over with Lexi, a tall blonde.

'Today is all about orientation. We want to get you settled in and ready to get stuck into what is quite a punishing training schedule tomorrow,' said the major. 'Sergeant Banks will show you where everything is. The accommodation huts, the mess tent, the necessary, the various teaching areas. First up, though, you will go to distribution and be supplied with two sets of clothes each. These are loose, practical items designed to make your time here easier. They allow a good range of movement for physical training. Once the grand tour is over, you will get changed and report to the main lawn for a run—'

Several groans greeted this announcement.

Major Stapleton raised her voice above the noise. 'If you are to serve your country to the best of your ability, you need to be as fit as possible. I suggest an early night after supper.' She eyed everyone in turn. 'The training will be hard, but I believe you can do it. Good luck.' She turned to the sergeant and handed him back the clipboard before leaving the room.

The sergeant tucked the clipboard under his arm and clapped his hands together, the harsh noise cutting through all the grumbles. 'Right, you lot. Follow me.' He led us out through the French doors onto a wide flagstone patio edged with a decorative balustrade. Wide steps took us down to cross a generous area of lawn to where a squat wooden cabin was half hidden by trees. The sergeant ground to a halt. 'Wait here. No talking.' He pointed to me. 'You, go in first.' He pointed to Jo. 'And you.'

Inside, a private handed us each a pile of clothes. 'Try these on for size.' She gestured towards two curtained areas. 'You can change behind those.'

There were two pairs of loose practical trousers, similar in style to those I'd seen Maria wearing back at home. The fabric was tough and hard-wearing. The only real difference to the Land Army uniform was the colour. One pair was a dull olive green, the other grey. The bundle also contained two plain flannel shirts, each a bland grey-green, a thick dark brown woollen jumper, two pairs of grey socks and a dark green headscarf.

I slipped off my ATS uniform and tried them on. Stepping out from behind the curtain, I tied my hair back with the scarf as the woman circled me, checking overall fit. 'Yes, you'll do.'

The other curtain was yanked back in a dramatic fashion. Jo struck a pose, her eyes sparkling with mischief. 'Do you have this in a nice bright yellow? I'm not sure bile green is my colour.'

The private grinned. 'The point is to blend in, not stand out.'

Jo sobered. 'I understand that.' She tugged at the wide legs of her trousers and sighed. 'A uniform is a uniform. Although—' she gave my clothes an appraising stare '—they're not exactly *uniform*, are they?' She was right. While our drab outfits were similar, they were not identical.

'Perhaps that is the point, too,' I said. 'Uniforms are identifiable. We're supposed to be easily overlooked. Forgettable.'

'Huh!' Jo sniffed in disdain. 'Something I've spent my life trying to avoid.'

'Somehow, that doesn't surprise me,' I said. 'You're just going to have to get used to it.'

She shook her head in mock despair. 'The things a girl will do for her country.'

There was a knock on the door. 'Get a move on, you two,' bellowed Sergeant Banks. 'We don't have all day.'

Jo's lip curled. 'He's such a sweetie pie, isn't he?'

'Here.' The private smothered a laugh and handed Jo a pair of strange-looking shoes. 'You need something on your feet.'

'Oh goodness,' said Jo. 'These are that new style of shoe I read about in the paper. They're from America. Specifically designed for running.'

I examined the pair I'd been handed. Constructed of a dark green canvas upper with rubber soles, they had long criss-crossed black laces running from toe to ankle enabling me to tighten them snugly around my foot and ankle. Scuffs down one side told me I was not their first owner. I'd never worn anything like them before. They were incredibly comfortable.

Another knock sounded at the door.

'Come on,' I said. We gathered up our clothes and scurried outside.

10

That first run at Haverhill was challenging in many ways. Recent stormy weather had turned the ground into a quagmire. The path had been well used by previous groups of runners who had churned up thick, gloopy mud that dragged at our feet. I set off with a spring in my step, delighted at the prospect of running with other women. Surely it was a promising sign that the first task we'd been given as part of this training program was something that I knew I could do?

The initial leg was a long, intimidating grind uphill that left hearts pounding and muscles straining. Several runners had streaked ahead. Given that it was an unknown course, I felt it wiser to stay with the main pack. Thanks to my intense workload at Ashworth, I'd not had a chance to exercise properly for several weeks, and while I ran from the house to the bay and back whenever I could, I hadn't done any long-distance routes since before the war. Maintaining a steady pace took concentration. My lungs burned with the effort of sucking in enough air. Cresting the brow of the hill, I slowed, noticing that, while Jo and Fliss were forging ahead and Connie was also holding her own, the other two women from our hut were lagging behind. As we'd not been told it was a race, it seemed wrong to leave them to struggle on alone. I slowed and waited until Louisa, the faster of the two, caught up, and then I fell into step alongside her.

'Hi,' I said.

Sweat darkened her red curls, plastering them to her head. She threw me a quick grin and puffed out flushed cheeks. 'Sorry. Can't talk. I daren't stop, neither. Never get started again.'

I grinned and dropped my pace to let her plod ahead.

Behind me, a squeal of pain rent the air followed by loud cursing. Lexi had slipped and fallen.

I hurried back and offered her my hand. 'Are you all right?'

'Does it effing well look like I'm all right?' she said, her accent revealing cockney origins. Ignoring my hand, she scrambled to her feet. Mud streaked right up one leg and the side of her body. She brushed at it but only succeeded in making things worse.

'Oh dear,' I laughed, trying to make light of it. 'We'll have to hope there's lots of hot water so we can get cleaned up when we get back.'

'I hate the blasted countryside. Give me streets and pavements over mud any day of the week.'

'Really?' I asked, glancing around. 'But it's so beautiful.'

Suddenly her eyes locked on mine. 'What are you doing back here anyway? All bouncy and energetic and *perfect*.' That last word was spat out. 'You could be at the front. The only reason to lurk at the back is to laugh at failures like me.'

'I wasn't laughing at you,' I gasped, beginning to wish I'd kept my mouth shut. 'I was just trying to be friendly.'

'Well don't. You heard the major. We're not supposed to socialise.'

I frowned. 'Checking if someone needs help hardly counts as socialising.'

She glared at me, her hands on her hips, her chest heaving. 'I don't need help.'

Why on earth was she being so prickly? I raised both hands, palms out. 'Look, I am sorry if—'

'Just leave me alone, will you?' She gestured ahead at where Louisa was disappearing around a corner in the track. 'Please. Go.'

'Fine.' I shrugged and settled into an easy loping stride that quickly left her behind.

While the remainder of the course was less challenging on a physical level, I was shaken that Lexi had misinterpreted my actions. I really hadn't been laughing at her. Why would she snap at me like that?

My childhood at Ashworth had been quite isolating thanks to Father's controlling ways. I knew girls from the village. I'd seen them going around in groups, chatting and laughing, but I'd always been on the outside looking in. Coming from what the locals termed 'the big house' created a gulf that was impossible to cross thanks to their assumption that my life was one of gilded privilege. If only they knew. There were certain advantages to my situation, I knew that, but appearances can be so deceptive. Fortunately, Tommy was my best friend as well as my brother, and I hadn't really needed anyone else until he left. And since the war had started, opportunities to mix with other women my age had been limited further. It was probably just as well Major Stapleton didn't want us to socialise. I clearly wasn't very good at it.

As I followed the ridge line to the south and then down through a section of forest to curl back towards our starting point near the huts, I resolved to tread far more carefully with my new companions. Running through the trees reminded me of home and thoughts of home brought my brother to mind. It wasn't much of a leap on from Tommy to Edward. I wondered how he was, where he had been posted, and what he would think if he knew what I had done.

* * *

Thoughts of Edward were still with me hours later as I shivered and hunched further down under my blankets. Hut 06 was typical temporary military accommodation, a Nissen hut constructed of prefabricated corrugated iron in a semicircular dome sat on a brick foundation with a wooden floor. Six metal-framed beds with thin mattresses ranged along one side. Each bed had a trunk at the foot for our kit and there was a desk and chair on the wall opposite. It was sparse and functional, perfectly suited to a large turnover of military personnel. My stomach rumbled. I thumped my lumpy pillow, ignored the smell of mildew and the click-clack of something small with claws scurrying over the metal roof outside, and tried to go to sleep.

Louisa's voice came out of the darkness. 'That sigh sounded like it came from your boots. Are you all right, Wren?'

'Yes, thank you,' I said, wishing I sounded more certain. Not knowing any details about my hut mates, other than their first names, was a little weird. 'It's been a long day.'

'You're telling me, love.' That was Jo. Her husky tones and her wicked sense of humour coloured everything she said. It was no wonder I had taken to her so quickly. To my relief, she seemed to like me too. So far, at least.

Another muttered comment slipped into the darkness. This time from the direction of Connie's bunk to my left. Her voice mirrored her nature; it was timid and cautious. 'Are you missing someone? Your man perhaps? I met a fella at a dance recently. He's an RAF officer. He's lovely and ever so handsome.'

'What's his name?' I asked.

'I don't know.' She sounded sad. 'He did say, but it was so noisy, and then we were dancing. I kept meaning to ask him again but I didn't know how without sounding rude. I'd give anything to see him again.'

'I'm not missing my chap,' said Jo, with a rueful laugh. 'He's gorgeous but he's more trouble than he's worth.'

'Isn't that often the case?' asked Louisa.

I grunted. Why Edward was filling my head, I couldn't say. I still couldn't believe that we'd almost kissed that day we heard about Tommy. The memory of being so close to him, those mesmerising eyes of his gazing into mine, just wouldn't go away. I kept feeling his warm breath on my face, the butterflies in my stomach.

'Is your man handsome, Wren?' asked Connie.

There was definitely something about him. A magnetism I couldn't explain, but that was not something I was ready to share. 'No,' I said.

'Ugly, is he?' said Louisa. 'That can work.'

'Oh no.' I could feel my cheeks burning in the darkness. 'I don't mean he's not handsome, because he is. I mean, he would be… if he existed, but he doesn't.' I mentally kicked myself. It was definitely time to stop speaking. 'What I mean is, I don't have a man.'

Jo cackled. 'We believe you.'

Lexi's grouchy tones butted in. 'Can you lot shut your traps? I'm trying to sleep.' She'd been last back from the run and had then spent ages trying to clean herself up in the scant bathroom facilities before arriving at the canteen for supper with only minutes to spare before they stopped service. Slumping into the only spare seat, she'd done nothing but scowl like a grumpy giant at me across the table, shutting down any friendly overtures I tried to make. I found such behaviour unnerving and had barely made a dent in my lentil and bean stew. Hence my rumbling stomach keeping me awake.

'Lexi's right,' I said, hoping to placate her. 'We should sleep. We've another five-mile run before breakfast, remember?'

11

The second run was just as wet and muddy. Familiarity with the route allowed me to take greater advantage of the breath-taking views of the hall from the ridge top this time. It was easy to see why a stately home had been chosen to house the training facility. The main lawns were hugged by immense broadleaf trees, their branches bare, but heavy with the promise of spring leaves about to emerge from the bud. These were interspersed with a variety of evergreens and a thick bushy undergrowth. In combination, the vegetation provided a natural screen for the many Nissen huts accommodating recruits scattered through the woodland. Marquees and bell tents used for larger functions, like the canteen, were dotted into small clearings. Their green, grey and brown camouflaged canvas panelling helped blend them into their surroundings.

The fresh air and exercise cleared my head. By the time I was changed and sat in the canteen with a bowl of saltwater porridge and a mug of tea, I was beginning to feel much more myself. All errant thoughts of Edward had been banished and I was ready to tackle whatever the training program might throw at me. I examined my surroundings with interest. One end of the tent was for meal service, with staff dishing out from behind trestle tables to recruits queuing up with trays. Numbered tables, one for each hut, were spaced at regular intervals in the remaining area. The atmosphere was sombre. Interaction between groups minimal.

I eyed the empty chair at our table. 'Where's Lexi?'

Louisa shrugged. 'Still running.'

'She'll have to be quick or she'll miss breakfast,' said Jo.

'You'd think she'd be good at running, wouldn't you?' said Connie. 'What with those long legs of hers. Not like my short, stumpy ones. I'm a useless runner.'

'No, you're not. And anyway, everyone runs differently,' I said. I suspected that Lexi's technique wasn't helping her, but it wasn't appropriate to say anything. 'My brother says: the best thing to do is to relax into your stride, to listen to your body's own rhythm and work with that.'

'Relax? He's kidding, isn't he? How are you supposed to relax?' grumbled Louisa. 'All I hear from my body when I'm running is that my feet hurt.'

I laughed. 'That's often what I hear too.'

Fliss waved her spoon. 'We have self-defence training later on today. I reckon a lot more of us will be hurting after that.'

I scraped the last of my porridge from my bowl, excitement fizzing in my chest at the prospect of learning new skills. Skills normally not taught to properly brought up young ladies. Excellent.

Lexi stalked in, helped herself to a bowl of porridge and threw herself into her chair.

'Hi, Lexi,' I said, striving for a welcoming tone. 'How are you this morning?'

She glared at me and shoved a spoonful of food into her

mouth. My heart sank. Was she really still cross with me, or had she just got out of bed on the wrong side?

'You're just in time, Lexi,' Connie murmured. 'I was afraid they'd stop serving and you'd be hungry all day.'

Lexi's shoulders relaxed and she shot Connie a grin. 'Heaven forbid!'

I watched her from under my lashes as she ate and chatted with the group. Was I imagining it? She seemed perfectly amicable with the other girls but, whenever I opened my mouth, she blanked me, allowing my words to fall into an awkward silence – just long enough to make me wonder if I had spoken at all. Then she'd change the subject. If it was deliberate, it was masterfully done. No one else seemed to notice. I glanced down at my hands, my cheeks growing warm, not really sure what to do.

Jo nudged me. 'You're quiet. What's up?'

I dredged up a smiled and nodded. 'I'm just tired.'

Lexi swallowed her last mouthful with relish and got to her feet. 'We'd best get on, hadn't we?' Gathering up her dirty dish and spoon, she headed for the clearance station.

'Have you seen the schedule?' asked Connie, falling into step with her. 'Languages, coding, stealth, whatever that is, shooting *and* explosives training. It's intense.'

Everyone else followed, chatting and clearing the table. I tagged along at the back.

'What are we starting with?' asked Lexi.

'Telecommunications,' said Connie. 'I wonder what that's all about.'

Louisa tipped her head on one side. 'Probably radios and telephones and things.'

Crossing the lawns to the house, I could feel my spirits sinking. If I couldn't get on with Lexi, there was a real risk that my relationships with all the girls would suffer. Hurrying to keep up with the others, I ran up the stone steps and into the hall. Several large rooms on the ground floor had been converted into classrooms, each filled with rows of mismatched tables and chairs. Lexi grabbed a table near the front. She turned her shoulder, refusing to acknowledge me as I slid into a seat nearby, making me wish I had sat somewhere else. Fortunately, once the lesson got underway, I was transfixed by all the new information and forgot all about her.

A serious-faced instructor introduced herself as Sergeant Armstrong. 'The fastest way to send and receive messages these days is via radio. That's why the radio is such a lifeline. In the next two hours, you will build a radio from its basic component parts. You will learn how to fix it when it goes wrong. You will learn how to make spare parts. You will practise assembling and disassembling a radio in record time and how to hide the pieces in plain sight. If the worst comes to the worst, you must know how to sabotage a radio so that it cannot be repaired and used by the enemy.'

Delivered in a flat monotone, the weight of the underlying message hit home. A hundred nervous butterflies started dancing inside my chest. There was so much to learn. It was all so important. I stole a glance at my fellow students. Were they feeling the same potent cocktail of anticipation and, dare I say it, apprehension?

Footsteps echoed in the corridor. A figure walked past the open doorway. I caught an impression of dark hair, broad shoulders and a limp. I froze. It couldn't be. There was no reason to think that Edward might be here.

Connie gave me a sharp nudge and a concerned look.

I shot her a quick smile of reassurance and dragged my focus back to radios.

12

Three hours later, we all poured out of the lecture room and into bright sunshine outside.

'That was very interesting,' said Fliss.

'It really wasn't.' Louisa groaned. 'My brain hurts.'

With our heads whirling with technical specifications for both wired and wireless communication strategies, and the prospect of an intense session on self-defence next, lunch back at the cafeteria was a subdued affair. A slice of national loaf, which usually tasted of cardboard, was marginally improved with a scraping of dripping and a SPAM fritter. The food filled our bellies but did little to lift our spirits. It was clear that this course was going to be as tough as the major had intimated. It would stretch us all and I couldn't help wonder, for the first time, what would happen if I wasn't up to it. I saw Lexi eyeing me speculatively and shook the thought away.

'It's going to take time to process what we just learned,' I said. 'There's so much information. It's hard to keep it all straight. I'll have to do some extra reading, I think.'

'Teacher's pet,' muttered Lexi.

Fliss didn't seem to hear her. 'I can explain it all again to you later, if you like, Wren.'

'That would be amazing,' I said. 'Thank you.'

'Can you explain it to me, too?' asked Louisa.

'Sure,' said Fliss. 'I'd be happy to.'

Lexi rolled her eyes and looked away.

I forced myself not to react. Perhaps if I pretended that everything was fine, things would settle down. Taking a leaf out of Lexi's playbook, I changed the subject. 'We have a session on self-defence this afternoon, which should be interesting.'

'I've never done self-defence before,' muttered Connie. She tugged at her shirt and trousers. 'Do we wear this for it?'

'I should think so. It's loose and flexible,' said Fliss.

I wrinkled my nose and mused, 'I imagine we need to be ready and able to fight at a moment's notice, regardless of what we're wearing.'

Jo snorted with laughter. 'Can you imagine politely asking an attacker to wait until you've changed out of your ball gown.'

Connie gave a wobbly smile. 'Everyone here is a lot bigger than me.' There was genuine trepidation lurking in her eyes.

'You may be small, but you're fast,' I said. 'Remember, you got hand-picked for this unit the same as the rest of us. They must think you're up to it.'

A handbell sounded.

'Come on,' said Fliss. 'We need to be on the back lawn.'

We cleared our dishes and hurried outside.

Connie gave a low moan when she caught sight of the instructor. I could see why. He was huge and dressed head to toe in black. He watched each of us in turn as we lined up around a wide circle marked on the grass with sandbags.

'Don't worry, Connie,' I muttered. 'Once Sergeant Muscles

over there has taught us a few tricks, we'll be deadly weapons. There'll be no stopping us.'

'YOU!'

I jumped. A low snigger sounded off to my left. I was certain it came from Lexi, but daren't check because Sergeant Muscles was pointing straight at me. My face flamed. Heck! Had he heard me?

I raised a hand to my chest. 'Me, sir?'

'Yes, you.' He beckoned. 'Come here.'

I shuffled forwards.

'Punch me,' he said.

'I beg your pardon?'

He slapped himself in the midriff. 'Punch me. Hard.'

'Are you serious, sir?'

'Don't argue,' he barked. 'Just do it.'

I'd never punched anyone in my life. Not properly. Play fighting with Tommy when we were little didn't count. I clenched my fist and threw it in the direction of his middle.

He sidestepped and gave a brief tug on my wrist that increased my momentum, sending me lurching forward to land flat on my face in the dirt, spitting out bits of grass.

He planted his foot firmly on my back and growled, 'Like Private Pitiful here said; once I've taught you a few tricks, you'll be deadly weapons. But you've got a lot of work to do first.'

That low snigger came again. I swiped hair and dirt from my eyes and looked up to see Lexi enjoying every second of my humiliation, smug satisfaction stamped all over her face.

The instructor continued, 'I am Sergeant Davis. I am going to show you how to use your opponent's own body weight and actions against them. When I'm finished with you, you will be able to counter attacks from someone significantly bigger and stronger than you. Even if you are as small as this recruit here—'

he pointed at Connie who shrank back, her eyes wide '—you will be able to break any hold and run. You will be able to dodge and disarm your assailant. But what you won't do is call me Sergeant Muscles.'

He lifted his foot from my back and offered me a hand. 'Is that clear?'

'Yes, sir. Sergeant Davis, sir. Sorry, sir.' I scrambled to my feet, my cheeks burning.

'Get back in line. Let's get to work.'

I hobbled back to my place. A familiar figure near the main house caught my eye. Edward. It was definitely him. Watching the self-defence class. It was too far to make out the expression on his face, but not far enough *not* to be able to register fury emanating from the stiff set of his shoulders. Louisa gave a low hiss. I snapped my attention back to Sergeant Davis.

'I can see from the pathetic effort Private Pitiful just made—' he cast a glance my way '—that you all need to learn how to punch. Let's start with the basics.' He held up his hand. 'Form your punch like this. Curl all four fingers into your palm. Do NOT put your thumb on the *inside* of your fingers. If you do, it will break. Curl your thumb across the outside of the midsection of your first finger.'

He went around each of us, checking that we had done it correctly and then pointed at me again and then at the sandbag at my feet. 'Bring that.'

It wasn't a sandbag. The large leather sack was stuffed with something relatively light making it firm yet springy.

'Hold it up, chest high,' he said. I did as he asked. A second later, he threw a punch into the bag that nearly knocked me off my feet again. Staggering back, I was surprised to realise I was unhurt. He glanced around at the class. 'Watch what I'm doing. Hold your fist just above your hip, knuckle side down, palm side up. Thrust out from the hip towards your opponent's solar plexus. That's the soft bit just under the centre of the rib cage. In one motion, as you punch, turn your fist over so that the fingers and palm side is face down. This twist adds power. Stepping forward as you punch adds yet more power. Like this.' He matched actions to words, demonstrating several times, making it look effortless. Each time a punch landed I was knocked back several paces, in spite of the fact that I was ready and braced for impact. 'Remember, keep that wrist straight. If it bends, it will break.' He paused to let that sink in. 'Right, you lot. Pair off and get punching.'

The next chance I had to look back at the house, Edward was gone. It didn't matter. I didn't have time to wonder what he was doing. Sergeant Davis clearly had it in for me because he paired me up with Lexi who, with her height, definitely outmatched me.

'Don't go easy on each other,' he said. 'I want to see real punches. Not namby-pamby nonsense.'

A gleam of wicked amusement in Lexi's eyes, left me in no doubt that she was fully prepared to oblige. I planned to return the favour.

The whole class progressed quickly from punching to blocking, then a triple combination of deflect, move and strike options. The pads were effective, but they were not enough to stop injury. My face and arms stung from all the times I had failed to block or dodge Lexi's blows. Add in a barrage of snide comments from her to accompany each attack and I was relieved when the self-defence session was over. I slipped away from the others and ducked into the trees edging the far side of the lawn, desperate for a moment to myself to nurse my wounded pride. I had not gone more than ten yards when a large, familiar figure stepped into my path.

'Edw— I mean, Captain Landers.' I hoped he couldn't hear my heart thumping wildly in my chest. 'I'm surprised to see you here.'

He fixed me with a steady stare. 'Not as surprised as I am to see you.'

'Is this your new posting?' In defiance at his disapproving air, I maintained a sociable tone, as if we had met unexpectedly at afternoon tea.

'No.' The furrow of his brow deepened. 'They haven't settled on a permanent position for me yet. I keep being sent off to different places.'

'I see. Why are you here?'

'I've been asked to teach a class this afternoon. The regular instructor has been taken ill. I'm en route to Devon. This was on the way.'

'Did you have a pleasant journey?'

He waved a dismissive hand. 'I'm more interested in what on earth you think you're doing here?'

I noted with interest that the gorgeous green of his eyes intensified when he was cross. 'What does it look like I'm doing? I'm training,' I said.

A muscle worked in his jaw. 'You're supposed to be safe at Ashworth.'

'Says who? You? What about what *I* want?' I'd had a small taste of what Major Stapleton's plan had to offer me and the one thing I knew was that I wanted more. Regardless of what Edward thought, I knew that I had made the right decision to come here.

'Damn it, Wren, this isn't a game.'

The back of my neck prickled. What gave him the right to patronise me? 'I do know that.'

'Have you any idea what you're mixed up in?'

'Have you?' I fired back. My hands curled into tight fists at my sides. Men always seemed to think that women were feeble, helpless creatures who needed the world explained to them. Now that I knew how to punch properly, I was sorely tempted to demonstrate exactly what I was mixed up in.

He gave a disarming bark of bitter laughter. 'No. Not really. And *that's* what worries me. All I know is that this is some major hush-hush project. It's got special ops, most secret and highly confidential written all over it.'

I put a hand to my chest, feigning shock. 'Has it?' Was this my first test? It was entirely possible that Edward *didn't* know what we were all doing at Hannington. I needed to be careful what I said.

'All that security means this is really dangerous, Wren. I can't protect you here.'

I shook my head in exasperation. I was here to learn skills and do something useful. I couldn't do that with someone hovering over me getting all precious about my safety. 'I don't need you to protect me. Look.' I pointed to bruises blooming along my forearm. 'I'm learning to protect myself. Which is exactly what I want.'

'It's not the same.'

'No, it's not. It's better,' I insisted. After just one session of self-defence, I felt taller somehow. I needed to practice, of course. But, should a fight start now, I was much better equipped to deal with it than I had been a few hours ago.

He gestured towards my face. 'From the looks of things, you're not very good at it.'

'Not yet, no. For heaven's sake,' I snapped. 'What part of *I'm learning* don't you understand?'

'But you don't need to.'

'I *want* to.' I was almost shouting. Frustration, hurt pride and mental exhaustion bubbled over altogether and I lost what tenuous control I had. Shoving him in the chest, I stepped forward, instinctively mirroring the punch-and-follow-through technique I'd been taught in class. It gave me the advantage of surprise.

Edward stumbled backwards. His foot caught on a tree root. Unable to move his bad leg fast enough to re-establish balance, he crashed to the ground. He wrapped both arms around me and pulled me over with him. I landed in an undignified heap on his chest wondering what on earth had happened.

Fireworks shot through me as I registered large portions of me in direct physical contact with him. It was a most disconcerting sensation. I tensed and pushed away, intent on regaining my feet. 'I'm sorry. I didn't mean to hurt you, I...'

'Stop squirming.' His arms tightened. 'I'm not hurt.'

Unable to move, I gazed down into his face, wondering if he felt unsettled too. This was neither the time nor the place. I pushed against him, but to no effect. 'Edward. For goodness' sake! Let me go.'

'Not until you tell me how you came to be here. Or can I guess? You went to Harrods, didn't you?'

I couldn't meet his gaze. I couldn't tell him anything. No matter what he said. 'I don't know what you mean.'

'I warned you not to. Even Tommy warned you not to.'

'Don't you *dare* bring Tommy into this,' I hissed, molten fire blasting through me. The mere thought of Tommy made me want to cry. I couldn't let Edward cut through my defences that easily.

'Why not? He wouldn't approve of this any more than I do.'

'You don't know that for sure.' My nostrils flared. 'Anyway, Tommy isn't here.'

He let out an exasperated hiss. 'All the more reason for you to listen to me.'

'You pompous ass.' Anger powered my struggles and I almost broke free.

His arms locked into iron bands and he gave a great heave. Before I knew it, we were rolling. Then, he was on top, pinning me down. It didn't hurt, but I couldn't move. Those beautiful eyes of his gazed into mine. His face mere inches away.

The breath left my body. My heartbeat went into overdrive. I couldn't think. He was so close that with a mere fraction of movement he could kiss me.

A bell rang in the distance.

He growled in frustration and pulled back. 'What's that?'

'It's the canteen,' I mumbled, dragging my scattered wits into a semblance of order. 'It's time to eat.'

With remarkable agility considering his injured leg, he stood and offered me a hand up. 'You'd better go, before you're missed. You don't want to get in trouble with your superior officers.'

I brushed leaves and dirt from my clothes.

'Please reconsider, Wren,' he said, picking a twig from my hair. 'That woman you were paired with back then wasn't exactly pulling her punches.'

'Do you think I don't know that?' Lexi had not gone easy on me, but I'd dealt her some hard knocks in return.

'Tell them you've had a change of heart,' he urged. 'Ask to be transferred somewhere safer.'

There had been a time when any serious form of contribution to the war effort would have been enough for me. Not any more. My stubborn streak was digging its heels in. There was no turning back. 'Tommy didn't take something safer, and neither will I. I want this. And, do you know what? I *need* it. For the first time in my life, I can control my own destiny. I'm learning things I'd never get the chance to learn anywhere else.'

He rubbed his chin. 'Why is learning such a big deal?'

'You wouldn't understand. No one stopped you going to Oxford because of your gender.'

'I know, but—'

'There is no *but*.' I focused on a point to one side of his head and searched for the words to explain, my voice low and halting. 'I have *never* had a purpose before. I've always been in the way. Father, when he isn't criticising me, looks at me as if he's not quite sure where I came from. I am fed up with being useless.' I lifted one shoulder and let it drop. How could I possibly explain how much I needed to be part of something meaningful? He could never understand the lack of something that he had always had.

The frown was back on Edward's face. 'I'm sorry.'

'I don't need your sympathy. I don't want *anyone's* sympathy. What I want is this.' I stabbed a finger at the ground. 'This place. Here and now. This chance to prove myself. I'll be damned if I back out now.'

Silence followed my words. He rubbed the back of his neck and sighed. 'I admire your determination, Wren. You're going to need it. They're going to push you hard. I mean really hard. These sorts of training schedules are designed to work out how tough you are. How resilient under pressure. How adaptable to change. Not everyone will make the grade.'

'I know.' I shivered at the thought. 'Do you know what happens to those who fail?'

He shrugged. 'Without being fully briefed on what exactly is going on here, I couldn't say. But I did overhear some of the officers when I arrived. They didn't know I was there and were speaking quite freely about how only a fraction of you recruits are expected to pass. They are already talking of getting rid of some of you so they can concentrate on the better candidates.'

I bit my lip. I couldn't lose this. It was too important. 'Getting rid how?'

'I've no idea. I imagine you'll just get sent back to your previous post. Or maybe transferred sideways to something like the Land Army.'

A heavy lump settled in my chest. The Land Army definitely hadn't featured in my plans. And no way would I let them send me home.

13

'You're quiet, Wren. Is something bothering you?' Connie spoke around a massive mouthful of Woolton pie. Minus any suggestion of meat, the filling beneath the pastry was packed with cabbage, turnip and swede. It was surprisingly tasty.

Given how intense the afternoon had been, I was ravenous, yet I couldn't shake a sense of impending doom. I poked my food with my fork. 'Did you know that most of us aren't expected to pass this training scheme? That they're already looking for ways to weed people out?'

Louisa sniffed. 'Stands to reason, doesn't it?'

'Does it?' asked Fliss.

'Of course, it does,' butted in Lexi in a *how stupid are you?* kind of tone. 'That's why we've been given so little information. It's why we're not to get too close to each other. They don't think most of us are up to snuff, and the less we know about what's actually going on here, the better.'

The colour drained from Connie's face. 'That does make sense.'

'I know,' I said. 'I really don't want to fail at this.'

Lexi snorted, her lip curling.

I slammed my fork down. 'What *is* your problem, Lexi?'

'You,' she said. 'You're my problem.'

'Why?'

'Keep it down, you two,' hissed Fliss. 'People are staring.'

I darted an anxious glance around. We were definitely drawing attention.

Lexi cursed, shoved herself away from the table, dumped her empty plate at the clearance station and left.

I leapt to my feet and followed, breaking into a run to catch up with her. 'Don't just walk away from me. We need to sort this out.'

'Oh, leave it, Wren, will you?'

I grabbed her arm, forcing her to stop. 'No, I won't. You don't like me. Fine. But what did I do?'

She rounded on me. 'It's not what you've done. It's what you *are*.'

'Eh?'

'Look at you. You think you're perfect, don't you?'

Perfect? If only she knew. No one had ever described me as perfect. 'What are you talking about?'

'How dare you criticise my running technique to everyone.'

'I didn't... I—'

'You did. Connie said that you said I have to *relax* and *settle into my stride*.' She poked my chest with a pointy finger. 'If you have something to say about me, you say it to me. To my face. Do you hear?'

For goodness' sake. No wonder she was cross if she thought I was talking about her behind her back. I cast my mind back. What on earth had I said? 'I swear, Lexi. I wasn't talking about *you*. I was talking about running in general.'

'Like I'd believe that.' She whirled away. 'I didn't come down in the last shower.'

'It's true.' I hurried after her. 'All I've done is try to be friendly. That first day, you fell over. I tried to help. You didn't appreciate it so I backed off. I am sorry if I upset you. I didn't mean to. Please, can we just clear the air?'

'You think you're better than me. You think you're better than everyone with your posh accent and your fancy-pants name. *Wren.*' She spat the word as if it tasted foul. 'It's not even a real name.'

That was a bit rich considering Lexi wasn't exactly conventional either. 'It's a nickname. It's short for Serenity.'

'If that's not snooty, then I don't know what is. Are you landed gentry, or something?'

'Wren?' Behind me, Jo's voice was heavy with concern.

My face burned when I realised that the others had caught up with us and were listening. Suddenly I was a child again, watching all the village girls play, knowing that I wouldn't be welcome if I tried to join in because of who my family were. Once the recruits knew, any chance of being socially included would disappear. It was better to get it over with, rather than maintain false hope.

'My father owns a manor house and some land, yes,' I muttered.

'There you are then.' She put her hands on her hips with an air of triumph. 'See?'

'See, what?' I asked. 'Are you saying that you hate anyone who isn't from the same social class as you?'

'No. Of course not. That would be ridiculous.'

'Then what?' I shook my head. 'The whole point of this place is to train women from all walks of life, so we can work together to protect our country.'

'She's right, Lexi,' chipped in Jo.

Lexi faltered, dashed a hand over her face and sighed. 'Look, I'm just tired. Can we leave it?'

'Can we at least agree to be civil?' I asked.

She shook her head. 'There's no point. You won't be here long. In my experience, toffs are too soft for this sort of thing.'

I stiffened at the implied insult. 'I'm not soft.'

'If you say so.'

'I do.' I stepped closer, my hands balled into fists. 'Would you like me to show you?'

'Hey, hey.' Fliss moved between us with both hands up, palms out. 'You two need to stop this before you get us all kicked out.'

Lexi scowled and stomped away.

'Don't listen to her, Wren,' said Jo. 'She's probably just as jittery about this whole training program as the rest of us are.'

I took a deep breath and released it slowly, battling to douse white-hot rage burning my core. How dare she call me soft? 'I don't care what she says. I know how tough I am.'

Connie sidled up, a troubled expression on her face. 'I didn't tell her you were talking about her, Wren. I promise. I was just trying to hand on that bit of advice you mentioned about running. I am so sorry.'

I shook my head. 'It's not your fault. I get the feeling Lexi was looking for a reason to be angry with me. I'm not sure why, but it's clear there's nothing I can do about it.'

Louisa laughed. 'She's right about one thing, mind, you do talk a bit posh. Other than that, though, I reckon you're all right.' She checked her wristwatch. 'Come on. We need to get to class. It's the last one today. If they're looking for reasons to get rid of us, like you said, we'd better not be late.'

14

The evening class was back in the main house. I had not had a chance to check the schedule to find out what subject we were learning. The moment I walked into the room, it didn't matter. Edward was stood at the front of the room watching everyone file in. My heart leapt into my mouth. He'd said he was here to teach but I hadn't expected it to be us. From the look on his face, neither had he.

I slipped into a chair near the door and tried to bring my scattered wits under control. The recent clash with Lexi had stirred up a hot mess of conflicting emotions, leaving me feeling agitated and vulnerable. I was trying so hard to fit in, and yet Lexi still saw me as an outsider. The others probably did too. The last thing I needed was everyone finding out that I knew one of the instructors. I was going to have to tread carefully.

The noise of scraping chairs and tables settled once everyone had arrived.

Edward waited until all eyes were on him. 'Can anyone tell me the difference between a code and a cypher?'

It was a simple question. I was surprised when there was no response from the class.

'Anyone?' he said, his face impassive. Edward was well aware that I knew the answer. He would expect me to reply if no one else did.

Silence stretched into discomfort. Nausea filled my belly.

He raised a single eyebrow and scanned the room as if prepared to wait all year.

My chair creaked as I raised my hand. 'Usually a code is created by exchanging words. One word might be used in place of another word, for example. It can be done with whole phrases or sentences too. A cypher transforms the individual letters, either by swapping them around or relating them to completely different symbols. Basically, you are making an unreadable format or language with a cypher.'

'Exactly,' he said. 'They can be used together or separately in order to add layers of security to a message.'

Edward gestured to a line of chalk characters written on a large wheeled blackboard. 'This is a recent communication from the enemy. Decrypting it saved hundreds of British lives. Can anyone tell me what it says?'

Silence.

'Anyone?' He stared at each student in turn until his gaze landed on me.

I closed my eyes and prayed that he wouldn't call on me again. Not in front of everyone. When I opened them again he was holding out a piece of chalk towards me. 'How about you?'

A scoff from across the room told me exactly where Lexi was.

Edward's attention darted from me to her. 'Ah. A volunteer. Excellent.' The chalk swung towards her. 'Don't be shy. Come to the front.' More silence. 'That's an order from a superior officer.' I'd never heard him use such a commanding tone before.

A chair scraped the floor. Hesitant footsteps approached and Lexi came into my line of sight. She took the chalk and stood before the string of numbers and letters, a red stain creeping up the back of her neck. The steady tick-tick-tick from the clock on the wall grew louder as she shifted from foot to foot.

Edward sighed. 'Would anyone else like to try?'

There were reluctant murmurs and shaken heads all around. Edward's gaze fell on me, his face impassive. 'You?'

I swallowed and stood up. Ignoring the daggers Lexi threw at me as she handed over the chalk, I focused on the board. If there was one thing I felt relatively confident about it was basic coding. This one didn't follow any standard I'd seen before. Loath to stand in silence like Lexi had, I started talking through what I knew. 'If it's an enemy transmission, I'll assume that the answer is not written in English.' I glanced at Edward for confirmation.

He nodded, his face giving nothing else away.

I grunted and studied the sequence again. 'It doesn't work monoalphabetically, and it's not transposition. Could it be...? Hmm. No. Interesting.' Conscious of Lexi's eyes boring into my back, I fixed Edward with a challenging stare. 'There is not enough information here. This message can't be decoded without a key or some other form of assistance. It's far too sophisticated.'

He grinned. 'You're right.' He turned to the rest of the class. 'The art of communicating with secret messages has moved on in leaps and bounds since the Great War. The enemy are using complex machines with sophisticated keys. As fast as we break them, they change tack. When you are deployed, you won't be expected to break enemy codes. We have people doing that.'

'So, what do we do?' The question came from the far side of the class, I couldn't see who.

'You need to be able to recognise an enemy transmission when you hear one. Then, make careful note of it, exactly as it is, and pass it on up the chain of command as fast as you can. To do that, you will need a solid understanding of both coding and cyphering.' He glanced at the clock. 'We're going to spend the next couple of hours going through the basic principles.'

True to his word, he drilled the whole class on basic Morse code and then increasingly complicated alphabetical substitutions and key codes until everyone had a good working knowledge. By the time we were done, we all staggered from the room, our heads awhirl with dots and dashes, and strings of numbers, letters and symbols.

15

'Where did you learn coding, then?' asked Jo, as we queued up for breakfast the next morning.

I shrugged, not wanting to admit to my obsession with numbers. 'My brother was into maths puzzles when we were children. He taught me. We developed our own special code. We used it to send each other secret messages that Father couldn't understand. It was fun. I suppose, it becomes second nature after a while.'

'That Captain Landers is a bit of a dish, isn't he?' said Louisa as we shuffled along the line.

Jo grinned. 'His limp makes him very mysterious. I wonder what happened to him.'

Keen not to get into a discussion about Edward, I asked, 'What have we got on this morning?'

'We're back in the classroom,' said Connie, tugging a copy of the schedule from her pocket. 'It says explosives training and then we've got guerrilla warfare. Goodness. They sound jolly alarming.'

Jo rubbed her hands with glee. 'Explosives? Excellent. I love a bit of chemistry. Blowing stuff up is always fun.'

'Where did you study chemistry?' I asked.

'Study?' She huffed. 'Don't make me laugh. Where would I get the chance to study anything other than home-making and all the other boring stuff we girls get offered. Oh look!' She pointed at the food being served. 'Bacon with bubble and squeak. Delicious.'

It did smell good. I accepted my helping and followed her over to our table. 'You sound like you already have a good working knowledge of explosives. What do you think we're going to cover?'

She shrugged. 'Who knows. But if it's anything like the lesson we had on radios, they'll probably teach us how to build improvised devices from everyday ingredients. You know, using fertilisers and such.'

I didn't know and was impressed that she did. I wasn't sure how I felt about creating things that could hurt and possibly kill, but this was war. I was going to have to get used to it.

Connie's eyes were huge. 'You mean we're going to build real bombs?'

Jo shook her head. 'I doubt we'll build anything dangerous today. We'll probably learn the basics of making them, rather than actually construct them. It's amazing how much damage you can do with a bit of gelignite and some shrapnel in a biscuit tin.'

Connie made a small whimpering sound. 'I don't think I want to know how you know that.'

'Four older brothers, a father and two uncles,' said Jo, her tone matter-of-fact. 'All in the military.'

I couldn't help wondering what we women could achieve on our own merit if we weren't restricted to knowledge passed on from handy male relatives. 'You know,' I said, swallowing my last mouthful of bacon, 'it strikes me that we all already have different areas of expertise.'

'How do you mean?' said Louisa.

'Well,' I said, 'Fliss understands the electronics, Jo seems confident with explosives.'

'And you understand coding,' interrupted Connie. 'I haven't any useful skills.'

'That's not true,' I said, wondering why she was always putting herself down. 'I saw you drawing last night during the coding session.'

She hung her head. 'Oh, that was only a scribble to help me think.'

I laughed. 'It was a scribble that was the spitting image of Louisa.'

'Was it?' Louisa's head shot up. 'Let me see.'

Connie shook her head. 'It's back at the hut. I'll show you later.'

'And you translated that French message yesterday evening, too,' I said.

'She's right,' said Louisa. 'You sound like a native.'

Connie lifted a dainty shoulder. 'My grandmother is French and her father was from Austria. She's always spoken to me in either French or German. But languages are easy. You just put a bunch of sounds in the right order.'

'That's definitely one way of looking at it,' said Louisa. 'How's this for putting a bunch of sounds in the right order?' She pursed her lips and the sweet whistle of a robin filled the air.

All noise in the immediate vicinity hushed. Heads turned.

'That's incredible,' said Jo.

I leaned closer. 'Can you do anything else, Louisa?'

She cupped her hands into a ball in front of her mouth. A low cooing sound emerged.

'I know that one,' I said. 'That's that coastal bird that comes in the winter. Oh, what's it called?'

'A great northern diver,' muttered one of the women at the next table. 'Gosh! That reminds me of home. Do it again.'

Louisa complied.

'Can you do a song thrush?' another woman asked.

A ripple of light, pretty notes filled the air.

'That's beautiful,' said Fliss.

'What about a wood pigeon?' The request came from another table.

I sat back and watched as Louisa switched to a gentle coo reminiscent of warm summers in the country. Several women approached our table with requests.

'Louisa,' exclaimed Jo. 'You're a natural mimic. How do you do it?'

Louisa raised one shoulder. 'I don't know. I just can.'

'Can you show us how?' asked Fliss, her eyes dancing with delight.

'I can try. The northern diver is an easy one. Look, you cup your hands like this.' She formed a hollow ball shape. 'And you press both thumbs together like this, so that there's a tiny diamond shape between them. Then you blow.'

Huffing and puffing from multiple quarters followed, along with snorts of merriment.

'Hold on... hold on... I think I've got it,' said one woman. A wobbly hooting emerged to a round of cheers.

Louisa laughed. 'Yes, well done. All you need to do now, is practice.'

More hoots, gaining in strength, came from the crowd around our table and before long the whole mess tent was filled with the noise of a flock of great northern divers. For a short time, everyone was laughing and chatting together before dispersing back to their own tables.

'See?' I said to Connie once it was just us again. 'That is what I mean, we all have different skills. I think we're missing a trick if we don't pool our resources. We could teach each other all sorts of things. Like when Fliss helped me, yesterday.'

'It's not a bad idea,' said Louisa. 'We could review things in the evenings before we go to sleep.'

'Is it worth it?' asked Jo.

'I think so.' I nodded. 'I mean, who knows where we're going to get sent after here. Even if we don't pass this training, they'll make use of us somewhere. Knowledge is power. We've no idea what we might need to know in order to survive. What do you think? Shall we do it?'

'There's no harm in a few hours of extra study,' muttered Jo. 'My bunk is so hard, I'm not getting much sleep anyway.'

'Watch out.' Connie nudged my arm. 'Captain Dishy just arrived.'

I didn't dare look. What on earth was he doing in the women's mess tent? I ran a finger across the surface of the table, examining the grain of the wood as if it were suddenly the most fascinating thing on the planet.

'He's coming over,' squeaked Louisa.

She didn't need to tell me. The prickling at the back of my neck told me he was behind me before he appeared in my peripheral vision. Edward nodded a greeting to my companions before touching my shoulder.

'Do you have a moment?' he said.

The other girls exchanged glances. Eyebrows were raised. I was on my feet before I knew I was going to comply, my face flaming. The weight of multiple curious looks followed us as we left the canteen.

'With respect,' I said, my heart beating so hard that I was sure he could hear it, 'I'm not sure it's good for us to be seen associating with each other. You're an instructor and I'm... well, I'm nobody.'

'You're not nobody,' he said, pulling his cap from his head and tucking it under his arm. 'But you're probably right about not being seen together.'

So why on earth was he here? Was he trying to make trouble for me?

'Don't worry. It's not going to be a problem. I'm leaving in half an hour.'

'Oh.' Unexpected regret crept around my heart. He might have pompous opinions, but he was still a connection to Tommy. Plus, there was the strange backflip that my stomach did whenever I saw him. I'd miss that. 'Where are you going?'

'Hopefully to learn what my permanent posting is. I wanted to say goodbye and good luck.'

'Thank you. You didn't have to.' But I was so glad he had.

'It felt wrong to just leave.'

I should have left it there, but curiosity got the better of me. 'Why?'

'I wanted to apologise for overstepping the mark before. It's not my place to tell you what to do. It's just...' He took two paces away, pulling his cap from under his arm and twisting it around by the brim. A series of expressions that I couldn't identify raced across his face.

'Edward? You're worrying me. What is it?'

He gave a low growl. 'You confuse me, Wren.'

I didn't know what to say to that.

'You're not like other women,' he said.

'Tell me something I don't know,' I said, stepping away, inky sadness pooling around my heart. I knew I was different; I didn't need Edward rubbing it in. I stared at the ground. 'Father is always reminding me of my lack of accomplishments.'

'That's not what I mean.' He paused as if searching for the right words. 'You're brave and determined. And...'

It took me several seconds to register his words as praise. I glanced up in surprise. This had never happened to me. And I couldn't let him stop there. 'And what?'

'Bloody obstinate. You're the most exasperating, incredible woman I've ever met.' That was said with an accompanying eye roll.

The bashful grin on his face made me laugh out loud. He laughed as well. Our shared merriment triggered bubbles of happiness that skipped through my veins. I shouldn't care what he thought of me. But, somehow, his good opinion meant everything, and in that moment, I felt as if I could take on the world and win. 'You realise that I am going to take that as positive encouragement, don't you?' I said.

'Oh, you should. You definitely should.' He smiled. Our eyes locked together and we stared at each other in silence. I wanted to stay in that moment forever. Then his face dropped and he stepped back. 'You are also Tommy's sister.' He grimaced and slapped his cap onto his head. 'Which is *my* problem, not yours.' He stood to attention and saluted. 'Keep safe, Private Ashworth. I hope we meet again.'

Before I could return the salute, he was gone. I stood rooted to the spot, shocked by the abruptness of his departure and his final words. *'I hope we meet again.'* The cold reality that we might not see each other again for a long time, if ever, sank in and I shivered.

16

Edward's parting remark weighed on my mind. Why should me being Tommy's sister be a problem for him? Fortunately, there was so much to learn that I had very little time to dwell on the frustrating man. Instead I concentrated on developing as many new skills as I possibly could. Spending time with the other girls in the hut doing extra revision sessions proved to be a lot of fun too.

'So, these are your sticks of gelignite,' said Jo, laying a series of thick twigs along the top of her bunk in a line. She held up a piece of string. 'And imagine this is Cordtex. You pass it through each stick in turn like a string of sausages.'

Connie moaned. 'I miss sausages.'

'So, do I,' said Louisa with a snigger.

'Louisa!' Fliss dissolved into scandalised giggles. 'Behave yourself!'

'What did I say?' asked Louisa, her eyes wide.

'Shush, you lot,' said Jo. 'This is important. Remember. You need to leave about nine inches of string between each sausage.'

There was another small moan. I nudged Connie.

'Sorry,' she whispered. 'But, for the record, I meant real sausages.'

'So did I,' said Louisa, a wicked twinkle in her eyes.

Fliss shot them both a look, the corners of her mouth twitching. 'Trust me, Connie, you don't want to eat this sort of sausage.'

The room dissolved into raucous cackles. I clutched my stomach, trying to catch my breath.

'Oh! Come on, girls,' said Jo. 'Do you want to know about this, or not?' The exasperation in her voice made everything funnier. It took us a while to compose ourselves. She crossed her arms and waited.

'Sorry, Jo,' I said, striving to present a suitably serious expression. 'Please carry on.'

'Right. You stuff the sausages into a length of old cast-iron pipe...' She paused. We all ducked our heads, biting our cheeks, not daring to catch each other's eyes. 'And there you are. One booby trap pipe bomb ready for action.'

Lexi turned away to throw herself on her bunk and stare at the ceiling. 'You don't find bits of cast-iron pipe lying around just anywhere, mind. Even the iron railings have been melted down for tanks.'

Trust her to find something critical to say. Jo had put a lot of effort into helping us all. I worried that Lexi's dismissive comment might hurt her feelings.

'I saw plenty of bits of old pipe in the rubble after bombing raids in London,' I said. 'It just depends where you are and what you can get your hands on.'

Lexi yawned, turned away and bashed her pillow into a more comfortable configuration. It seemed a casual move, but I knew it was a display of disdain aimed at me. It was really hard not to react. I bit my tongue. If I said anything, it would only end up making me look bad.

'Adaptability,' said Jo. 'That's the key. If you know what the basic ingredients are, you can fashion all sorts of explosive devices.'

'Like what?' asked Connie.

I noticed Lexi turn her head a fraction so that she could still hear us.

'If you've got access to potassium nitrate, charcoal and sulphur, plus some sort of fuse, or even a narrow wire that you can pass a short electric current through,' said Jo, 'then all you need is to pack it all into something, for example, a biscuit tin.'

'Doesn't charcoal burn really slowly?' I asked.

Jo nodded. 'That's why these devices can be unpredictable. Whatever you do, don't ever go back to one after you've set it. As soon as that slow burn reaches all the other ingredients...'

'Boom!' said Connie, her face pale.

'Exactly.' Jo shrugged. 'You can add shrapnel to the tin too. It can be as simple as small stones if you haven't got ball bearings or nails or anything else. The whole thing together is pretty lethal.'

'I guess it's destruction on two levels,' said Louisa. 'The main explosion causes a fireball, and the shrapnel sprays out like bullets in all directions.'

We stared at the string of twig sausages on the table in silence. There was no hint of our previous amusement remaining. I desperately hoped I would never have to use the knowledge. I could only guess that my companions' thoughts were running along similar lines to my own. 'Well,' I said. 'That's one lesson I am never going to forget. Thanks, Jo.'

She grinned. 'You're welcome.'

A heavy knock on the door made us all jump. Sergeant

Banks poked his head in. 'Constance. Felicity. Pack your kit. You're both being reassigned. Report to the main hall in half an hour.' He was gone before anyone could speak.

We stared at each other in alarm.

Connie went white. 'Reassigned? Reassigned where?'

Edward had said this would happen. I'd expected to have more warning.

A creak sounded from Lexi's bunk. She swung her feet to the floor, her face serious. 'Best of luck with wherever they send you.' The sincerity in her words made me think that this sudden development had shaken her as much as it had me.

Connie's shoulders slumped. 'Four weeks. I made it through four weeks of training. They started sending other girls away ages ago. I kept thinking it would be me, but it wasn't. I stupidly began to think I might make it. And now it's over.' She shook her head, her eyes on the floor. 'I knew I wasn't good enough.'

I wrapped an arm around her and gave her an encouraging squeeze. 'You are good enough. Don't ever believe otherwise.' I wished I could convince her of that and hoped that wherever she was sent, she would be appreciated for the kind and funny person she was.

'They've probably seen how amazing your language skills are,' said Jo, 'and need you somewhere else.'

'Exactly,' I said. 'And, wherever they send you, you'll still be serving your country.'

'You'll be brilliant at it,' said Louisa. 'You too, Fliss.'

Fliss wrinkled her nose. 'Thank you, but you don't need to worry about me. I already know where they're sending me.'

'What?' Jo gave her arm a mock punch. 'Have you been holding out on us?'

Fliss pulled a face. 'We're not supposed to share information. Remember?' She shrugged. 'But, without giving too much away, I met Major Stapleton a couple of years ago, shortly after war broke out. I think she was already planning this secret army of hers; it's just taken her a while to put all the pieces into play. I knew when I came here that I wouldn't be staying for the whole six weeks. I was only here to pick up some specific skills. I've enjoyed meeting you all, though, and I wish you luck for whatever is to come.'

Stunned silence filled the cabin. None of us had expected that. Although, it made sense when I thought about it. Fliss had always seemed more confident and self-contained than the rest of us, a calming presence in the background. Part of the group yet also slightly apart from it.

Connie's shoulders slumped. 'That means I'm the only failure round here.'

'No, it doesn't,' said Fliss. 'Major Stapleton has a plan up her sleeve for each one of us. That's why she chose us. We all have a part to play. We just have to trust her.'

Connie nodded, her face solemn. 'If you say so.'

'Come on,' said Louisa, giving Connie's arm a bracing rub. 'We'll help you pack.'

We jollied Connie along, as we stowed her things in her kitbag, but the idea of parting was painful for all of us. As I hugged her goodbye, I had an idea. 'How about we arrange to meet up after all this is over?'

She dashed a hand over her face. 'You mean, after the war?' The wobble in Connie's smile triggered an ominous warmth behind my eyes.

I blinked furiously. 'Yes.'

'We can't,' said Jo.

'Why not?' I asked.

'We're not supposed to share personal details, remember,' said Fliss.

'We don't need personal details,' I said. 'Let's agree to meet in London. Nelson's column, Trafalgar Square at midday on May 1st of whichever year comes straight after the end of the war. We can meet the second year too, just in case some of us are delayed the first time around. And the year after.'

'That's a great idea.' Louisa grinned. 'Let's do it.'

'Yes. Let's,' said Fliss.

Connie smiled. This time it reached her eyes. 'I'd like that.'

17

With Connie and Fliss gone, the atmosphere in the hut intensified. Any one of us could be next. I was determined to last the final two weeks. Time seemed to speed up with the days slipping past in the blink of an eye as we all worked longer and harder, and took every opportunity to practise all aspects of the training sessions we attended. With Jo and Louisa's help, I worked on hand-to-hand combat and started landing on my backside less and less. In turn, I was able to help them with other things.

'So, how come you're such a good shot?' asked Louisa, as we walked back to the hut after a session on firearms. The smell of burnt gunpowder from the spent cartridges clung to us, stinging our nostrils.

'It's part of life where I grew up,' I replied. 'My brother and I spent a lot of time with the local gamekeeper. He taught us how to handle a shotgun.'

'For shooting pheasant?' asked Jo.

'No.' I pulled a face. 'I couldn't bring myself to actually kill anything. I just practised firing at pine cones balanced on logs.

That sort of thing. But Tommy and the gamekeeper shot rats mainly. Occasionally rabbits for the pot. Sometimes deer if they were old or sick.'

'Bunnies and deer.' The dismay in Jo's voice was clear. 'But, they're so cute.'

'They are,' I agreed. 'But in the forest, especially with the deer, it's important to cull the population to keep the rest of the herd healthy.'

'Well you've got a good aim,' said Louisa.

I was glad that they were teaching us to shoot a variety of firearms. While I was confident with a shotgun, a handgun was a completely different kettle of fish. I was going to need a lot of practice. Women were not supposed to be in active combat but, if Major Stapleton's prediction of a German invasion came to pass, there was no knowing what we would have to do to survive. I wanted as many skills at my fingertips as possible.

Jo opened the door to our hut. 'We've got a session on stealth later. Is that something your gamekeeper taught you too?'

I followed her inside. 'We spent a lot of time tracking. You have to move really quietly for that. I guess the main principles can be transferred to covert movement anywhere.' A picture of Tommy and I as ten-year-olds trying to sneak up on each other in the forest sprang to mind, bringing with it a wistful sense of longing. Was I ever going to see him again?

'Go on then,' said Louisa, slumping down onto her bunk. 'What are your five top tips? Let's see if we can all give whoever is teaching us a surprise with our expertise.'

'All right.' I blew out my cheeks, sorting through information in my mind. 'Stealth is about not being seen *and* not being heard. So, for starters you need quiet clothing in both senses: what you can see and what you can hear.' I tugged on my shirt.

'This kit they've given us is good. It's not loud, not in a visual sense. The colours are dull and fade into the background.'

'Ugh!' Jo shuddered. 'Fading into the background is against my religion.'

I grinned. 'And the fabric itself doesn't crackle when you scrunch it. If you can move in a way that doesn't rub cloth against itself to make a swishing noise or a rustle, that's really important.'

'Like this?' Louisa sprang to her feet and mimed walking up and down with her arms and legs wide apart so her trouser legs didn't rub against each other.

I laughed. 'Kind of. Only, if you walk down the street like that, you're going to attract attention. Everyone will think you're loopy.'

'They'll think that anyway,' teased Jo. 'They've just got take one look at you, Lou, to know you're away with the fairies.'

Louisa poked her tongue out. They both laughed. Their daft antics made me feel warm inside. Building genuine friendships on this training scheme was something I hadn't anticipated. I wanted to hold these moments close, so I could remember them later.

'What you're saying makes sense, Wren,' said Jo. 'Even if it doesn't make me like this outfit any more. What else can you tell us?'

I scratched my head. 'You must always pay attention to your surroundings. That's where the forest will differ from other places.'

Jo narrowed her eyes. 'What sort of things are we looking for?'

I cast my mind back to Ashworth, picturing the trees, the undergrowth, the ground cover. I had loved the parts of my childhood that had been spent out of doors, away from the pressures of trying to be a sensible young lady. The words of the old gamekeeper who had taught us to track herds of deer echoed down the years.

'Be careful of anything that will make a sound if you come into contact with it,' I said. 'In the forest, that might be a low-hanging branch or a bush. Brushing against them makes the leaves rustle. And if you tread on twigs on the ground they might snap. You always want to slide your foot underneath things like that. Make sure you're putting your weight directly onto the ground.'

'Rather like not stepping on a squeaky floorboard or a loose step on the stairs,' said Louisa.

'Exactly,' I said. 'If doing that makes a noise, then find another way.'

'We had a creaky stair back home,' said Jo. 'If I stepped really close to the wall, where it was supported, rather than right in the middle, it didn't make a sound.'

'See?' I said. 'You've got this licked already.'

'Aye, aye.' Louisa raised an eyebrow at Jo. 'How come you were sneaking up the stairs? Or were you going down? Were you going out to meet a fella, perhaps?'

Jo blushed. 'None of your beeswax.'

I glanced from Jo to Louisa and back again, trying not to giggle. Would I ever feel confident enough in a friendship to tease someone like that?

'Basically, you just need to go slowly and deliberately,' I said. 'And, if you have to do something that will make a noise, wait until something else happens that will mask the sound.'

'Like my dad snoring,' muttered Jo.

Louisa snorted with laughter. 'You were definitely meeting a fella.'

18

Whether it was our shared knowledge or simply good luck, Jo, Louisa and I managed to stay together for the remainder of the training course, with Lexi hovering on our periphery. The number of other girls present in class dwindled steadily. No one said anything about the empty spaces in the mess hall. Instead we concentrated on consolidating information. Days were packed with knife-defence techniques, pistol training, rifle drills, explosives manufacture, use of grenades, orienteering, stealth, aircraft and ship recognition, and so much more than I had ever thought possible; to the point that I thought my head would explode.

The final afternoon at Hannington was upon us before we knew it.

Louisa burst into the cabin, her eyes wide with apprehension. 'We're all to meet on the main driveway in an hour. We have to go to the supply cabin first.'

'Did they say why?' I asked.

She wrinkled her nose. 'Apparently, we're all being issued with special kit for wherever we're going.'

'Lovely,' said Jo. 'Yet more puce-green and grey to wear.'

Louisa bounced on her toes, full of nervous excitement. 'There are six covered trucks out front. I reckon they're for us.'

'Where do you think we'll be sent?' said Jo.

'Wherever it is, there's no way any of us will get to stay together. So, don't go getting your hopes up,' muttered Lexi.

I bit back a sharp retort, telling myself that she was probably nervous about what was happening. 'We don't have to be together to support each other. The important thing is that *we* know that we've got each other's backs. Always.'

Lexi tutted. 'You talk such rubbish, Wren.' She grabbed her bag, and nodded at Louisa and Jo. 'Good luck,' she said and stomped from the hut.

Jo put a hand on my arm. 'Don't listen to her, Wren. You're right. It doesn't matter where we get sent. This war can't stop us being friends.'

'Exactly,' said Louisa, fastening the toggles on her bag. 'They can't stop us thinking about each other and wishing each other well.'

'We'd better say goodbye properly now, though,' said Jo. 'In case we don't get a chance later.'

A jagged lump in my throat made speech almost impossible as I gave my first real friends in the world a farewell hug. I wasn't ready for this to end. I could only hope that at least some of us were going to move on to the next phase of training together.

19

An hour later, sat on a wooden slatted bench, right at the back of a canvas-covered army truck, a tightly packed rucksack at my feet along with my gas mask box tied to the outside of it with string, I squashed down a wave of panic that threatened to swallow me whole. There were seven other women in the truck, all from different cohorts. Only one was from the group I had arrived at Hannington with: Lexi. Apprehension spread through my middle as I peered through the canvas flap at the rear of the truck and watched Hannington Hall recede in the distance.

We journeyed through the night. Barely able to see anything in the darkness. No one spoke. Being thrown around in the back of the truck every time the wheels hit a pothole made it almost impossible to rest. At one point, it seemed as if we were being driven around in circles, which might have been a deliberate ploy to disorientate us. I gave up trying to mentally plot our route. Wherever we were going was a long way away. I tugged the lapels of the dull brown woollen coat I'd been issued closer together in an attempt to ward off the encroaching chill. Leaning my head back against one of the wooden support beams holding up the canvas cover, I settled into a fitful doze.

Hours later, fingers of dawn spread through the sky. I peeped through the canvas flap again and watched the world wake up. Eventually, the brakes squealed. I grabbed the bench to stop sliding sideways into the woman next to me as the truck came to a stop. A door slammed.

'Come on, you lot,' came a shout. The deep voice was far too cheerful for such an early hour. A sergeant I'd never seen before poked his head through the flap. 'Wakey-wakey, sleeping beauties. Rise and shine.'

Groans were stifled and limbs, stiff from the hours sat still, stretched. One by one, we scrambled down onto a narrow gravel track that cut through isolated moorland. Thick woodland lurked on one side of the road, and a wide expanse of dry grass, heather and broom on the other. Beyond that, fields rolled away into the distance, criss-crossed with drystone walls and dotted with sheep.

The sergeant pounded the side of the truck once we were all out. The engine revved, the horn sounded and the truck drove away.

'Follow me,' he said and set off into the trees along what looked like a random animal track.

Eyes gritty with exhaustion, I shouldered my rucksack and fell into step, swaying slightly at the unaccustomed extra weight. We marched deep into the wood until the sergeant stopped at the edge of a small clearing. He glanced around, then pushed between a thick set of bushes and crouched low to the ground to roll back a section of fabric camouflaged with dried sticks and leaves. Underneath was a circular metal hatchway set into a concrete plinth. He hauled the hatch cover open to reveal an iron ladder descending into the earth.

Murmurs of surprise rippled through the group.

'Down you go,' he said.

I saw Lexi recoil. She fixed the sergeant with her signature stare. 'You're having us on. There's no way we'll all fit down there.'

'You're having us on, *sir*,' he barked. 'And, you *will* fit, because I have told you to.' He pointed down into the hole. 'Now get a move on.'

One by one, we descended the ladder. The rucksacks on our backs made it awkward, but with a bit of wiggling, it was possible to ease down into the concrete chamber below. It was much larger underground than I expected, although, as each new body arrived at the bottom of the ladder, we were forced to shuffle closer together. There was a lengthy pause before Lexi finally deigned to join us. Whether she was having trouble manoeuvring through the hole or just being obtuse, I couldn't tell. When she finally arrived, she stared around in disgust, like a queen in close proximity to dirt for the very first time.

I clamped my teeth together. Why did she always have to be difficult?

The sergeant was the last down, pulling the hatch closed behind him. Once it was secure, he tugged on a slim rope, which I could only assume flipped the fabric outside back over the hatch to hide it. Without daylight I had expected to be plunged into darkness. Instead, a series of small electric lights glowed. They were secured in metal cages attached to the ceiling and lead out of the chamber into a corridor. The sergeant shouldered past Lexi. I pressed back against the wall to allow him through.

'This way,' he said.

The corridor led deeper into the earth to a second, larger passageway. I noted concrete supports interspersed with reinforced steel sections of wall and roof. The sheer size of such a hidden facility was an amazing feat of engineering. How was it possible to have so much underground? Doors peppered the walls at regular intervals. Eventually, the sergeant stopped, opened one and waved us in. 'Wait in here.'

The room was large with a long table at one end. Alongside a large teapot, cups and saucers and a bowl of apples, sat a large plate of sliced national loaf and fish paste sandwiches and a smaller plate of honeyed biscuits. The warm, sweet aroma from the latter made my stomach rumble.

Lexi stowed her rucksack at the side of the room and dived on the teapot to pour herself a cup. 'What?' she demanded, seeing that all eyes were on her. 'Who else is this for, if not us?' She reached for a sandwich. 'I say we eat. There's no telling when we'll next get a chance.'

Something in her voice and the set of her jaw struck me as odd. She'd always been prickly but I'd never seen her so on edge. Her defiance held a touch of something I couldn't quite put my finger on.

'She's got a point,' I said, taking an apple and sinking my teeth into it. 'We can always apologise if we're wrong.'

One by one, people reached for sustenance, drifting towards wooden chairs arranged around the room. We ate in silence.

The door opened again and Major Stapleton walked in. Immediately, we all stood to attention, the atmosphere tense with anticipation.

'Ah, good. You've arrived. At ease.' The major showed no interest in the fact that we had all armed ourselves with refreshments. 'Do any of you have any idea where you are?'

We all exchanged blank looks.

'Excellent.' She gave a nod of satisfaction. 'Sit, please.' There was a compliant scraping of serviceable chairs. 'The good news is that all of you passed every aspect of the first phase of training with flying colours. Well done. You are the best of the best.'

'Can we ask what happened to the others, ma'am?' asked a small dark-haired woman from the back of the room. 'I get that this is all highly confidential, but people kept disappearing over the last few weeks. It would be nice to know that they're all right.'

Murmured agreement rippled around the room.

The major gave a brisk nod. 'It's a fair question. I can assure you that everyone is fine. There are many layers to this special operation. We simply reassigned cadets to different projects as each of their specific strengths became clear. There was no point forcing them through the rest of the program when they are going to be more useful to us in a different area. It's as simple as that.'

'What happens to *us* now, ma'am?' asked Lexi.

'Now, we get down to the hard stuff.' Major Stapleton pulled a clipboard from under her arm. 'You will be working in pairs for the next week. After which time, if you perform as I expect, you will be fully briefed about this special operations project and your part in it for the road ahead.'

'What exactly will we be doing?' Lexi's tone was short, which surprised me. She was usually very respectful to the officers.

The major didn't appear to notice. 'Each pair will be assigned a small underground bunker, much like this larger facility you are in at the moment. That is your operational base. There you will find enough survival equipment to withstand an extended period of time. Whilst there, you will build yourselves a radio and monitor the airways. You are expected to decode incoming messages, follow orders and complete any tasks you are set. You will eat, sleep and live underground, except when ordered to leave the bunker to carry out missions.'

'What missions, ma'am?' asked a woman at the back of the room.

'Dummy assignments that will occupy your time whilst enabling us to test your resilience and initiative. For the most part, the top brass refuse to consider that women can be involved in active combat in this war. Hence, we are assigned supporting roles like drivers, secretaries and nurses. But, I know we can do far more. To that end, I plan to push you, to see exactly what you are made of.'

I glanced at Lexi, half expecting some pithy comment to be forthcoming. Her eyes were fixed on the ground.

'If you perform well over the next week, then you will be inducted into one of the most top-secret projects of the war effort so far. If not, then you will be reassigned.' Major Stapleton opened a notebook. 'These are your pairs.' She started to reel off names.

I listened with a growing sense of dread as I realised exactly who my partner was going to be. From the look on her face, Lexi was clearly as delighted at this development as I was. Fortunately, we both had the sense not to say anything.

'You were issued with extra clothing at Hannington,' the major continued. 'You will have noticed the colour. This is deliberate. Can anyone tell me why?'

'Does Churchill like women in muddy green and grey?' joked the woman at the back.

Major Stapleton smiled. 'Even if he does, that's not the answer I'm looking for.'

'For crying out loud,' muttered Lexi, before raising her voice. 'It's camouflage.'

'Exactly. These outfits will allow you to blend in to most settings. Your aim is to pass unobserved wherever you are. When you left Hannington, yesterday, you were also issued with a rucksack. This wasn't just so that you could pack your clothes to come here. In your rucksack, you should have a torch, matches, a map, two twenty-four-hour ration packs similar to those issued to our men on active service, mess tins, matches, a compass, a length of lightweight rope, a water bottle and some provisions.' She unclipped some sheets of paper from her board and started handing them out. 'I am giving each pair a copy of their individual orders. You will see two sets of co-ordinates. The first is where you are now. The second location is your assigned bunker. The rest is up to you.' She looked at each of us in turn. 'I will see you in four days. Good luck.' With that, she turned and left the room.

Murmurs broke out and the group split into couples to read their orders. Instead of joining me, Lexi hoisted her rucksack onto her back and wandered over to the table of food.

I followed, watching her help herself to another sandwich. 'More food?' I asked.

'I eat when I'm stressed,' she muttered. 'Anyway, it makes sense to take some of this with us. Have you seen the contents of the ration packs? Dried meat cubes, oats, powdered tea and those weirdly hard chocolate blocks that don't really taste of chocolate at all.' She stuffed a couple of honeyed biscuits into one pocket and an apple in the other. 'Come on. You know I'm right.'

I tucked an apple into my pocket. 'Happy now? How come you're stressed, Lexi? I know you don't like me. Believe me, I'm not over the moon about being paired up with you either, but you're not usually this... abrasive with other people.'

'It's not about you.' She darted a furtive look at the other teams. 'Look, can we just get out of here?'

'Fine.' I grabbed a biscuit and headed back towards the hatch with her.

20

Above ground, Lexi stalked off into the forest.

I scampered behind her. 'Slow down. You know better than to just pick a direction and storm off. We need to work out where we are. Come on, Lexi. You'll get us lost.'

She ground to a halt, dropped her rucksack and rummaged in the side pocket for her map. 'What am I looking for?'

I reread our orders and called out the first set of co-ordinates. 'That's where the main facility is,' I said, edging closer to see the map, fully expecting her to snatch it away so that I couldn't. 'We must be here.' I pointed to a spot about a hundred yards from the hidden hatch. 'See that stream. That's just behind us.'

'And where are we heading?'

I read out the second set of co-ordinates. Together, we searched the map.

'There.' She stabbed a finger at the right location and then checked the scale. 'Bleeding Nora, it's miles away. That'll take hours.'

'We'd better get going.'

She scanned the trees, a muscle working in her jaw. 'I'm a city girl. It was bad enough adjusting to all the trees and stuff at Hannington. This forest is something else.' She shuddered. 'It's not natural.'

'I hate to break it to you, Lex, but that's exactly what it is. Nothing can be more natural than nature.'

'Don't call me Lex. And you know what I mean. It's not *normal* then. And neither is living in a hole in the ground.'

I clenched my jaw. I wasn't looking forward to the whole hidden bunker thing either, especially with her. *She* couldn't be the reason I failed this. 'I'm sure you can rough it for a week. I know I can.'

'You? Rough it? Really?'

'For goodness' sake, Lexi. I'm not the precious little princess you think I am.'

She shrugged. 'If you say so.'

'Look,' I said. 'We're stuck with each other for four days and there's nothing we can do about it. Shall we at least try to be civil?'

'Fine,' she said and set off into the forest, her pace making it clear that she would be more than happy to leave me behind if I couldn't keep up.

I matched her step for step, determined not to let her get to me. 'It was a good idea of yours to suggest we eat, back then,' I said. 'And to take extra food before we left. I didn't expect them to throw us straight in to another test almost as soon as we arrived.'

Lexi grunted, examined the map again and then altered course. 'This way.'

I gave up trying to talk to her after that and instead studied our surroundings as we walked. The route took us uphill, across several large fields and then back into woodland, where we skirted a series of small glades. Looking up, I could see dark clouds massing overhead and shivered. I hurried after her. 'Let's hope we're inside and under cover before that storm hits.'

We upped our pace. My calves and back ached with the exertion. Thick leaf litter cushioned our footfall. Periodically, we stopped to double-check our route with map and compass. Crows cawed in large untidy nests, swaying high above us in the bare branches of the oaks. Every now and then, the forest thinned out, replaced by bushes so dense we were forced to push a path through prickly gorse and heather.

Eventually, Lexi paused, scanning the undergrowth. 'It's somewhere near here.'

'I don't see anything.' There were no traces of any human presence. 'It must be camouflaged.'

'Duh! Of course, it is.'

A fat raindrop splattered onto my head, followed by another, and another. *Perfect timing.* 'Let's be systematic about this,' I said. 'We need to hurry before we're completely soaked or we'll freeze. Who knows what supplies we'll actually have down there to help us warm up or dry off.'

Lexi glared, but didn't disagree.

'I doubt it will be too close to the stream we just passed because that isn't practical. There would be a risk of flooding,' I continued. 'So, it must be hidden alongside, under or behind something.'

'I'll check those bushes over there, and those rocks,' said Lexi. 'You search behind that fallen tree.'

The tree trunk was almost as wide as I was tall. Judging from the colony of moss growing along its length, and the interlaced swathes of ivy anchoring it to the ground, it had fallen many years before and lain undisturbed ever since. I paced along one side from uptorn roots to broken branches, and back down the other side, inspecting the ground. I was about to move on when my boots caught on a collection of twigs and I stumbled. There was something strange about the ground. I squatted, brushing away leaves to reveal a sheet of camouflage netting similar to the one on the hatch at the main bunker.

'Here,' I shouted, pulling the fabric aside to reveal a hatch. It was heavy. The hinge groaned as it lifted to reveal a dark, damp hole. 'Do you want to go first?' I said.

Lexi stared at the opening for several beats.

'Come on, Lex, we're getting soaked.'

She stepped back and shook her head. 'You go.'

I pulled the torch from my pack and scrambled down the ladder, landing with more haste than grace in a cramped space made from concrete blocks and a galvanised corrugated iron panel roof, similar to the Anderson shelter at Ashworth Manor. Deep shelves stacked with boxes lined one wall.

'What can you see,' called Lexi.

'Not much. Hang on. It's some sort of supply cache.' I dug in some of the boxes. Tins of food. Blankets. Small spades. Even a tub of gelignite. Useful, but not what I was expecting. A snowball of despair rolled around in my chest, getting bigger and bigger. This couldn't be it. We needed proper shelter. There was no way we could both fit in a space this size for five minutes, let alone four days. Running my eyes over every inch of wall, I noticed a faint crack underneath the bottom shelf. It disappeared behind a large packing case. Dragging the case out revealed a square hole in the wall just big enough to crawl through. I struggled out of my rucksack and scrambled through, pulling it behind me. I emerged in a larger space. It was long and narrow, only slightly wider than me if I stood with both of my arms stretched out. There was a set of bunk beds on one side with two desks opposite, each with a paraffin lamp, and a chair. There was a door at the far end.

I lit one of the lamps and made for the door. On the other side was a pantry area with a single gas hob. There were air vents in the ceiling. A second door led on to a space that contained a lidded bucket. No prizes for guessing what that was for. A square hatchway in the far wall opened onto a cramped tunnel that led off into the darkness. Cool fresh air touched my cheeks, telling me that it must lead up and out. An escape route perhaps, should the main entrance be discovered, or maybe it was merely for ventilation. Even though it was large enough to crawl along, I wasn't tempted to do so.

I was surprised that Lexi hadn't followed me down, peppering me with tetchy questions and sarcastic remarks. I retraced my steps and clambered back up the ladder, calling out, 'It's fine. I've found it. It's small, but there's a lot packed in. Bunk beds, a pantry stuffed with tinned food, a cooking area, and a necessary.' I poked my head up through the hatch. 'Are you coming down?'

It didn't look like she had moved a muscle in all the time I'd been gone. She stared at me, wet hair plastered to her head.

'Lexi? What's wrong? Get down here out of the rain.'

'How small?'

I blinked raindrops from my eyelashes. 'Sorry?'

'How small is it?'

'Come and see.' I registered her ghostly pallor. 'Oh... Lex. Are you claustrophobic?'

'No. I just don't like small spaces.'

Now wasn't the time to argue over definitions. This must be why she'd been the last to enter the main underground facility earlier on. She was scared. Genuinely, properly scared. Poor thing. The whole time we'd been underground with Major

Stapleton, she'd looked kind of pasty and off her game. I'd put it down to the long journey and lack of sleep. A fear of confined spaces explained so much. Sadly, while I wasn't particularly fond of Lexi, as my partner, her issues were now my issues. And if *I* wanted to pass this training program, I was going to have to help *her* pass too.

I threw her an encouraging smile. 'I misspoke. It's not small. It's quite roomy, actually. You have to get past the entrance bit, which feels small because of all the boxes. Then, you have to duck under a shelf and then it opens out into a sizeable room. Come see.'

She shook her head.

'This is the only shelter we have for the next four days, Lex.' I kept my tone soft and cajoling. 'It's fine, I promise. This is no different from the main complex. And you were all right there.' I mentally crossed my fingers. 'Come on. Pass me your rucksack, then you'll find the ladder easier.'

She slowly slid the straps from her shoulders. I grabbed it. 'I'll be back in two shakes,' I said and disappeared below to store her bag on one of the bunk beds before scrambling back up the ladder. She still hadn't moved. 'All sorted,' I said. 'Just follow me. You'll be fine. You can come straight back up if you don't like it.'

She took a step towards the hatch, and stopped. She was actually shaking.

'Please try, Lexi. I can't do this without you. According to our orders, our first task down here is to build a radio. It's way more complicated than the ones we worked on at Hannington.' I crossed my fingers behind my back. 'You're much better at that than I am.'

'Fibber,' she muttered. 'You're just trying to distract me.' A small ember of interest flared in her expression in spite of her words.

I shrugged. 'Yes and no. I'm serious about the radio. It's got me stumped. Come and check it out.'

She edged towards the hatchway.

'Tell you what,' I said. 'As soon as we're settled down here, and the rain has stopped, we can come back outside and practise some self-defence. You'll feel much better once you've thumped me a few times – you know you will.'

Her eyes narrowed. 'Don't tempt me.'

Sensing victory, I tipped my head back the way we had come. 'I mean it. There was a clearing a few hundred yards back that would be perfect for it. And, who knows? Maybe you can give me some tips.'

She scowled. 'Why are you being nice to me?'

I sighed. 'Why do you think? We're stuck with each other for the next few days. And I don't know about you, but I want to pass this thing. We stand a better chance of that if we work together. So, come on.' I backed down into the storage area and waited.

She inched down the ladder. I could hear her breath coming in rapid gasps by the time she made it to the bottom. I demonstrated how to get into the main living space. She gave a small whimper, ducked low and pushed on to join me, where she stood stock-still, gazing around, her eyes wide like a startled rabbit.

I lit the second paraffin lamp. 'Which bunk would you like?' The question was intended to distract her rather than because I really cared. Limp pillows and scratchy grey blankets made neither one look particularly comfortable. 'I think the top one is roomier. The ceiling is quite high.'

'Yes. The top one. I'll have that one.'

'Fine, and which desk? The one nearest the way out?'

She nodded.

'Good choice. Look.' I gestured to radio components stacked on her desk. 'Can you build that and check in with base to find out what our orders are?' I grabbed a couple of water canisters hanging from a hook and slipped a small brown bottle of water purification tablets into my pocket. 'I'm going back up top to get some water from that stream. Then I'll make us both some hot, sweet tea.'

Lexi nodded, slid onto the chair and started rummaging through the electrical components with trembling fingers.

Back up the ladder, I paused to listen and make sure there was no one else around before hurrying to the stream. The water was cool and clear, and smelt perfectly fine to drink; even so, I added two small white tablets to each full canister just to be on the safe side. I returned to the bunker and made sure we'd left no tracks on the ground around the hatch, before pulling it closed behind me and tugging on the rope to deploy the camouflage netting. In the time that I had been gone, Lexi had built the radio. Listening intently to the headset, she searched in the desk drawer for pencil and paper and started scribbling.

'Morse code,' she said. 'Co-ordinates for a drop site. We're to collect a message.'

I passed her a map.

She scanned it. 'Here.' She marked an X and stood up. 'Come on.'

'Now?' The thought of another hike so soon filled me with horror. 'I haven't even made the tea yet.'

'It can wait,' she said, a mutinous set to her lips. 'We have a couple of hours before dark and we have to follow orders.'

'Fine,' I said, well aware that her enthusiasm had more to do with getting back outside than anything else. She was starting to sound more like herself again and, while I found her usual abrasive outlook wearing, I preferred that to watching her have a meltdown. 'I guess we'll move faster without our rucksacks, so it shouldn't take too long. But we should eat something.'

She tugged an apple and a biscuit from her pocket. 'Sorted. Let's go.'

'Hang on. It's still chucking buckets up there. Here. Catch.' I hooked a couple of oilskins off a peg on the far wall and threw one to her. 'Let's go.'

21

We hiked in silence, staying alert to our surroundings. Eventually, the rain stopped and weak sunshine peered through the clouds. The route wound along minor forest paths through the trees and across streams. Birds chattered overhead. After about twenty minutes, Lexi ground to a halt and frowned at the map.

'Can I see?' I held out a hand.

Her grip tightened, crumpling the paper. Then, she relented and passed it over. 'You always have to be in charge, don't you?'

'No, I don't,' I muttered, busy orientating myself.

'Yeah, you do.'

'I just like to know we're heading the right way.'

'That's what I mean.' The faintest touch of amusement coloured her voice.

I ignored her. 'It's just out of this woodland, up over that rise and then on to a crossroads. There's a hamlet beyond.'

'I know,' she said. 'Because *I* was reading the map.'

I rolled my eyes. 'Fine. I have control issues when it comes to maps. There. I've said it. Happy now?'

'Yes.' She flashed me a sudden grin.

I'd never seen her smile before. Not properly. It transformed her face. My irritation evaporated and I gave a tentative smile back.

'Come on. Let's go,' she said.

'What did the message say about the drop site?'

She pulled a face. 'We're to check the gate near the crossroads.'

'There are fields all around the crossroads and they all have gates.' I sighed. 'We'll just have to try each one in turn.'

'What about people? There are bound to be some. We're not supposed to draw attention to ourselves.'

I folded up the map and handed it back to her. 'Let's dump these wet coats somewhere. We can come back for them, after. It's not like we're in uniform or anything. We can pretend we're locals out for a stroll, lean against a few gates, have a chat. That sort of thing.' I threw her a sardonic look. 'We could even pretend to be friends.'

Her nostrils flared, making it plain that she'd rather have a tooth pulled. She tucked the map back in her pocket and set off. I caught up with her near the crossroads. A farm truck passed by. The driver peered at us through the windshield, his brow crinkling with curiosity.

'Slow down,' I muttered. 'We're supposed to be strolling, remember? You look like you're on a route march. Relax.'

'I am *not* an actress,' she hissed.

I nudged her, giving an exaggerated laugh, as if she'd said the funniest thing in the world. 'You don't need to be. Just talk to me.'

'What about?'

I laughed again and tucked an arm through hers. 'Anything.' She stiffened at my touch, but I could feel her making a concerted effort to loosen up. We strolled along the drystone wall lining the road. There was another engine sound in the distance behind us, the noise growing louder.

'Go on,' I said. 'Ask me something.'

'All right. How do you know that captain?'

I'd not expected such a direct question. 'Which captain?'

'The sexy one with the limp, back at Hannington.'

I stumbled, searching for a casual tone. 'I don't know who you mean.'

'Yes, you do. The one who taught us coding.'

'Ed— I mean... um.'

'See?' she said, with glee. 'Ed. Dear old Ed. I *knew* you knew each other.'

'I suppose we do. Vaguely.'

'Poppycock,' she scoffed. 'I saw the way he looked at you.'

'What do you mean?'

She rolled her eyes. 'Like he'd starve to death if you weren't there.'

'Don't be ridiculous.'

'That man is in love with you, Wren.'

I paused mid-step, my mind going into freefall. Edward? In love with me? No. He couldn't possibly be in love with me. He didn't really know me. I cast my mind back to our last encounter. He had spent most of the time telling me off. Although at the end... well... he had said some lovely things. I'd replayed his words in my head many times since. Usually in the dead of night. They made me feel as if I could accomplish anything. Could Lexi be right? Could he be in love with me? I didn't know what to think. The very idea made me feel all fidgety, as if a million butterflies were fluttering about inside me. It was too enormous to comprehend. And I had other things I needed to concentrate on.

'No, he isn't,' I said, in a tone that brooked no argument, and carried on walking. I ran an idle hand over the top of the first gate we came to, checking for any anomaly in the wood that might give away a secret hidey-hole. 'What do you think we're looking for?'

Scanning down the wood, she bent and pretended to retie her shoelace, whilst checking the wall around the post for loose bricks. 'Nothing here,' she murmured. 'Let's try the next one.' This time she was the one looping her arm through mine. 'So, go on. How do you know Captain Ed, then?'

'He's a friend of Tommy's.'

'Tommy?'

'My twin. Edward came to tell me that he was missing in action.'

'Oh.'

We'd reached the second gate by now, and it was my turn to tie my shoelace. A faint groove in the post, just above the lower hinge caught my eye. 'I've got something.' I eased the blade of my pocket knife into the groove and a section of the post popped out, revealing a small compartment. Palming the piece of paper inside, I slipped it and my knife back into my pocket, replaced the wood and stood up. 'Let's head back. We can read it when we're under the cover of the trees.'

Lexi fell into step beside me. 'How did your captain get injured?'

'He's not *my* captain,' I huffed. 'And I don't know how he got injured.' That didn't mean I hadn't wondered though.

'Trust me. He's definitely *your* captain.'

'Give over, Lex.'

We ambled along the road to a stile, climbed it and headed back to the woods. As soon as we were out of sight of the road I handed Lexi the slip of paper.

She scanned it. 'It basically says we're to send out a radio message tonight and wait for a response.'

'What's the message we have to send?'

'That bit is coded but there was a sheet of cypher keys back at the bunker. I'll work it out when we get back.' She tucked the paper in her pocket.

I glanced at the sky. 'It'll be dark soon. We'd better head back now. I'll make us something hot to eat and you can send that message.'

We walked back in silence, my thoughts full of Edward. Lexi was wrong about him loving me. Yet, the thought of him as *my* captain caused a surge of warmth in my chest.

As we approached the hatch, Lexi muttered, 'I'm sorry.'

I frowned. 'Sorry about what?'

'Your brother. You said he was missing in action,' she said. 'I'm sorry. I hope he's... well, wherever he is, I hope he is safe.'

Hot tears simmered behind my eyes. I pushed them back. Getting all sentimental wasn't going to help my focus. 'Thank you.' I glanced over my shoulder to check we were alone, and then bent to pull back the camouflaged netting. She stared at the hatch, biting her lip.

'You can do this,' I said. 'Just like you did before.'

'Distract me. Tell me about yourself.'

'I've already told you way more than I should. We're not supposed to get to know each other, remember?'

'They mean don't say where you're from and stuff like that. All I know is you have a brother somewhere and your sexy captain is called Edward.'

'He's not my—'

She flapped an urgent hand. 'Please, Wren. Just talk. As soon as I'm past the first bit, I'll be fine. It's just really... small.'

'What do you want me to say?'

'Tell me about how you got into coding.'

'That's easy.' I laughed. 'It was the best way to totally infuriate Father.'

She stared at me as if I'd grown another head. 'Why would you want to do that?'

'It's a long story.'

She started down the steps after me. 'And the coding?'

'We're twins, my brother and I. We had our own secret language and the whole coding thing started from that. Father hated that we could communicate and he didn't know what we were saying.'

'Do you not get on with your dad, then?'

I ducked into the main bunker. 'I love him, but he's... challenging. He thinks women should sit quietly in the corner and be decorative.'

'That's not unusual. A lot of people have strong opinions on what women should and shouldn't do.'

'True.' I shrugged. 'Anyway, he'd have an apoplectic fit if he could see me now. This definitely doesn't come under his definition of ladylike behaviour.'

We arrived in the main living space. Lexi's skin was grey and clammy. Concerned that she might pass out, I nudged her onto the nearest chair. 'Here, let me show you what our secret codes were like.' I grabbed a pencil and paper and started writing. 'We each had our own codename, like this. His was TATATA. It's just his initials. TA for Thomas Ashworth. I... uh!' I ground to a halt, mentally kicking myself for revealing my surname. In trying to help Lexi, I'd just handed her a way to cause serious trouble for me. If she told Major Stapleton, I could be thrown out. All this would have been for nothing. The thought of failing made me want to curl up in a corner and cry. I couldn't believe I had been so stupid.

Lexi didn't react. Perhaps in her anxious state she hadn't noticed. 'So that makes your call sign SASASA, then?'

'Almost,' I said. The only thing to do was to carry on as if nothing was wrong. If I kept wittering on about this silly childhood game, Lexi might forget what I had said. 'Father is the only one who calls me Serenity. Tommy calls me Wren and he thought WAWAWA was hilarious. He said it sounds like a baby crying.'

'He's right.'

Relieved to see colour returning to her cheeks, I perched on the bottom bunk and kept talking. 'Anyway, Tommy would put my call sign at the start of a message and then he'd put his at the end like a signature. Although, come to think of it—' I scratched my head '—there was only us sending messages, so I guess we didn't really need to do that at all.' I smiled at our childish naivety.

'It sounds fun.'

'It was. Anyway, after our call sign at the start, the next bit of the code told us which key to use to break the main body of the message.'

'Like what?'

I tipped my head on one side. 'We had several of them. All from Jane Austen Novels. *Northanger Abbey* would be JANA. *Pride and Prejudice* JAPP.'

'So, if I had the right novel, I could decode your message.'

'Not exactly. You don't know what the key actually is, and even if you did know it, the message would be written in our secret twin language, which probably wouldn't make sense.'

'Bleeding Nora,' she huffed. 'No wonder you annoyed your father.' Silence fell in the bunker for a moment. Then, she said, 'I like Jane Austen novels.'

'Me too.' I grinned. Maybe Lexi and I had more in common

than I'd thought. 'Now, come on, we need to decode that message and find out whatever we need to do next. And we need to eat.'

She tugged the slip of paper out and got to work.

A mere three paces from the bed took me into the mini kitchen where I mentally catalogued supplies packed onto the shelving unit attached to one wall. Opposite that was a small table with a bowl and jug, and a camping stove. It took some time to work out how to assemble the compact trifold field stove and light the fuel disc. As a heat source it wasn't the most efficient, and warming a can of soup proved tedious. Conscious that fumes underground could prove fatal, I opened the hatch to the escape tunnel, grateful for the cool waft of fresher air that drifted in. Eventually, I returned to the main room to find Lexi poring over a map. She looked up as I set a mug of steaming soup on the table.

'Thanks,' she said.

'You look serious.'

She cocked her head towards the radio. 'Another message came in while I was sending out ours. We have new orders for tomorrow.'

'And?'

She took a swig of soup, returning her attention to the map. 'There's a supply column passing through the area late tomorrow afternoon. We have to reach it undetected, access the fuel supply and leave a dummy bomb marked with our call sign, to prove that it was us who did it.'

'We can do that.'

She wrinkled her nose. 'It's not that simple. We have to race all the other operational base teams. There will be a single red flag in the cab of one of the other trucks accompanying the fuel tank. Apparently, the first team to take that flag wins.'

'Which is more important, the fuel or the flag?'

Lexi shook her head. 'Does it matter? We need to do both.'

'But if we can't, if something goes wrong, I wonder which one we should concentrate on.' I gave myself a shake. I was probably overthinking it. 'Forget it. We'll work it out.'

Lexi gestured to the map. 'You haven't seen how much ground we have to cover. It's a long way. I don't know about you, but I'm beat.' She had that wide staring-eyed look that you get when you're close to physical collapse and the next thing that happens might prove to be the last straw.

I scanned the map. 'You're right, it *is* quite a trek. The best thing to do is to get a few hours' kip now. Then we can set off really early. If we move at a steady run, we can cover a fair old distance.'

She snorted. 'You've seen me run. I can sprint; I'm really fast over a short course. But when it comes to long-distance running I might as well be going backwards.'

'I can help you with that, if you let me. There are different techniques—' I broke off, seeing a hard light appear in her eyes.

'Does it get exhausting?' she asked, a sudden edge to her tone.

I paused, conscious that I had stepped out of line somehow. Had I damaged our fledgling relationship? 'I don't understand.'

Her nostrils flared. 'This perky, can-do attitude of yours.'

'I... uh...'

'You were always so chummy and positive back at Hannington. I found it annoying. But the others didn't seem to.' She sounded quizzical rather than cross. As if she was trying to understand something. 'In fact, you built quite a cosy little team around you, didn't you?'

'You could have been part of it, if you wanted.'

'I wouldn't know how. I'm not like you.' She let out a heavy sigh. 'You have a brother. You're close to him. You've even got a father who cares enough to boss you about.'

'Yes, but—'

'No!' She held up a forefinger. 'You might not like what he says, but at least he's there. Not everyone is that lucky, you know.'

I bit my lip. She had a point. Compared to a lot of people, I was very lucky. 'Have you no family?'

She dashed a hand over her eyes before shaking her head. I resisted the urge to fill the silence that stretched between us. Instead I waited, hoping she would go on.

'I've been on my own from the word go. I ran away from the orphanage as soon as I could,' she said, sticking her chin out, as if daring me to judge. 'Take it from me, the backstreets of London aren't somewhere you go around trusting people. Not if you want to survive.'

'I'm sorry. That must have been tough.' I paused. 'You can trust me, Lexi.'

She shrugged. 'In my experience, trust is for fools. There's always a catch.'

'Not with me there isn't. I just want to help.'

She gave a sigh. 'I can't do this.' She waved a hand to encompass everything: the bunker, her soup, the radio, me. 'I need it all to stop. I'm so damn tired.' She scrambled up onto the top bunk, pulled the blanket right up and turned to the wall.

Lexi had always been disagreeable towards me. I hadn't ever expected to like her. Yet, watching her struggle to hold it together hit me hard. It reminded me that we never know what baggage other people are dealing with. Perhaps all her crankiness came from a fear of not fitting in. Or, worse, of failure. I could appreciate both of those.

I put a tentative hand on her shoulder. 'I'm not trying to be perky when I say this, Lexi, but, for what it's worth, I think you're really strong. And I think you can do this.'

She wriggled fractionally away from my hand.

'You're right,' I said collecting up our soup mugs. 'We need to rest. Then, we'll be able to think straight. You don't have to like me, Lexi. Hell, most of the time even *I* don't like me.' I gave a bitter laugh. 'But, I promise you that you can trust me. We need each other. If we work together, we can nail this thing.'

There was no answer.

I set the alarm on my wristwatch. 'I'll wake you just before dawn. If you decide to come with me, that's great. If not, I'll go alone.' I paused. 'I really hope you come, Lexi. I don't think I can do this on my own.'

22

Sleeping underground brought with it a total absence of external noise that I hadn't anticipated, as if we were cocooned from the world and everything in it. My watch rang out from beneath my pillow where I had stowed it to muffle the noise in case it gave away our presence to someone who might happen to be outside the bunker. I shut it off, blinking sleep from my eyes, and tried to remember where I was. My nose was cold. The air smelled damp. I was reluctant to emerge from my scratchy nest of blankets. A small rustle came from across the room. Lexi was already up and examining the map, her torch trained close to the paper.

'What are you looking at?' I mumbled.

'Our route.'

The decisive snap to her answer told me that weak and wobbly Lexi from the night before had been banished. Gritty, single-minded, totally in control Lexi stood in her place. I swung my legs over the side of the bed and lit the main lamp. 'Right, then. Let's take light day packs. I spotted a couple of small haversacks in the kitchen yesterday. They're the perfect size. We need ration packs, water, torches, rope; useful things that won't weigh us down.'

'Good idea,' she said, taking the bag I handed her. 'Then, we should get going.'

Out in the forest, as early morning birdsong filled the air, I struck out in a steady half-jog. 'I suggest we try walking and running.'

'Explain,' she demanded, falling into a jog beside me.

'We run for two minutes and then walk for two minutes. The walk will give us time to recover from the running but it also means we don't stop.'

'Fine.'

'If we set our pace right from the start, we should be able to keep going for hours, if necessary.'

'Hours?' Lexi squeaked, already floundering.

'Relax your shoulders and settle down into your stride,' I suggested.

'Eh?'

'You're trying too hard,' I murmured. 'It's not a race. That's what always beat you back at Hannington. You'd set off at top speed and then not be able to keep going. This is about endurance. The key is to work with your body, not against it. And remember to breathe.'

'I am breathing,' she squeaked.

'No, you're gasping like a landed fish. There's plenty of air. You need to regulate your intake so it's smooth and controlled. Find a slow, deliberate breathing sequence that works with your stride.'

'Easy... for you... to say.'

'Try this. Breathe in for three strikes of your feet and then out for the next three strikes. Then repeat. It will help you regulate and settle into a rhythm. That rhythm is the critical factor when it comes to sustaining your pace.'

We ran for two minutes and then dropped to a brisk walk, before running again. We alternated in that way for nearly half an hour and I listened to Lexi's breathing settle in tandem with her stride. Eventually, she was able to speak and run at the same time. She threw me a sardonic glance. 'You know something, Wren?'

'What?'

'You're even more annoying when you're right.'

I laughed. 'So are you.'

'Ha! Damn right I am.'

The genuine smile on her face added an extra spring to my step. 'Come on,' I said. 'Let's keep going.'

We covered a fair distance, running through the forest, side by side in companionable silence, occasionally stopping for water or to check the map.

Eventually, Lexi dropped to a walk and said, 'I think we're nearly there. According to the map, the woodland ends just over that rise. From then on, it's open countryside. We'll have to be careful not to draw attention to ourselves.'

We approached the final treeline a few minutes later.

'What do you suggest?' I asked.

'We've made good time. We're not far from where the convoy will pass through. Let's take a break here, while we've still got some cover, and have something to eat.'

'Good plan.' I skipped off the path towards a huge oak tree. The trunk forked at waist height, providing a useful foothold for scrambling up onto the lowest branch. 'Let's climb up here a bit. We'll have a better view.'

Lexi watched me, then tucked her map away and followed suit. 'I've climbed lots of things, but never a tree.'

I chuckled. 'I've never raided a fuel supply convoy before.'

She took a swig of water from her flask. 'A day of firsts all around, then.' Pulling a ration pack from her rucksack, she handed me a small, silver-wrapped packet. 'Here. Have some delicious meat cube to keep you going.'

'You're so kind. Thank you.' I matched her mocking tone, glad that our truce seemed to be holding. 'Actually, this doesn't taste too bad.'

She nodded gnawing off a corner of her own meat cube. 'It's tough and a bit salty, but it does the job.' She swilled it down with water.

I pointed to a dirt track that cut across the expanse of land that ran parallel to the treeline. 'Is that the road the convoy will use?' There was little to no cover available once we left the trees, other than tall grass and the odd bush or rock. Unease slithered up my spine. It would be tricky to approach anything in that terrain unobserved. If we were careless, there was a serious risk that this could be over before we even started.

'I think so. The intelligence we had is that the convoy will pass by at around four, and pull into a farmyard about a mile further on for the night. The fuel is supposed to be in the rearmost truck.'

'And the flag?'

She wrinkled her nose. 'I don't know. One of the other two.'

Damn it. Even with the exact information it would have been a difficult task. My nerves jangled with apprehension. We couldn't afford to mess this up. There was no telling how many more chances we would get to prove ourselves. I checked the time. 'It's nearly three thirty now.'

'The question is,' said Lexi, 'should we try to reach them while they are moving or wait for them to reach the farmyard.

Once they've settled in for the night they're more likely to be off guard? What do you think?'

'Depends how fast they're travelling,' I said. 'In theory, if we're close to the road, we could hop on while they're still in motion but—'

Lexi slapped my arm and hissed, 'Look.' She pointed out into the sparse grassland.

I squinted, murmuring, 'What am I looking at?'

'That's the other group. The pair with the chatty lady from the main bunker.'

'I think her name is Enid,' I whispered.

'Trust you to know her name. Did you swap addresses too?'

'Yes, we're going to have tea tomorrow.' I could feel Lexi's eyes boring into me and tutted. I watched the two shadows slipping from bush to bush in the direction of the road. 'I wonder what their plan is.'

'Duh! Good old Enid and her pal are getting close enough to the road to jump on one of the trucks. Which is what *we* should be doing.' Lexi started scrambling down to the ground.

I grabbed at her arm, my fingers closing on thin air. 'Hang on. Lex, wait.'

'No. Get a move on. If we don't hurry, they'll beat us to it.'

I cursed under my breath in frustration. Why wouldn't she listen to me? I hurtled down the tree after her. I wasn't sure why I did what I did, I simply knew I had to stop her. There was something about the grassland that didn't add up. As Lexi prepared to dash out from the cover of the woodland, I threw my arms around her waist and dragged her down behind a bush. Putting one hand over her mouth, I whispered, 'Shh! Please, Lexi. Trust me.' I scanned the horizon. That's when I saw it. 'There. Look. Over at that old tree trunk. See? Can you see the sunlight is reflecting off something?'

She followed my direction. 'Is that...?'

'Binoculars, I think. Someone else is watching.'

'Who?'

I shrugged. 'I don't know. Could be another operative pair like us. Or, it could be a patrol.'

'What do we do?'

'The only choice we have is to watch this play out and then decide what to do.'

She scratched her head. 'If it's another pair like us, then one of them could beat us. Or both of them could.'

She was right. Losing out to one of the other teams would be nauseating. Even so, my instinctive need to be cautious overrode all else. We couldn't afford to dash off with a half-formed plan. It was too important.

'That's possible,' I said. 'But let's think about the bigger picture here. At least they're on the same side as us, as opposed to the convoy, who are supposed to be the enemy.'

'I suppose so.' She scrunched up her nose. 'I still want to win, though.'

'I know, but wouldn't you prefer that the mission is a success, even if one of them beats us, rather than we all end up captured?' Bile burned my throat at the thought of being caught. This might only be a dummy drill, but it felt so real. I took a deep, steadying breath.

She frowned. 'You're saying we just wait?'

'For now.'

Fortunately, it wasn't long before a low drone started in the distance. It quickly morphed into the distinct growl of diesel engines, and a column of trucks rumbled up the track. Watching their progress, I couldn't tell if the odd fizzing sensation in my limbs was excitement or nerves. As the last vehicle drew level with a particularly large clump of gorse bushes, two figures broke cover and ran towards the tailgate. My heart leapt as adrenaline surged through me. It was all I could do to hold my position and watch. Were they going to make it?

Several things happened at once.

Another pair emerged from behind some rocks and also made a dash for the trucks. Both seemed likely to reach their target until two guards armed with rifles leaned from the rear of the last truck. No shots were fired. The women slowed, abandoning their attempt and turning back for cover. A hidden patrol of soldiers rose from the grassland and surrounded them.

'Hmm,' said Lexi. 'It looks like you were right. I vote we go for plan B. What do you reckon? We creep up to this farmyard they're supposed to stop at, scout around a bit and then plant the bomb and grab the flag?'

'Agreed.' I kept my eyes trained on the women being herded in the wake of the convoy as it disappeared into the distance. The soldiers weren't exactly treating their captives gently. Something dark solidified in my core at the sight. We might be role playing but this wasn't a game. The consequences of failure should we ever have to complete an operation like this for real might well be fatal. Grim determination settled around my shoulders like a heavy cloak. If I could find a way to free those captives, I'd do it.

23

It took us over an hour to cover the distance to the farmyard. We took a circuitous route to ensure that we weren't being either followed or observed. The gathering dark of early evening helped obscure our movements.

'There should be at least one other group of operatives out here,' muttered Lexi, slipping into a puddle of shadow behind a length of drystone wall. 'How come we haven't seen anyone?'

'I'm more concerned with not running into a patrol,' I whispered back, running my eyes over the collection of buildings ahead. 'Look. The farmyard is almost completely enclosed. A house, two stone barns and a wooden stable.' They formed a square, rather like a courtyard, with one route in and out. 'This isn't going to be easy.'

Lexi pointed to one corner, the furthest from the entrance to the courtyard. 'How about we head for the back of that barn? We need to get close enough to work out where those trucks are. Then we can work out a plan.'

Taking care to stay low, we crept into place. A narrow gap between the two barns allowed us to edge close enough to gain a reasonable view of the courtyard. Hidden behind a vast wooden rainwater barrel, we watched as each of the three vehicles were manoeuvred into position. The first two vehicles were tucked into the barn to our left. The truck with the fuel was in the barn to our right. The doors to each barn were closed and armed guards stationed outside. The four captured operatives were herded into the wooden stable beyond the barn to the right. The guards shoved them to hurry them up. I ground my teeth and seethed, as two women stumbled and almost fell because their hands were bound tightly behind their backs.

I tapped Lexi on the shoulder and beckoned for her to follow me away from the farmyard. Staying low, we crept back out onto the grassland to a ditch behind a clump of gorse bushes and hunkered down out of sight.

'What do you reckon?' whispered Lexi.

'It'll be tricky. I reckon getting the flag is do-able. That barn door looks rotten. I'm not so sure about the fuel truck though.'

'The problem is, as soon as we hit one, we lose the element of surprise for the other.'

'Which do you think is the most important?'

She blew out her fringe. 'Probably the fuel. Only, that flag is important, too. I know this is a drill, but it could represent important documents or something, information that would help the war effort. We just don't know.'

I hadn't thought about that, but she was right. 'I suppose we could divide and conquer.'

'Split up, you mean?'

I shrugged. 'It would be easier if there were more of us. Why don't we see if we can find the other pair of operatives and team up with them?'

Lexi's mouth formed a perfect 'O'. 'Are you mad? That's exactly what we're *not* supposed to do.'

'Is it? What did our orders actually say?'

She scowled, thinking. 'That we had to plant the dummy bomb and that the first group to the flag wins.'

'So, it didn't say that we couldn't team up.'

'Not specifically, no, but... don't we want to win?'

'It's not about winning, though, is it? What if the real test is to think about the bigger picture? This is about advancing our side's position in the war. Making sure the enemy can't use that fuel against our troops and potentially retrieving vital information. Working together increases our chances of doing both. I know you don't trust easily, Lex, but please run with me on this? If we are going to succeed, we need the other teams.'

She huffed. 'Fine. Only how are you going to find them? It's dark and we're stuck in a hole in the middle of nowhere with no radio and no idea where they are.'

'I bet they aren't far away, though.' I grinned and cupped my hands together before my mouth and let out a warbling hoot.

'You're kidding!'

I wriggled my eyebrows. 'The great northern diver probably isn't native to wherever we are, but I doubt the soldiers in the courtyard know that.' I waited a beat and then hooted again. A few minutes later, I did it again.

We listened.

Nothing.

I tried one last time. Almost immediately, a hoot came back.

'Well, I'll be damned. It worked.' Lexi peered into the darkness. 'Do it again.'

I complied. Over the next five minutes, the responding hoot got closer until, eventually, there was a hiss. 'Where are you?'

'Over here,' I hissed back. 'In the ditch.'

Two women scrambled down beside us.

'Fancy seeing you here,' said the first, a wiry woman with a bright smile and mud smeared across her face. 'I'm Bessie and this is Jean.' She gestured to her partner, also slim, lithe and covered in mud. Like us, both women had their hair tucked out of sight beneath the dull coloured headscarves issued at Hannington.

'I'm Lexi. She's Wren. We figured we could team up.' Lexi's tone was brusque, as if she expected to be rebuffed. 'Are you up for that?'

Bessie grinned. 'Good idea. We've three secure buildings with three sentries on guard, all of whom can see each other. You got a plan?'

'Yes, actually.' Lexi sounded so certain. 'Can you two deal with the flag?'

Bessie nodded. 'I think so. I saw a couple of windows on the far side of that barn with no direct line of sight to them from the front. We should be able to force one open.'

'Good,' said Lexi. 'We'll go for that fuel truck.'

'How?' I asked, a flash of annoyance at the fact that tasks were being divvied up without my input making my tone sharper than necessary. 'There are no handy side windows on that barn. I checked.'

She looked at me as if I was particularly dense. 'Easy. *I'm* going in through the roof.'

'What?' I said. 'There's no way you can climb those walls.'

'You climb trees. *I* climb buildings.'

'There's nothing to hold on to,' I said. 'No ledges, footholds or anything.'

Lexi threw me a sardonic glance. 'I've been cornered in a lot of alleyways. There's always something to grab on to if you're desperate enough.'

'Desperate or not,' I replied, 'there's no way *I* can climb a sheer wall.'

The unconcerned shrug she gave, indicating that my failings weren't her problem, grated on my nerves, as did her breezy response. 'Looks like it's just me, then. Anyway, one person has less chance of attracting attention.' She rummaged in her rucksack and pulled out a coil of rope. 'I spotted several missing roof tiles. Once I am up there, I can slip inside, tie this to a beam and lower myself down. I'll come out the same way and use the rope to abseil down to the ground.'

'What do I do?' I asked.

She grinned. 'Keep watch.'

'That's not a bad shout,' said Bessie. 'Having someone keeping an eye out for any movement in the courtyard would be useful. You could create a distraction if necessary.'

'But I...' Unable to find words, I closed my mouth with a snap.

'You wanted a team, Wren,' said Lexi, a wicked gleam in her eye. 'You got one. Live with it. Remember the bigger picture. You can't always be the hero.'

I put both hands up in mock surrender. 'Fine. I'll run interference from the courtyard. Once you're both done, you better send me a signal to let me know I can retreat.'

'Wood pigeon? Diver? Or, song thrush?' asked Bessie. She demonstrated all three, a grin teasing the corner of her mouth.

'Song thrush will draw too much attention at night. Wood pigeon from you,' I said. 'It's nice and low, easily overlooked. And northern diver from Lexi. Just one call.'

'Right,' said Bessie. 'Then what do we do?'

Lexi turned a don't-be-dim look on her. 'We each slip away into the night from where we are, of course.'

'Yes. Best not try to meet back up before leaving,' said Jean. 'Bessie and I will retreat to our base and you to yours.'

'Agreed,' said Lexi. She turned to me. 'I'll leave from wherever I make it back to the ground. I'll head for that tree we stopped at earlier. We can meet and hide out there until the coast is clear, then start back to the bunker.'

'Right.' I looked at each of my companions in turn, wondering if they were buzzing with the same nervous energy that I was. 'If we're all on board with this plan, we'd better get going. Good luck.'

24

The half moon overhead cast deep shadows that we took advantage of as we slipped back towards the farmyard. Hiding behind the same water barrel as before, I watched in amazement as Lexi shimmied up the side of the barn to my left. Taking advantage of tiny nooks and crannies between the stone blocks as toe and finger holds, she soon disappeared out of sight onto the roof. I closed my mouth with a snap and dragged my attention back to the courtyard. A slight shift in the shadows beyond the barn to my right reassured me that Bessie and Jean were on target. There was nothing I could do, apart from watch and wait.

All was still. An owl hoot rang out somewhere nearby, making me jump. Thank goodness we hadn't chosen owl calls as our signal.

I shifted from foot to foot, the chill night air seeping into my bones. My heart thumped in my chest so hard, I wondered if the guards could hear it. A door banged. Light briefly spilled from the farmhouse and then disappeared. Boots scraped stone. A figure marched across the yard towards the barn on my left. I held my breath. *Don't go in. Don't go in.* There was no way to warn Lexi someone was coming. I cast around for a stone or something to throw. *Create some sort of distraction* was the only thought in my head as my mind tumbled into a freefall of paralysing panic. What would Edward say, if he could see me now? Heavens, this was only a drill and I was falling apart. What would I be like with the real thing?

I closed my eyes and counted to ten, focusing on the last time I'd seen him. He'd said I was the most incredible woman he'd ever met. The memory suffused me with warmth. I could do this. I stiffened my spine, mentally ordered my internal jitters to behave and opened my eyes to scan what was happening in the yard.

The marching figure halted and grunted at the guard. There was a rasping sound. The brief flare of a match. A pinpoint glow from a cigarette. The guard rumbled a reply. The figure turned and walked towards me. I ducked and held my breath. He passed mere inches from my hideout as he approached the sentry to my right. More muttering followed before he wandered over to the stable and chatted to the guard there as well, before disappearing back into the farmhouse.

I released a long slow breath, willing my heart rate to settle as the minutes ticked by. Eventually, I heard the low call telling me that Lexi was clear and heading back. Good. Now it was over to Bessie and Jean.

Never very good at waiting, I allowed my gaze to drift to the wooden stable across the yard. There were four operatives held captive in there. Perhaps I should take a look. Realistically, I knew I should stay on task, but everything was going to plan. There was no harm in a little investigation while I waited. Slipping around behind the barn, I kept to the deep shadows, taking slow, steady, careful footsteps, and approached the stable from the rear. The wooden slats that made up the sides of the building were in a poor state of repair. Time and rot had nibbled away at the edges, leaving gaps that allowed me to see inside. I made my way along one wall, peeping in to a series of stalls. The first two contained horses. In the third, four women sat on the floor, hands and feet bound.

I edged along the wall and examined each wooden plank, trying to ease my fingers into gaps and tug. If I could find enough loose ones, perhaps I could slip inside. Yes, there. The plank creaked as I eased it away from the rusting nail holding it in place. I paused, listening intently. Nothing happened. I snuck back to peer into the yard. All was still. The guards were in place. The farmhouse quiet.

The low coo of a wood pigeon drifted across the night air to me. Bessie and Jean were done. Good. There was nothing to lose. I crept back and worked on the next plank, using my pocket knife to overcome resistance. A horse stuck its muzzle in the hole and let out a soft whiffle. I gave the warm nose a gentle pat and pushed it away before wriggling through the gap onto the straw-strewn floor. Slowly getting to my feet, hardly daring to breathe, I peered out of the stall into a central corridor. The coast was clear. I tiptoed along to the end stall and ducked in, holding a finger to my lips as I made serious eye contact with each woman in turn. With shaking hands, I sawed away at each set of ropes until all were free. They rubbed wrists and ankles, stifling groans.

'Shh!' I hissed. 'Follow me.'

One by one we slipped out through the gap in the planks and slunk away from the farmhouse buildings back towards the ditch. It wasn't until we were all under cover that the trembling hit me. Fear and elation in equal measures proved a potent cocktail. Had I really done that? I sank onto a rock and waited for my legs to stop feeling like they were made of jelly.

'Thank you,' whispered Enid. 'What do we do about the mission?'

I gave her a thumbs up and a wobbly grin. 'The others have it covered. All we have to do is to get out of here.'

A harsh shout filled the air.

'Sounds like they're on to us,' I said. 'We'd better split up. Stay low, keep quiet. Good luck.'

The four women headed out onto the grassland in pairs, moving with determined purpose, gliding from shadow to shadow like wraiths. There one minute, gone the next.

I stayed behind, waiting, listening to the bustle of activity in the courtyard, unsure whether to head off straight away or stay where I was. The more of us out there trying not to be seen, the greater the chance we would draw attention.

Doors banged. Footsteps hurried. Orders were shouted.

'Fan out,' came one gruff voice.

'Get a move on,' said another. That one sounded very close by. I shrank back into the darkness and slowed my breathing.

'They're only a bunch of women,' muttered a third. 'They can't have got far.'

That last one made me grin into the darkness. *Only a bunch of women. Ha!*

I crouched lower in the bottom of the ditch, making myself as small as possible. Tucked out of sight, screened by gorse, I watched the search unfold with growing satisfaction. There were no shouts of triumph from the soldiers. Eventually, they slunk back, grumbling and swearing, with no sign that any operatives had been recaptured. I waited until the farm had settled back into silence before emerging from my hiding place and using the stars to guide me back to the treeline. At the base of the oak, I looked up to see Lexi's pale face staring down.

'What did you do?' she demanded, her voice low and

intense. 'I dealt with the fuel truck, then I heard Bessie and Jean's signal, so I knew they were clear with the flag. Ten minutes later, all hell breaks loose. Then I get back here and you're nowhere to be seen.'

'I got held up.'

She frowned. 'I couldn't go back and find you. There were troops everywhere.'

'Aw, were you going to come and rescue me? Lex, that's so sweet.'

'Don't call me sweet,' she huffed. 'And don't go thinking we're friends or anything.'

'I wouldn't dream of it,' I said.

'I was only concerned because *I'll* look bad if *you* go getting yourself captured.'

'If you say so.' I smothered a grin. 'Anyway, I'm here now. Shall we head back?'

She grumped and grumbled her way down the tree, landing on the ground beside me with a gentle thud. 'So, go on then. What did you do?'

'I let the other teams out.'

'What?' Lexi's outraged squeak hurt my ears.

'Shhh!' I said. 'There might still be soldiers prowling around.'

'Why take such a risk?' she hissed. 'You could have compromised the whole operation.'

'Oh, come on, Lex. I couldn't just leave them. And anyway, I waited until you were done before I did anything. Plus, I figured they couldn't chase us all down. The more people running away the greater the chance we could escape in the chaos.'

'You're unbelievable, you are.' She shook her head but amid her disapproval I sensed respect. 'Come on,' she said. 'We'd better go before you decide to do anything else ridiculously stupid.' The ghost of a smile flashed across her face. My soul gave a happy little skip. Whatever she said, we were friends. Prickly friends, for sure, but definitely friends.

My delight was marred by the knowledge that we only had a few days or so left to enjoy that friendship. All too soon we would return to reality, to Major Stapleton and the true purpose of her women's secret army. There was no knowing where we would be posted. There was a very real possibility that I might never see Lexi again.

25

Two days later, in her office in the main underground facility, Major Stapleton sat behind a large desk and studied me intently. Stood to attention, my gaze fixed on the wall behind her, I waited.

'How do you think your mission went, Private Ashworth?'

I lifted my chin, and straightened my already straight spine. 'We followed orders, Major.'

She cleared her throat. 'You're not concerned that you... improvised?'

Warmth burned my cheeks. 'I didn't do anything risky, ma'am. At least, not until I was sure that our main objectives had been achieved.' I risked a glance at her face, saw her lips purse, and I hurried on. 'I know we were not supposed to have any communication between groups, but I figured the more of us fighting the war the better. It made sense not to leave captured operatives behind. If that was wrong, then I'm sorry... no... No!' I swallowed, the urge to tell her the truth overcoming my sense of self-preservation. 'Actually, I'm not sorry, ma'am. It was the right thing to do.'

She frowned. 'You do understand that keeping the individual cells of this project separate is for everyone's protection, don't you?'

'Yes, I do.'

'You were lucky this time. You got away with it. In future, however, I caution you against similar impulsive actions.' She sat back in her chair and crossed her arms. 'You've surprised me, Private Ashworth. I did wonder, when we first met, if you would be tough enough for this.'

'I am,' I said, putting as much conviction as I could into the words. The last few weeks had taught me many things, the most important of which was that I was far stronger than I had ever thought possible. 'I know I am.'

'Yes. I rather think you are.' She glanced down at the papers on her desk. 'I deliberately teamed you up with Lexi. I expected you two to clash. I wanted to see if you could work together, or if you would let your differences interfere with your mission.'

'We got along fine.'

She raised a single enquiring eyebrow. 'Is there anything about Lexi that you think I need to know?'

'Like what, ma'am?'

'Like, how she functioned underground?'

I froze. Alarm bells started ringing in my head. That question was too pointed. The major's expression too steady. 'I'm not sure what you mean, ma'am.'

'Our evaluations indicate she is not too happy in confined spaces. Did you see anything that might support this?'

Oh, no! How was I supposed to answer that?

'Private Ashworth?' Major Stapleton's tone had developed an edge of steel. 'I need absolute honesty from those under my command.'

Nausea flooded my belly. I couldn't betray Lexi. Yet, there

was no changing the fact that she might prove a liability for an underground mission, which might in turn put her and others in danger. Whatever choice I made would be wrong. The only way forward was to tell the truth and hope for the best. I swallowed down the lump that had suddenly appeared in my throat. 'Lexi was uncomfortable when we first entered the bunker, but she handled it. She was a huge part of the success of our operation.'

The major scribbled a note in a file.

The bitter taste of regret filled my mouth. 'Please, Major. Don't fail her. There's no way we'd have been able to hit that fuel truck successfully without her. She scaled the barn. I couldn't have done it. She was amazing.'

The major kept writing, her face yielding no clue to her thoughts.

'She's an excellent operative, ma'am,' I persisted, hoping I hadn't just scuppered my spiky friend's chances. 'Way better than me.'

'Your spirited defence of your colleague is noted.' She gave a small smile. 'She'll receive a suitable posting. I'm just making a note not to force her down any rabbit holes. The real question is, what am I going to do with you?'

I chewed the inside of my lip and waited.

She leaned forward and fixed me with a stern look. 'You must never repeat what I am about to tell you to another soul.'

'You have my word, ma'am.'

She placed her elbows on the desk, her hands clasped together. 'As I mentioned to you before, I have been tasked with building a network of highly trained female personnel in key locations along the British south and east coast.'

'You called it the Special Duties Section.'

'Yes. The army has devised a number of programs that will

deploy troops of men in the event of invasion, but this particular project is intended to make use of the many special talents of our women. The ultimate aim is for both men *and* women to work together in a co-ordinated British Resistance, should our shores be overrun by the enemy. However, they are being set up separately for obvious security reasons.'

'I see.'

'You are now officially a part of one of the most secret operations in this war, Private Ashworth. Superficially, you will receive a relatively mundane posting. One that will draw no attention. The whole point is for you to be utterly forgettable. And while you are being underestimated by everyone around you, you will be the eyes and ears of the resistance, keeping a lookout for potential enemy incursions.'

'You mean spies.'

'Yes. We have reports coming in all the time of spies attempting to infiltrate local communities to send information back that could facilitate a full-on invasion. Your work will be vital in stopping that happening.'

I shuddered at the thought of the Nazis gaining a foothold in Britain, but stayed silent.

'Should, heaven forbid, the enemy successfully overrun us, we need people like you to remain in post as long as possible. Be as unobtrusive as you can. It's a fact of life that a low-ranked female officer will, more often than not, be overlooked. As such, you can gather vital intelligence.'

'And if I am not overlooked?' The thought of capture made my toes curl.

The major steepled her fingers. 'Then, assuming you can avoid internment, you retreat underground to your assigned bunker. Stay there as long as possible. Support and co-ordinate resistance activities in the area.'

'So, there'll be a team of us?'

'Yes and no. There will be others, but you won't know who they are. That way, should you be detained, you won't know enough to upset the apple cart.'

'I see.' The prospect of torture was never more real than in that moment. Her implacable tone sent shivers down my spine.

'But for now,' she continued, 'we need your eyes and ears focused on spies.'

'And where are you assigning me?'

She produced a map from a drawer. 'Ashworth Manor.'

My heart turned into a solid lead ball at her words. 'What? I mean... pardon, I...' Try as I might, I couldn't keep the disappointment from my voice. I'd wanted to escape Ashworth. Had I really just gone through all that training only to be sent straight back home? My cheeks grew warm and a thick murky fog of disappointment settled around my heart. 'I'm sorry, ma'am. But, what did I do wrong?'

'Nothing.'

'You said I'd be sent to a strategic location,' I said.

'Ashworth Manor *is* a key strategic location.'

'It's a maternity home?' I mentally kicked myself on hearing my tone echo Father's disdain when discussing Ashworth's allocated role.

'In times of war, appearances are often deceptive, Private Ashworth. You should know that by now.' The major paused, her steady gaze ensnaring mine, as if she were trying to say something more without actually saying it.

'Are you telling me that the maternity home isn't real?'

She tipped her head on one side. 'Not exactly. The maternity home is precisely what it appears to be. There just happens to be more going on than meets the eye. A lot more.'

'Such as?'

She sighed as if I was being obtuse. 'Subterfuge to confound the enemy operates on multiple levels. For example, it can be as simple as the removal of signposts at crossroads, making it difficult for strangers to find their way. Alternatively, it can be more complicated like running more than one operation from the same site.'

'And Ashworth is one of those sites.' The more I thought about it, the more it made sense. Ashworth might be tucked away on the edge of the New Forest but it had great connections with London, Southampton and the west. Operating multiple projects from the one location would be entirely feasible.

'Precisely. Very few people will be aware of all of its functions. Which is why we need one of our best operatives in place. That's you. Your position as the daughter of the house working as a secretary for the maternity hospital, will give you access to all areas. More so than anyone else we could put in place. You grew up there. You know the wider community and the area and are more likely to spot if something is slightly off-key. Local knowledge is invaluable.'

'I see.'

'The officer in overall command of the hospital will also be responsible for a number of other projects scattered through the forest, including arranging supplies for a large network of hidden temporary airfields, and several other facilities. He will spend much of his time occupied with those projects, leaving you to keep the show on the road at his office at Ashworth.'

'Why isn't the officer stationed at one of the airfields?'

'Airfields are too obvious a target. Whereas Ashworth, as a maternity home, won't be of high priority to the enemy. Hence, all the important communication for the area will come into Ashworth. Which is what makes your position there so useful.'

'I understand.' An idle thought crossed my mind: Father

would hate me being so involved. That fact alone, to my shame, made the posting more appealing.

'You know everyone in the area,' continued the major. 'Everyone *thinks* they know you. You can easily pass under the radar. You'll be able to check drop sites, watch the coastline, people-watch and keep your eyes and ears open, all without raising any suspicions. Given your history of running morning and evening, no one will be bothered if you continue to do so. Similarly, your habit of disappearing off to read in your room in the evenings will mean that no one will miss you if you are off monitoring radio communications.'

Her knowledge of my previous daily movements still surprised me, although heavens knew why, given the conversation we were having.

'In short—' she lowered her voice '—you will be underestimated by everyone just as I suspect you always have been. And *that* is what I'm banking on. Because having the bunker under Ashworth Manor staffed in the event of enemy invasion will be critical.'

I couldn't stop my eyes bugging at her implication. 'What bunker? Where?'

She gave a soft laugh. 'I thought that would get your attention. What do you think the engineering corps stationed at Ashworth have been doing?'

'Mapping the area to find new locations for airfields.'

'That was one of their tasks, yes.' She paused as if waiting for me to catch up.

'Oh!' I said. 'That was only part of it.'

'Indeed. Among other projects, turning Ashworth into a maternity home has caused a lot of upheaval. While that has been going on, my engineers have built and equipped an underground bunker for you. It can be accessed via the priest hole in your father's study.'

'How did you know about that?' The priest hole, built into the walls of Ashworth Manor during the late sixteenth century to hide a Catholic priest from Oliver Cromwell's puritans, was a closely guarded family secret passed down the generations from father to son. By rights, even *I* shouldn't know about it. Tommy had told me in a defiant effort to cheer me up after a particularly brutal verbal clash with Father. I hadn't believed him; not until he'd actually shown it to me.

'I make it my business to know,' replied the major. 'The priest hole now hosts a hidden trapdoor. There is a second entrance to the bunker concealed some distance away in the forest, connected via an escape tunnel. But—' she held up a finger to emphasise her point '—while you should find everything you need down there for a lengthy stay, I hope you won't ever need to use it. *If* the enemy gain a foothold in the area and build a stronghold at Ashworth, and *if* you become compromised, then *that* is the point at which you should retreat underground and not before.'

'And once I'm underground,' I said, understanding dawning. 'I can creep up into the priest hole and listen.'

'Exactly. Because your father's office, now the maternity home commander's office, will have state-of-the-art telecommunications equipment in it. Any invading force are likely to want to use the space as a communications hub as well. They won't necessarily realise they are being watched.'

'And if there is no invasion?'

'Spies.' The major's lips settled into a grim smile. 'You watch out for them and report anything suspicious.'

'I see.'

'On a superficial level, as well as providing the commander with administration assistance, your work will involve helping the matron with hospital records and generally being useful. It is important to keep careful lists of arrivals and departures. You will note which mothers and babies are being evacuated, where they are going. You will make the necessary arrangements for that to happen. Meanwhile, you will also patrol the coastline morning and evening, and keep watch for any shipping movements off the coast. Engage in everyday life in and around the manor and the village, and keep an eye out for anything or anyone unusual.'

'Anything else?'

'In your bedroom you will find a hidden compartment with a service-issue revolver.'

'Where?' I asked.

'I'll brief you on that shortly. Also concealed are radio components for those times that you can't access the bunker without being seen. Report anything suspicious to us via coded communication and listen for incoming messages from us with updated orders. Monitor the general chatter on the airwaves. Ashworth is near the coast, so you may pick up enemy transmissions. Forward these on. There are a number of drop sites in or near the grounds of the manor. We may send dummy messages via these for you to relay over the airwaves to confuse enemy communications.'

I gave a slow nod, mentally filing away all those tasks.

'Should the enemy successfully invade, Private Ashworth, your orders are to stay put. Keep all lines of communication open for as long as you can so that we can co-ordinate full-scale resistance activities in the area. The bunker is stocked with enough supplies to last approximately six to eight weeks.'

I swallowed. *Effectively buried alive.*

She leaned forwards, her voice intensifying. 'If you are

forced underground, hold your position as long as possible.' She ran a hand over the map of Ashworth. 'Be assured that you are part of a much wider network, Private. Working together, we will ensure ultimate victory. Now, let me show you the section of coast you'll be patrolling.'

I stepped closer for a better view, my knees feeling suddenly wobbly. Somehow speaking of potential invasion at Ashworth, of all places, solidified the danger faced by the whole country.

'Here.' She pointed to Ashworth Bay. 'This section of coast is particularly vulnerable.'

'How so?'

'To the west you have Highcliffe, which is well defended. In addition to razor wire mines and anti-tank stakes, not to mention admiralty scaffolding offshore, there are multiple manned pillbox gun emplacements. To the east is Hurst Castle, which is similarly catered for. No one in their right mind would try landing there. Then, there is the Chewton Bunny area.'

'There's no point trying to land an invasion there,' I said. 'The cliffs are unstable. There are regular slips, not to mention quicksand.'

'Which brings us to Ashworth. A relatively small section of woodland, tucked away, not easily patrolled or accessed thanks to dense undergrowth.'

'Meaning defences are not quite as robust as elsewhere.' I'd surreptitiously watched the coastal defences being installed and knew exactly what was where; from the placement of mines to the lengths of razor wire and other anti-tank measures.

'Indeed. The cliff is too unstable to mount permanent guns but a small Alan Williams turret as a temporary gun shelter is now in place.'

That was news to me, but so much was happening at Ashworth, it didn't surprise me.

'The Home Guard should patrol regularly,' she said. 'They have access to a relatively powerful machine gun that can be operated from the turret if needed. The route from the sea into the forest is easily accessible because the cliff height dips significantly at that point.'

'That's true.' I shook off a rush of unexpected sentimentality. 'And I grew up sailing the local shoreline, so I know the beach shelves quickly. There's a deep channel just offshore. Troop ships could land.'

Major Stapleton's features settled into grim lines. 'A small sub could also lurk unobserved to either pick up or drop off enemy agents. That, Private Ashworth, is why we need you.'

Having the manor's vulnerabilities pointed out so bluntly was a sobering experience. I left that meeting with my head spinning. I hadn't wanted to go back to Ashworth. The whole point of working so hard to pass the training scheme had been to escape. But I could see why I was needed. And, what soldier anywhere in the whole damned war actually wanted to be where they were? In all probability, none of them. These were my orders. I had a job to do. I'd better jolly well get on with it and make the best of the situation.

26

It felt strange to walk up the drive from the gatehouse to Ashworth Manor with a small pack on my back and my kitbag in my hand. I felt like a totally different person to the one who had left only two months previously. Once again clad in my ATS uniform with my hair neatly twisted into pin curls beneath my cap, I missed the loose, practical garments I had been wearing since arriving at Hannington. I wasn't the only thing that had changed. Ashworth had undergone a transformation of its own.

While the shell of the house looked the same, the driveway was a hive of activity. Three army trucks, parked in a pool of April sunshine, were the focus of significant activity. Medical equipment was being unloaded by uniformed personnel. A small, gently rounded woman in a white cap was busy directing operations, issuing instructions whilst ticking things off on a wooden clipboard. She wore the blue and white, fine-striped, A-line dress and white apron of a nursing auxiliary. Another similarly clad nurse was assisting a heavily pregnant woman down from the back of an ambulance.

The nurse with the clipboard looked up as I approached, an open, enquiring expression on her face. 'Can I help you?'

'I'm Private Wren Ashworth. I'm here as secretary to the commander.'

'We've been expecting you. Welcome. I'm Nurse June Travers. It's good to see you. Honestly, we can use all the help we can get. It's bedlam just now. Everything is arriving at once.'

A short, stocky man dressed as a hospital orderly in dark trousers and a white smock top, approached, a large box in his arms. 'Where do you want this?' he demanded.

June checked the label against her sheet of items.

'Come on,' he grumped. 'I haven't got all day.'

'Hold your horses, Roberts,' she replied, her tone surprisingly mild. She started back at the top of her page. 'It must be here somewhere.' She reached the bottom of the list for a second time. 'No. It's not here. It must be for the next drop site. Put it back on the truck, please.'

He stomped off muttering something under his breath that I suspected was extremely rude.

June flashed me a wicked smile. 'That one hasn't learned that I always read much, much slower when he's rude and grumpy.'

'I wonder why that is,' I murmured, suppressing a giggle. I liked this woman already. 'I had better let you get on. I'm to give my orders to the commander. Do you know where can I find him?' I pulled the letter Major Stapleton had given me from my jacket pocket.

She wrinkled her nose. 'He hasn't arrived yet. I'm told he's got lodgings in Ambleford village. You'd better show that to Matron. She'll know what to do.' As she spoke, she pointed through the main door. 'Down the hall, third door on the right.'

The library. I smiled my thanks. Her focus was already back on her deliveries.

The hustle and bustle on the drive was matched by similar chaos inside the house. Two small children dashed past, a pregnant woman in hot pursuit, her cheeks rosy with exertion. Nursing staff walked with brisk purpose. I made careful progress down the corridor, peering through open doorways. The morning room, the day room and the dining room had all been repurposed. Magnificent paintings and ornate furniture passed down the Ashworth generations had been replaced with hospital fixtures: practical chairs, plain tables and iron bedsteads. The silk rugs had been rolled away leaving bare floorboards, years of careful polishing scuffed away by busy feet. Father would be livid. He would have taken some furniture with him to the lodge, no doubt, and made sure that all other precious heirlooms had been stored up in the attics, to be brought back down after the war was over.

I felt a curious sense of dislocation. This was my home but not as I had ever seen it before. Instead of the usual hushed oppressive atmosphere, the house felt alive, as if reborn with fresh purpose. A seed of excitement germinated somewhere deep inside me, like a tight knot of anxiety beginning to unravel. I wasn't the unwanted daughter of the house any more. I had a new place here and a job to do. Perhaps this wouldn't be so bad after all.

Squaring my shoulders, I hurried along to the library, glad to see the books and shelves still present if nothing else. Matron, an older woman with tired eyes and a hospitable manner, sat at a table with piles of paperwork before her. She glanced over my orders. 'Private Ashworth. As in...?' She gestured to the room around us. 'Ashworth, Ashworth?'

I gave a small nod, crossing my fingers behind my back that she wouldn't make a big deal about it.

She pursed her lips and reread the letter before looking up. 'Excellent. If you already know the house there's no need to show you around. Which is good because I can't spare an orderly to do that right now.' She waved a hand towards the door and the busy corridor. 'You can see, we're swamped.'

'Please, don't worry about me,' I assured her. 'I can sort myself out. I'm not here to cause you any trouble at all.'

'Good. That's what I like to hear.' She pulled a key from the bunch hooked to her waistband, her motions brisk and efficient. 'You are to take charge of this. The commander's office is across the hall. It is kept locked when he isn't present. As his secretary, you are the only other person with full access. I suggest you go and get settled in. Later, you can get something to eat in the canteen – that's down in the basement next to the kitchens. I'm told it used to be the old servants' dining room. I am sure you can find it.'

'Thank you.' With the main family dining room now full of patients, it made sense to feed everyone downstairs.

She frowned. 'I know that you are here primarily to support the commander. It would help if you could assist me as well, if you have any free time.'

'I'd be glad to.'

The smile she gave me took ten years from her face. 'Good. In which case, Private Ashworth, welcome.'

An auxiliary with another pile of paperwork arrived to claim her attention.

I slipped from the room and headed downstairs, where I sidled into the kitchen, hoping for a glass of water. The hustle and bustle there matched that above stairs. Two people wrapped in huge white aprons and white caps worked at the vast wooden table in the centre of the room, one peeling a mountain of potatoes, another rolling pastry. A third, her face flushed, stirred a huge stainless-steel pot that bubbled away on the stove. An orderly brought boxes of supplies in through the back door and stacked them next to the pantry. A woman, elbow deep in dirty pans at the sink, saw me loitering. She wiped her hands on a towel and came over.

'Can I get you something?'

'I was hoping for some water,' I said. My stomach let out a huge rumble. 'Goodness, please excuse, me. I've only just arrived. I've been travelling since five this morning and...'

The woman wasn't listening. She filled a glass at the sink, fished an apple from a bowl on the sideboard and handed them to me. 'Here. This'll keep you going. Staff meals are served in the canteen.' She pointed along the corridor. 'Just along there. At eight, one and six. There'll be three gongs half an hour apart. The first one is for patients, those that are able to walk around. The second and third gongs are for staff. Two half-hour shifts, so there's always someone watching the wards. Patients not well enough to come downstairs get trays in bed.'

'Thank you,' I said, but she was already back at the sink.

Clutching my glass, I took a bite of apple and wandered back up to the ground floor, to the newly built staff accommodation wing. My room appeared untouched in my absence. I looked at it with new eyes thanks to my recent conversation with Major Stapleton about hidden compartments. Locking the door behind me, I dumped my bag on the bed and crossed to the minuscule built-in wardrobe and crouched down to reach into the base. I shoved aside the wooden box that held my letters, my writing things and a few odds and ends. Running my fingers over the floorboards, I tested each in turn until one shifted under the pressure. Ah ha! Forcing my fingernails into the groove on either side, I pried two boards up to reveal a cavity below and pulled out the power supply unit for a small radio. It was exactly where the major had said it would be. She must have planned for me to come back here all along and the colonel's engineers had built the room to her exact specifications. My pulse danced an erratic tango of anticipation. This was really happening.

I glanced around. Where else had she said? The head of the bed. Just as with the floorboards, the panelling behind the bed revealed a second power supply unit, wireless components and a set of headphones. I tucked them back out of sight, promising myself that I would assemble everything later to check they worked. Moving on to the secret cubbyhole under the windowsill I pulled out a revolver and ammunition. Cold and hard, the weight in my hands made me shiver. I hurried to hide it again, my hands shaking, hoping I'd never have need of it.

I stared out of the window into the courtyard, a heavy sensation around my heart and an ominous prickle at the backs of my eyes. I was back at Ashworth. The place I had fought so hard to leave. Thank heavens Edward couldn't see me back where I started. He'd think me a failure. After all my wild assertions that I was going to do something important for the war effort, he would see what everyone was supposed to see: that I'd been sent back to Ashworth to type.

He wouldn't know there was a radio hidden in my room. He wouldn't know that I was genuinely doing what I set out to do. The last few weeks *did* happen. A lump appeared in my throat. I missed my friends and wondered what were they doing. Where had they all been sent?

Wherever they were, I hoped they were safe.

I shook myself away from the sense of melancholy. Ashworth or no Ashworth, this was a new beginning for me. A peculiar brew of anticipation and anxiety fizzed in my core. I wanted nothing more than to share everything with Tommy. We had always shared every major milestone with each other. His absence hit me anew, along with fear at what the future might hold. What if I couldn't do this? Or, what if something happened to me? Might Tommy come back from wherever he was and find me gone? He would worry so. My mind spiralled with possible disasters and I paced the tiny room, agitation making my heart thump and my fingers tremble.

A gong sounded in the distance.

My eyes fell on my diary nestled amongst my favourite books on the shelf next to the bed. In the past, when I'd felt like this and Tommy wasn't here to talk to, I had shared my thoughts in writing instead. On impulse I snatched it up, and read the final few entries.

Friday 23rd January 1942

A letter arrived, today, marked Private and Confidential. It's addressed to me, of all people. A Major Belinda Stapleton asks if I am interested in volunteering for some sort of mission. I'm to meet her at the public lounge in Harrods at 2 p.m. on Friday 6th February.

I'm not sure what to do.

Father would refuse to let me go if he knew.

I'm not going to let him stop me. I just need to find a way to get there.

* * *

Wednesday 28th January

I had a phone call from Tommy. He's in London. They're deploying him next week. On Friday 6th February.

He wants me to go up and see him off and is sending the fare.

What a coincidence! It's meant to be. I can go to Harrods after his train leaves and meet this Belinda Stapleton.

I wonder what it's all about.

Given the secret nature of the major's special operations unit, these entries weren't necessarily a good idea. I'd better destroy them. Yet it felt wrong to remove them entirely. I tugged the pages from the diary and tore them into tiny pieces. Then, on a fresh leaf, I rewrote those exact sentences again, but this time using Tommy's and my secret childhood language. No one would be able to crack it. At the end, I added:

Tommy, if you are reading this JAPP

Confident that he would know what I meant, I turned to my copy of *Pride and Prejudice* and began writing in the margin of the first page, still using our special cypher.

I signed The Official Secrets Act in a cluttered basement that smelt of damp...

Being careful not to give away names and specific locations, I outlined my adventure so far, for Tommy's eyes only. Writing helped me to put my thoughts in order. It was as if my twin was stood beside me, reassuring me, telling me that everything would be all right. I ran my eyes over the finished message, feeling calmer. I'd promised not to tell anyone. This didn't break that promise. No one would learn anything of value from a random collection of shapes; pattern running down the edge of a page in a book. Easily dismissed.

The second gong echoed in the distance just as a knock sounded at the door.

I snapped the book closed, tucked it back on the shelf beside the rest of Jane Austen's works, and unlocked the door to find June outside.

'I wondered where you'd got to,' she said. 'I've got half an hour for my lunch now. Would you like to join me?'

Feeling much calmer, I grinned at her. 'I'd love to. Thanks.'

27

Things had changed significantly in the staff dining room since I had last been there. It was strange to register how the original space had been knocked through into a couple of storage areas, presumably to make it big enough to accommodate the sheer number of staff and patients required. Bubbly and positive, June chattered about anything and everything as we queued up for plates of vegetable stew. 'Diana over there—' she tipped her head towards a nurse who was sat at a table to our left and engrossed in conversation with an orderly '—has a sweetheart based at RAF Lymington. She met him at a tea dance six weeks ago and fell head over heels for him. The officers all looked so smart in their uniforms. They made all the girls feel giddy. Including me.'

'Did you meet someone?' I asked, mopping up the remnants of my stew with a piece of dry bread.

'Oh no! Not me.' She laughed. 'My Billy wouldn't like it.'

'Billy?'

I listened with mild amusement as she told me her Billy was in the merchant navy delivering supplies to troops overseas. The pride in her voice was clear. I was drawn to her friendly and open manner, but given my mission, I couldn't afford to get too close to anyone at Ashworth. With a bit of subtle prodding from me, she let fall titbits of gossip about several staff members and some patients too, making me think that June might be a useful source of general information moving forward. I made a mental note not to confide anything in her, unless I actively wanted the entire Ashworth population to be fully informed within minutes of the information leaving my mouth.

All too soon, the third gong sounded and we had to clear our plates to make way for the next sitting. With a cheerful wave, June hurried back to the wards.

I glanced around the basement before I left. I'd rarely been down here before, when it was the domain of the housekeeper, the cook and the maids, so was not totally familiar with the layout. Nevertheless, it seemed different somehow. I tried to work out which parts of the basement were directly beneath which of the main rooms above. My eyes were drawn to a large shelving unit that had been built across the wall farthest from the kitchens. Had that been there before? I recalled Major Stapleton's description of the hidden bunker that was supposed to be here at Ashworth. If there really was a trapdoor in the floor of the priest hole on the floor above, it must go somewhere. Stealing a small section of the basement and hiding it behind a useful storage unit was entirely possible. Especially as there was no one left at Ashworth, apart from myself and Father, who would know. And if I struggled to see it, there was no way Father would spot it. The notion seemed incredible, yet the radio and the revolver were hidden in my room, exactly as the major had described. There was no reason to doubt the existence of a hidden bunker, yet I needed to see it.

The office key Matron had given me weighed heavily in my

pocket. Checking out a potential escape route in advance of an invasion made perfect sense. After all, who knew when I might need to access it in a hurry? The commander hadn't arrived yet. This was the ideal opportunity to snoop around.

I hurried back to my room for a torch before making my way to the study, moving as fast as I could without drawing undue attention. The key turned easily. I took care to lock the door behind me, tucked the key back in my pocket and surveyed the room. I felt like I was trespassing, as if I was still a small child and not allowed to be there. No significant structural changes had been made. Father's carved wooden desk with the polished leather inlaid top was gone. That was no surprise. It would be in his new office at the gatehouse. A wide serviceable table and chair occupied the desk's former position in the bay beneath the stained-glass window. No doubt the commander would use that. More office furniture had been added. To the right of the bay sat a smaller desk equipped with a gleaming typewriter. That must be for me. On the opposite side of the room, three metal filing cabinets stood to attention alongside another table with a radio and three Bakelite telephones, two black and one green one.

Who on earth needed three telephones? The major's words about Ashworth being a communications hub echoed through my mind. Yet more evidence of the importance of my undercover role.

I crossed to examine the panelling on the wall behind my desk, frowning at the contours of the wood as I scoured my memory. Tommy had pushed something to make the panel spring free. It was so long ago, I couldn't for the life of me remember what. Testing the wood, I worked my way down the wall at approximately the height that Tommy and I had been when we were twelve. My fingers ran up against a knot in the grain. I pushed, and then pushed harder. There was a click and the panel shifted. My heartbeat drummed in my ears. I glanced over my shoulder at the locked door. Sounds of muted activity outside in the corridor drifted over to me. I waited to make sure there was no sign anyone might come in.

It was now or never.

With my torch between my teeth, I used both hands to slide the panel aside until there was enough room to climb through the gap. I found myself in a space approximately six or seven feet high and two to three feet wide that ran the length of the wall. Once inside, I replaced the panel, praying I would be able to open it again from the inside. I shuddered at the thought of being entombed and paused to steady my breathing. The air tasted musty and old. The light of the torch picked up cobwebs as thick as ropes overhead. I supressed a squeak of dismay and refused to consider the potential size of their creators. Dust motes hung in the air, disturbed by my movements. Head down, I searched the floor. Major Stapleton had said one of the flagstones moved. I tested each one, trying to ease my fingers under the corners, searching for a lever. Inching along the narrow corridor, I worked in sequence until, finally, I found it. The lever moved. The slab hinged up and back – the action silent and smooth – to rest against the wall. I noted a handle on the underside and then stared down into a hole large enough to fit a person, and a set of irregular stone steps leading down.

Did I dare go down? I'd come that far. It made no sense to go back now.

Taking a deep breath, I shuffled down onto my bottom and lowered myself into the hole, my uniform hampering my movements. My mind flitted to Lexi. There was no way she'd cope with this. Even I was beginning to feel peculiar. Although, that could be due to a lack of oxygen.

A cold draught wafted up the steps, snatching at my ankles.

It smelled marginally fresher than the air where I was. I crept downwards, tugged the slab back into place over my head and said a quick prayer of gratitude that this was relatively easy to achieve without making any noise. The flimsy beam from my torch lit the way as I descended into a small chamber reminiscent of the entrance at our training bunker. Stacked with shelves laden with boxes of supplies, it was intended to fool the casual observer into thinking that this was all that was down here.

I dragged out a particularly large box from floor level and examined the wall behind it. Sure enough, there was a well-concealed trapdoor, and on the far side of that was the bunker. Equipped in an identical format to the one in which I'd just spent four days with Lexi. I stared around at bunk beds, desks and chairs, the kitchen and necessary. Major Stapleton had mentioned that there were other operatives in the area. I'd not been read into their details for security reasons. I had to assume that, should the worst happen, I might not have to shelter down here on my own. Seeing first-hand evidence of the extensive planning that must have gone into establishing and equipping a facility like this had a strangely calming effect on my nerves. Yes, this was serious. And yes, enemy invasion must be a genuine possibility if the special operations unit were building bunkers like this. But at least they seemed to know what they were doing.

I took a brief scout around the kitchen and found the entrance to the escape tunnel. There was no time to explore that. I'd just have to wing it if I ever needed it. I crept back the way I had come, climbing the steps back up into the priest hole. As I lowered the slab back into place, I heard something and froze.

Was that a throat clearing?

Someone was in the office. I was sure of it. I tiptoed down the length of the priest hole. Near the hidden panel, a small hole had been drilled into the groove of the ornamental woodwork. A tiny filament of daylight streamed through. Holding my breath, I put an eye to the hole. Someone was sat at the main desk. Try as I might, I could only see a pair of hands and the papers they were working on. Whoever it was cleared their throat again.

A knock sounded on the office door. I smothered a squeak of surprise.

The hands stilled and a deep voice said, 'Come in.'

I knew that voice. It couldn't be. Surely not?

The door opened and Matron spoke. 'We're not sure where your secretary is, Commander. Her bag is in her room and she had lunch with one of my nurses, but she doesn't seem to be anywhere in the building at the moment. I can only assume that she went out for some air.'

'I see, thank you. When she gets back, please send her to me. I shall be here all afternoon.'

'Yes, sir.' The distinct thud of the door closing as Matron left was quickly followed by the shrill ring of one of the telephones. The hands disappeared from view, a chair creaked, uneven footsteps sounded as the man moved around the desk and into my field of vision. He reached to pick up the receiver and spoke in a clear rich tone. A voice that made my insides melt.

Two things struck me. Firstly, Major Stapleton was right. Should an invading force set up shop here at Ashworth, there was a good chance that they would use this room for their operations. If they did, from my position in the wall, I would be able to hear every word spoken and gather vital intelligence.

Secondly, Edward was my new boss.

28

My choices were limited. I could stay where I was and wait for Edward to leave, or retreat underground to the bunker and use the escape tunnel. Neither option filled me with delight.

Edward finished his call and returned to his desk. It was clear that he was settled in for several hours of work. If he was expecting his new secretary to appear at some point in the near future, I was going to have to check out that escape tunnel after all. I retraced my steps down through the bunker and started along the tunnel, crouching all the way, cursing the physical restrictions of my uniform. The cramped passageway seemed to go on and on and I began to think that I might be lost underground forever. Just before my torch gave out, I reached a dead end with a metal hatchway overhead.

Taking a moment to gather my thoughts, I gingerly pushed it up a crack. Fresh air flooded in along with birdsong and the rustle of small animals in the undergrowth. I waited, to be sure there were no people around, then swung the hatch fully open and climbed out into low bushes. Securing both the hatch and a section of camouflage netting, I leaned against the fallen trunk of an immense oak tree and brushed cobwebs from my hair and dirt from my uniform. *I must look a complete sight.*

No wonder it had taken so long to get out. I was a long way from the main house, past the stables and up the hill, deep into the trees leading to the coast. Spitting on my hanky, I wiped my face and took several deep breaths of fresh air. It was time to head back and face the music.

The walk to the house gave me time to consider the Edward situation. The last time we'd met, I was sure he'd been about to kiss me. And I'd wanted him to. Not only that, he'd listened to me rattle on about wanting to do something important for the war effort. He had said I was brave and determined. And even though he'd called me the most exasperating woman he'd ever met, he'd also said I was incredible. He had seemed proud of me.

Now, here I was, back at home. A low-ranking secretary; working for him, of all people. Shame burned my cheeks. He would assume that I'd given up or, worse, that I'd failed to make the grade and been sent back home. How could he think anything else? And I couldn't tell him otherwise. It was nauseating. The whole situation made me ache with frustration. I wanted to shout the truth from the treetops but Major Stapleton had been clear. Even though it stuck in my craw, I had to stay silent.

Arriving back at the office door, I marched in. Edward looked up from his papers and sprang to his feet. He limped around the desk, a smile lighting up his features. 'Wren! How lovely to see you! What are you doing here?'

I stood to attention. 'I'm reporting for duty, Commander.'

He stopped short. 'I beg your pardon?'

'I am your new secretary, sir.'

'Are you?' Surprise skipped across his face. 'I received a

message to expect someone, but they didn't say who.' He took a step back, examining me from head to toe. 'You look like you've been dragged through a hedge backwards.'

I dropped my gaze, brushing at a streak of mud on my skirt. Could my humiliation get any worse? 'I went for a walk, and took a tumble.'

'Are you hurt?'

'No.' I shook my head. 'I'm fine. Thank you, sir.'

'You don't have to call me, sir, Wren.'

I locked eyes with him briefly, my gaze emotionless. 'I do, sir. I'm your junior officer.'

He pursed his lips. 'Then, technically, I suppose you do, but not when we are alone, I think. Please, be at ease, Wren. Talk to me.'

I gave a short nod and relaxed my stance. 'What do you want me to say?'

'I never thought to see you back at Ashworth. What happened?'

My lips smiled as best they could as I stared over his shoulder. 'I've learned that one has to take what one is given. This is as good a position as any.' It was the closest I could come to the truth.

He tried to capture my gaze with his but I refused to co-operate. I couldn't bear to see the inevitable conclusions he must be drawing. Witnessing him lower his expectations of me was too painful. Before he could say anything, I rattled on with fake cheer, 'I didn't expect you to be here, either. Last I heard you were a captain. And, now, you're a commander. You must be very proud. Congratulations.'

'Thank you. The honorific title, commander, goes with the position of senior officer in charge of any unit. Even this maternity home. Like you say, it's as good a position as any. Given my physical limitations—' he grimaced and gave his stick a little wave '—I have to take the postings I am given.'

'Life doesn't always turn out the way we think it will, does it?' I indicated the second desk and moved towards it. 'Is this one mine?'

'Yes. You should find all the equipment you need. I'm told that machine—' he pointed at the typewriter '—is the latest model. A Remington Noiseless, apparently. Top of the range and identical to the ones in Churchill's war room.'

'Lucky me.' My tone was almost as dry as my mouth. I ran my hands over the keys, my eyes creeping up to feast on Edward as he returned to his desk. It was so good to see him, especially looking so much healthier, and moving with such confidence. His broad shoulders filled his uniform to perfection. Even his limp was rhythmic and lithe rather than painful and stilted. Every inch of me yearned to throw caution to the wind and tell him the truth. Making a concerted effort to pull myself together, I sat down and searched the drawers for paper and a pencil. 'Shall we get started?'

* * *

Several hours later, I slunk back to my room, threw myself onto the bed and stared at a crack in the ceiling. My nerves jangled. Not revealing my true purpose at Ashworth to Edward made me ache all over. It was impossible to concentrate. Why did the man affect me like this? His voice, the turn of his head, the way he moved. All I could hope for was that, in time, my senses would adjust and come down off their current extra-high alert setting. For one thing, it made typing very difficult. I'd have to do better, tomorrow.

My limbs buzzed. I needed to burn off pent-up energy if I

was ever going to sleep. Pulling on loose trousers and a top, I slipped out of a side door intent on going for a run. I'd take the opportunity to check out my patrol route while I was at it.

The night was clear. The waning moon still cast enough silvery light for me to find my way. It didn't take long to settle into a steady, rhythmic pace along the familiar footpath. I kept my senses alert, ready to slip into the trees out of sight at the first sign that I wasn't alone. The forest at night had never scared me. Creatures went about their business, unfazed by my passage. Some were settling for the night, others just waking up. Bats dipped and dived overhead. Hedgehogs scurried through leaves. Owls called out in the deepening darkness. All too soon, the sparkle of moonbeams on water peeped through the trees. Ashworth Bay. Slowing to a light jog, I made for the western headland and gazed down at the sand and the gently lapping waves. All beaches along the coast were officially out of bounds and almost impossible to reach thanks to the defensive measures installed.

The urge to dip my toes in the water was overwhelming. I checked my surroundings. There was no sign of a Home Guard patrol in progress. I worked my way along the narrow headland to the small rocky outcrop overgrown with clumps of thick marram grass. Slipping off my shoes, I eased my way through the embrace of several prickly gorse bushes and began to climb down the cliff. It wasn't a path by any stretch of the imagination, merely a series of staggered ledges that Tommy and I had worked out how to negotiate as children. Before long, I was on the shingle, beyond the razor wire, stakes and mines.

I closed my eyes and dipped my toes into the sea, enjoying the simple pleasure of paddling. Cold water lapped at my ankles, the sensation of sand and small stones shifting underfoot. Taking a deep breath of fresh, salty air, I finally felt the tension in my shoulders slipping away. I could do this. I could work with Edward *and* keep my mission a secret. I'd take it one step at a time. All would be well.

The sound of a regular splash filtered into my thoughts. I scanned the waters of the bay. My heart leapt into my mouth. A swimmer carved through the water, arms alternating in a creditable front crawl, heading straight out to sea. For a fleeting moment I thought it was Tommy before my instinctive glow of delight solidified into cold, hard anger. Of course it wasn't Tommy. But who was it? And how dare they swim in our cove? More importantly, how the hell had they got through all the beach defences, let alone the scaffolding pipes that I knew had been sunk into the water at low tide? Hard on the heels of those thoughts came another more disturbing one. Why were they here? I covered my mouth with both hands, my mind racing. Could this be an enemy agent?

I scurried back to the shelter of the cliff, ducked behind a large rock and watched. The swimmer neared the buoy tethered furthest out in the bay. The regular overarm strokes slowed and the swimmer turned a wide half circle around the buoy before heading back to shore. Holding my breath, I kept my eyes locked on their progress, noting that the swimmer's technique, whilst good, was slightly uneven. One arm had a stronger pull than the other. The swimmer neared the shore and a head and a pair of broad shoulders rose from the water followed by a deep chest and muscular thighs. Naked as the day he was born, Edward strode onto the beach, reaching for a towel placed next to a pile of clothes. I couldn't tear my eyes away, even as my brain shrieked at me to leave before he saw me.

'There's no need to hide,' he called out. 'I know you're there.'

I shrank further back into the shadows, averting my gaze. My hands flew to my burning cheeks. Oh, God. Here I was, staring. What must he think? Perhaps if I stayed very still, and very quiet, he'd think I'd gone.

'Wren. Come on out. I know it's you.' He stepped into his trousers, securing them at the waist, and slid one arm into his shirt. Reaching around behind, he searched for the second sleeve. There was something awkward in the movement of his left arm that I'd not noticed before, and he kept missing his target. 'Blast it. Wren, for goodness' sake, are you just going to stand there, or are you going to help me?'

My body took over without instruction from me. I hurried to hold the shirt so he could shrug into it. A gasp died in my throat at the sight of the thick rope of scar tissue that glinted almost white in the moonlight. It ran up his back and over one shoulder. My fingers itched to soothe his hurt away. I clenched them into fists and stepped away.

'You do know this beach is out of bounds, don't you?' he asked, turning to look at me.

'I do.'

'I'm intrigued.' He tipped his head at the wire. 'How did you get through that?'

I shrugged, unwilling to give away my secret path down from the cliff. Major Stapleton had been clear about not trusting anyone, even him. His presence here was decidedly odd. 'How did you do it?' I asked.

'Like this.' He gathered up his towel and inched a path through the thick wooden stakes pointing out to sea. I followed him over to a large rock. He used a wide plank of driftwood to push down the razor wire and walked over it.

'Impressive,' I said skipping over behind him. 'And very brave. After all, three feet that way—' I pointed left '—and... well... boom!'

He followed my finger, a muscle working in his jaw. 'Mines?'

I nodded. 'Yup. There's a big warning sign up on the cliff.'

He grunted. 'I must have missed that. Although, I suppose it is to be expected.' He turned a quizzical gaze on me. 'How come you know where they are?'

'I watched them being laid.'

'I don't want to know how you managed that,' he muttered, pulling the plank of wood up behind us and allowing the wire to spring back into place. 'But, seeing as you did, you'd better lead the way from here.'

Two minutes later, we were safely back on the cliff path. 'What are you doing out so late?' His autocratic tone reminded me so much of Father, it snapped any semblance of amicable connection between us.

All my compassion for his injuries evaporated. 'What am *I* doing here? I'll have you know, I've been running along this coast for the best part of two decades. The real question is, what are *you* doing here?'

'The doctor recommended swimming to aid my recovery.'

'Did he also recommend dicing with death by anti-tank defences and a trigger-happy Home Guard?' I didn't bother to mute the sarcasm in my voice. 'If they come along here and see you out there, they could be forgiven for thinking you're a... a...'

'A what? A one-man invasion?' He laughed. 'I doubt enemy attack plans include sending individual troops out for a night-time swim off the coast.'

I crossed my arms. 'They'll think you're a spy.'

He held his hands up in surrender. 'You're right. Which is exactly why *you* shouldn't be here either. It's not safe.'

'Safe for you but not for me?' I asked.

'How would you defend yourself?'

Something snapped inside. How dare he act like I was

completely powerless. 'I'm not some helpless little flower. I learned a lot at Hannington. I can handle myself.'

'I still don't think you should be out here in the dark,' he insisted.

'Edward, I work for you but you don't own me. That means you get to say what I do during daytime office hours. All other times, including the evenings, my time is my own. If I want to come out for a walk, or a run, or even—' I gestured at the sea '— a swim, I will. Is that clear?'

He closed the gap between us, one hand closing around my upper arm, tugging me closer until I could feel his breath, warm on my face. The urge to move closer still ambushed me. My breathing was fast and shallow, my skin tingling in anticipation. I wanted nothing more than to tip my face up towards his.

'I missed you,' he whispered. 'Heaven help me. I can't stop thinking about you. You're my friend's sister and my junior officer. I shouldn't have feelings for you.'

'Feelings?' I whispered, electricity crackling through every part of me. My body swayed towards him of its own volition, like iron filings to a magnet.

'Please, Wren. I couldn't bear it if anything happened to you. I'm sorry things didn't work out for you at Hannington. Let me keep you safe.'

I shook myself free of him, the flames lit by his proximity doused by his words. Gathering my dignity around me like armour, I said, 'You're not listening to me. I can look after myself.'

'You must be disappointed to have been sent back here,' he said.

My jaw ached with the effort it took to stay silent, anger simmering in my core.

'But, Wren, I can't lie to you,' he continued, 'I'm glad you're here.'

'You're glad I didn't get the posting I wanted.'

'No. Not that.' He reached a hand out to me. 'I am glad that you are safe. I promised Tommy I would protect you and I can't do that if you're off heaven knows where, doing—'

I knocked his hand aside. 'I'm not some obligation handed to you by my brother,' I spat. 'What about what I want? I'm a person in my own right, with hopes and dreams of my own. If you can't treat me as an equal, then stay the hell away from me. Now, excuse me? I have a run to finish.'

'Wren? Wren, wait.'

I closed my ears, ducked into the treeline and broke into a steady jog. Taking care to maintain as silent a footfall as I could, I weaved between tree trunks and dodged behind bushes. With my knowledge of the area, I was soon able to shake off Edward's clumsy attempts to follow me. A combination of anger, frustration and disappointment kept me company for several miles inland, all the way from Ashworth Bay to the outskirts of the village of Ambleford. It was only then that I realised how late it was, and I turned for home.

29

The next morning, I arrived at the office with my emotions hogtied, braced for confrontation, only to find a note on my desk. Edward's spiky handwriting informed me that he would be away for a couple of days. He had meetings at two other military sites in the area: Bramford Hall in Ambleford and Whitely Manor south of Beckley Grange. He'd left me a list of tasks to complete in his absence and I spent the morning systematically working through everything, whilst taking telephone messages and filing paperwork. At one thirty, June tapped on the door and asked me to join her for lunch. The prospect of her company and her bright, friendly chatter was just what I needed to lift my spirits.

After a lightly spiced bowl of blitz soup – a warming concoction of cabbage, onion and carrots served with a dry but filling hunk of bread – I strode along the hall towards the office, ready to tackle the mountain of typing waiting for me. Turning the corner, I ground to a halt with a sharp intake of breath. The door to the study was ajar. I'd locked it. I knew I had.

Was Edward back?

I tentatively pushed the door fully open, surprised to see the grumpy orderly, who had given June a hard time the day I arrived, standing by Edward's desk. There was no one else in the room.

'How did you get in?' I demanded.

He spun around, eyebrows raised in surprise. 'The door was open.'

'No, it wasn't.' I frowned. 'I locked it when I left half an hour ago.'

'You can't have. Otherwise I wouldn't be in here, would I?'

His patronising tone put my teeth on edge. He was not a commissioned officer. There was no reason to allow him to talk down to me. I was damned if I'd let him get away with it. I narrowed my eyes and spoke slowly and clearly. 'It. Was. Locked.'

He shrugged. 'Someone unlocked it then, didn't they?'

Aware that we could go back and forth like that all day, I changed my tactic. 'Fine. Why are you here?'

He picked up a pile of papers from Edward's desk. 'Matron asked me to deliver these.' He thrust them at me.

A quick glance told me the documents included a list of patient names for the next evacuation transport, along with each patient's medical file. 'Thank you,' I said. 'You can go, now.'

He scowled at my dismissive tone. I locked eyes with him, my expression blank, and waited. After several beats of silence, he whirled on his heel and left, slamming the door behind him. I stood stock-still for several minutes, my skin crawling as if thousands of tiny ants were scurrying just beneath the surface. The door had definitely been locked. If *he* hadn't unlocked the door, then who did? More importantly, why?

***

I was still mulling over the conundrum when I finished my tasks late that afternoon. I carefully locked the office door, triple-checking that it was definitely locked, before changing and heading off for an early evening run down to the coast. The exercise and fresh air helped to clear my head and soon I emerged from the trees at the clifftop.

Gazing out to sea, I remembered Edward swimming the night before. The thought of diving into the crisp, cool waters stayed with me as I completed a full circuit of the forest paths Major Stapleton had asked me to patrol. I arrived back at Ashworth Bay in the gathering dusk and scanned the coastline for any notable anomalies. A crescent moon and a handful of twinkling stars rode low over the Isle of Wight. Bats flitted overhead. Stiff, spiky grasses spilled down the cliff line and the fizzing, rhythmic rush and retreat of water over shingle called to me. Certain that all was as it should be, I picked my way down my hidden cliffside path again, shucked my clothes and stowed them under a rock. Clad only in my white cotton unmentionables, I waded into the sea.

The water's silky embrace engulfed me. I edged with care over the underwater metalwork until I was far enough out to swim parallel to the shoreline unimpeded. Reaching the far headland, I ducked down into a tumble turn before starting back. The familiar exercise and muscle memory forced my body to release the tension it had hoarded during the day. I swam up and down until my limbs felt heavy and my head was empty at last. Turning onto my back, I lay like a starfish in the water, every inch of me completely relaxed. I stared up into the stunning expanse of sky and thought: *Tommy would love this.*

Suddenly, arms like steel bands latched around my middle. I was yanked against a rock-solid torso. Squealing, I jack-knifed, lashing out, squirming to break free. My vision blurred. Salt water stung my throat. Wet hands slipped on wet skin. Unable to find enough purchase to push away, I aimed a savage kick at my assailant's lower quarters. The water slowed the impact, but my blow hit with sufficient force. There was a grunt and the grip of those arms eased enough for me to wriggle free. I resurfaced, gasping for air, poised to break into a fast front crawl.

A deep voice rent the air. 'Stop. Wait.'

'Edward?' I gasped. 'What the hell are you trying to do? Drown me or terrify the life out of me?'

He coughed, shaking water from his eyes. 'I saw you from the cliff. Lying deathly still. I thought you'd drowned.'

'Don't be ridiculous,' I scoffed. 'I'm fine.'

'I can see that. Corpses don't usually fight back.'

'You sound disappointed. Oh!' My eye caught on the scars criss-crossing over his shoulder and down onto his chest. Unable to stop myself, I reached out.

He jerked back. 'Leave it. It's nothing.'

'It's not nothing. What happened to you, Edward?'

'I was lucky.' He gave a bitter laugh. 'If you can call being stranded in enemy territory with serious injuries lucky.'

I thought of Tommy, a heavy, jagged lump of worry lodging in my chest. What if he were stranded somewhere, injured, trying to get home? 'You made it back, when so many don't. Whichever way you look at it, Edward, that *is* lucky. And extremely brave.'

He didn't reply.

'I'm imagining all sorts of horrors, here,' I said softly. 'Please, tell me the truth?'

He was silent for several beats, treading water and staring out towards the island with an unfocused intensity that suggested he was seeing things that weren't really there. 'Parachuting behind enemy lines is always dangerous. Our mission was doomed from the start.'

'You were a paratrooper?'

He shrugged.

'What went wrong?' I whispered, aware that I probably shouldn't ask, but I needed to know. I had no idea what it was like to be in an active combat zone. I wanted to understand.

'We were betrayed. They knew we were coming.'

'How can you tell?'

'You have to bring the plane down to a low enough altitude for troops to drop successfully. Anti-aircraft guns were waiting for us. The mobile sort. They had been moved into position ready. We were hit almost immediately.'

'Oh my.' I shuddered at the thought. 'Couldn't your pilot turn around or fly higher?'

'He was dead. Bullets ripped through the plane, killing the crew and most of the company. Both engines were on fire. I had no choice but to bail and risk the guns on the way down. My chute was damaged but still worked well enough. I was burned, dazed and pretty much a sitting duck. They were taking potshots at me, two of which got me in the leg. By rights I should have died.'

If he had died then, I would never have met him. The very idea brought with it a groundswell of unbearable loss. 'How come you didn't?'

'Pure chance. A gust of wind carried me over a woodland. I took a gamble and cut my parachute free.'

'While you were still in the air?' He must have been really desperate to do something like that. Heights had never particularly bothered me, but there was no way I could have done it. How brave.

He nodded. 'The white silk was giving away my location. The wind took it and I fell. Luckily, I got tangled in the branches of a tree rather than hitting the ground. A brave local lad – he couldn't have been more than fourteen, I reckon – cut me loose and hid me in an abandoned barn until the enemy search for survivors was called off. When I was recovered enough, I made for the coast.'

He looked so utterly lost as he spoke. On impulse, I darted forward in the water and pressed a kiss to his lips. Before I could retreat, his arms slipped around me, pulling me close. He deepened the kiss. The heat of his mouth in contrast to the chill of the sea water was like a magnet. I wanted more. My arms crept around his neck. I'd never experienced anything like it before. I wanted to drink him in, to get so close that we merged into one. His strong hands ran up and down my spine, setting off delicious tingles that rippled through me from my head to my toes. I never wanted it to end.

Breaking the kiss, he gently touched his forehead to mine, and whispered, 'Promise me you won't swim alone at night, please?'

I tugged from his grasp, swirling vast armfuls of water into the gap between us. 'Don't start.'

'Well don't be obstinate,' he replied. 'Have I not just proved how dangerous it is here? I just swam right up and grabbed you. For heaven's sake, we just *kissed*.'

'Don't worry. *That* won't happen again.' No way was he getting to control me. I didn't care how good a kisser he was. I struck out for the far headland with a strong overarm stroke.

'Wren, come back!'

I glanced back over my shoulder. 'Ha! Make me.'

I'd watched him swim; I'd seen his uneven stroke. There was no way he could outpace me. Spurred on by a wicked delight in frustrating him, I powered across the bay. By the time I made it to the beach he was well behind. I grabbed my things and shimmied up the cliffside before melting into the forest to dress and jog home.

30

My brain replayed that kiss, over and over, all night. There was no doubt, my body wanted Edward. Edward! Tommy's friend and my senior officer. It was all wrong, yet the chemistry between us was undeniable. A delicious sizzling reaction that was impossible to ignore. But he clearly thought of me as some simpering wallflower in need of his protection. It was infuriating not to be able to tell him or show him otherwise thanks to my situation. If he couldn't respect me as an equal, there was no future for us.

After tossing and turning for hours, I rose determined to present a professional but distant demeanour in the office and to avoid Edward at all other times. It was the only way to stay focused and in control.

He was already at his desk when I arrived and looked up with a frown. 'Close the door, please.'

I complied, prickles of unease skating across my shoulders. Was he angry?

He got to his feet, rounded the desk and stopped a few feet

away. 'I owe you an apology. My behaviour last night was unprofessional and ungentlemanly. I should never have... uh...'

'Kissed me?'

He coughed. 'Exactly.'

'If you remember correctly, *I* started it.'

'Did you?' His brow furrowed some more. 'Oh! Yes, you did.' He coughed again. 'It doesn't matter. I should never have... well. Anyway. I am sorry. It won't happen again.'

Was he blushing? He was definitely blushing. 'I am sorry too,' I said.

'Good.' He gave a brisk nod and went to retrieve his coat from the coat stand by the door. 'We'll say no more about it. I have a number of errands this morning, but there is plenty to keep you occupied here. If you could answer any calls and take messages, that would be helpful. I am waiting for information on the Home Guard and a number of other dispatches as well.'

Before I could reply, he was gone, leaving me wondering if he really needed to be elsewhere, or was he deliberately avoiding me?

I passed the morning typing letters, sorting paperwork and taking telephone messages. It was steady, interesting work that gave me a good overview of the various military outfits operating in other requisitioned properties in the area. Matron sent messengers in periodically with queries about medical supplies and mother and baby evacuation arrangements.

Eventually, June stuck her head around the door and said, 'Are you coming to lunch? They baked honey biscuits, this morning. The smell has been driving me mad. I do hope there are some left.'

I locked the door and followed her to the canteen for bread and SPAM with a sliver of cheese as a treat. Whilst there, I managed to secure a tray of tea things and a small plate of honey biscuits, fresh from the oven, to keep me going for the afternoon. Returning to the office, I was surprised to see Father in the hall. An avalanche of guilt crashed through me. I should have paid a call to the gatehouse to see how he was, but the thought of facing a barrage of criticism had stopped me. Now, here he was. To my shame, my first instinct was to shrink back out of sight until he left. Then I saw the look on his face. Standing still, right in the middle of the hall, with the activities of the maternity home flowing around him, he seemed utterly lost. Orderlies ignored him as they bustled past with equipment. Nurses helped patients move between wards as if he wasn't there.

Bracing myself for inevitable censure, I hastened forward.

'Father. Hello. Here, if you could take this, I'll unlock the office.' Without giving him time to object, I thrust the tea tray at him and fumbled for the key. 'Please, come in.'

Inside, he hummed and hawed as he examined the changes to his study. I poured us both some tea and offered him a seat. He accepted his cup with a grunt and sat. 'You're back, then?' he said, his voice lacking its usual vigour. 'Finished junketing about the countryside, have you?'

'I have.'

'What did they teach you then?'

I lifted one shoulder and let it drop. 'Standard office protocol. Telephone etiquette, typing, general filing systems.'

'Huh! It's a waste of time training a woman but, I suppose, it will keep you out of mischief.'

What he would think if he knew the truth? It was strange not to feel my usual outrage at such comments from him. Perhaps the knowledge that I now had skills, way beyond anything he could possibly imagine, gave me confidence. Whatever he said, he couldn't belittle me. Nothing could take my achievements away. Even so, telling myself that didn't help as much as I had hoped it would. Inside, I was still a little girl who wanted to make my father proud. He was never going to know that I was putting my life on the line for my country. He was never going to know the real me.

He jerked a hand towards the telephones. 'Why do you need three of them?'

There was no need to dissemble. 'One is a secure line from the War Office. The other two are for general communication. One local. The other national.'

'Hmm. A secure line from the War Office, eh?' One bushy eyebrow quirked with interest. 'Talk to them much, do you?'

'Usually, it's Captain Landers they speak to. But, I've taken several messages, today.'

'Have you?' He peered at the stack of papers on my desk. 'What about?'

It felt wrong, but I had no choice. I stepped between him and the desk. 'It's confidential, Father. Marked *most secret*. You understand.'

His face fell. Then he helped himself to one of my biscuits and nodded. 'I do. I do indeed. Yes. Yes. Well. Who would have thought it? You handling important wartime information.' Did I hear a sprinkling of grudging respect? 'Very impressive,' he said. It almost sounded like he meant it.

Astounded, I cast around for something to say. 'How are you settling in at the gatehouse?'

'It's small and cramped, compared to here, but thanks to the modifications I talked Colonel Williams into making before he left, it is adequate.'

'That's good to hear.' It dawned on me that this was potentially the most civilised conversation we'd ever had. Perhaps we were moving into a new phase of our relationship. I resolved to go and visit him very soon.

'Of course, I'm not there much,' he continued. 'I'm a busy man. I've been supervising the extra vegetable gardens going in on the south lawns. Farmer Barnes needed direction. He doesn't understand about the importance of soil quality. I've been reading up about it.' The defiance in his tone spoke of an underlying desperation to be useful. I recognised that. I'd felt it myself prior to my connection with Major Stapleton. That need to be involved. To do my part.

'I'm sure Farmer Barnes is very grateful for your help,' I murmured.

'There's not much to do, now it's all installed, of course. We have to wait for the damned veg to grow.' He cleared his throat. 'I don't suppose...' He tugged a handkerchief from his pocket and blew his nose.

It was bizarre to be in this position. He clearly wanted something from me. 'You don't suppose what, Father?'

'Nothing, nothing.'

The telephone rang. I hastened to answer it. By the time I had finished taking a message, he was gone, leaving me wondering. What on earth could he want?

I worked steadily all afternoon, Father's lost expression preying on my mind. He was a relatively fit man for his age, and intelligent. He needed an occupation. Something to focus on. I was sure of it and when Edward returned, I decided to say something.

'I've been thinking,' I said, before he'd even had a chance to settle in his chair.

'Do I need to be worried?' A teasing smile danced across his face.

I couldn't help but respond in kind. 'Always.' I shook my head, fighting to stay on point. 'You know we had that message in yesterday, about the Home Guard in Ambleford?'

'Ambleford. Remind me. That's the village where the sergeant in charge is ill, isn't it?'

'Yes. It's about four miles directly north of here. Anyway, there was another phone call today. The sergeant has taken a turn for the worse. You've been asked to arrange a replacement.'

'I see.' Edward's eyes narrowed. 'Why do I get the impression you have a suggestion?'

'I think you should ask Father if he'll do it.'

He leaned his elbows on the desk and steepled his fingers. 'You're advocating for your father?'

'I suppose I am. Yes.'

'I thought you and he didn't get on.'

'Whether we do or don't, that doesn't negate the value he could bring to the Home Guard,' I said.

He sat back in his chair. 'True. But didn't he already turn down an invitation to be involved?'

'Yes, he did. But that was only for the small unit at Ashworth,' I rushed on. 'And it was ages ago. I think he thought refusing that position would mean he'd get offered something more important. Only that didn't happen.' I remembered tiptoeing around him for days after that particular incident.

'It's an interesting idea.' Edward got to his feet. 'Come along then.'

'Come along where?'

'Let's go and ask him.' He made for the door.

'You want me to come?'

'It's your idea.' He paused. 'Have you been outside at all today?'

I shook my head.

'Well, then. A walk to the gatehouse will do you good. Come on.' He marched out into the hall. I scurried in his wake, locking up behind us as I went. So much for my plan to avoid spending time with Edward.

31

We strolled down the drive in the sunshine together. Birdsong filled the air and the heady vanilla scent of early broom rolled off the heathland.

The gatehouse had been built in the latter part of the previous century. My great-grandfather had been determined to improve Ashworth using the plentiful dowry that came with his marriage to my great-grandmother, an American heiress. At the same time as commissioning the ornate red brickwork and imposing chimneys on the manor itself, he had insisted that a sizeable gatehouse along with huge brick pillars and an ornate wrought-iron gate be constructed at the point that the carriageway from the manor met the main road through the forest. The building was intended to house great-grandfather's mother-in-law on the mercifully few occasions that she deigned to cross the Atlantic on extended visits. As such, it boasted several sizeable reception rooms downstairs, with comfortable family bedrooms on the first floor, and a kitchen and scullery with a room out the back for a cook-cum-housekeeper to live in.

Father seemed surprised to see us and ushered us in with all haste. He had certainly made himself comfortable in his new home. The drawing room was furnished with a selection of pieces I recognised from my childhood: family heirlooms, silk rugs and wall hangings, all transported from the main house, giving it a cosy familiar feel.

'What can I do for you, Commander?' he said, inviting us to sit.

Edward settled into a winged-back chair near the fire and absently tapped his cane against his boot. 'It's rather more, what you could do for your country.' He paused to let that concept settle.

A light sparked in Father's eyes. 'I'm listening.'

'Your daughter suggests that you might be exactly what we need to sort out an issue with the local militia.'

Father's eyes darted to me. 'The Home Guard?'

'Yes,' I said, hastening to explain before he could misunderstand. 'But not the Ashworth Home Guard. Or, not *just* the Ashworth Home Guard.'

'There's a vacancy a little higher up that needs filling,' said Edward.

Father frowned. 'Where?'

'Ambleford and the neighbouring area.'

'I see. And what exactly has my daughter been saying about me?'

'That your years of military experience, and your knowledge of the area, means that there is no one better to command the respect of both local recruits and any additional military personnel posted here from other areas in the way that such a position would require.'

Father let out a long, slow breath. His shoulders, which had been up around his ears, started to drop away. 'She's not wrong.'

Edward let out a soft laugh. 'I am beginning to realise that she is rarely wrong.'

My heart skipped a beat. Had he just said that?

Father's eyes turned to me, brimming with confusion. 'Really? I've always found her rather headstrong and defiant.'

I ducked my head, praying for the ground to swallow me up.

'Her strength and resilience are admirable,' said Edward with an unmistakable warning in his tone.

'Maybe so, maybe so,' mused Father.

'We need someone to take over immediately,' said Edward. 'There's a batch of new recruits arriving from Salisbury next week. They need processing and knocking into shape, before being assigned to smaller units in and around the forest. Will you take the post?'

Father got to his feet. 'I will.'

'Excellent.' Edward stood too. 'We'll head back and Wren can set that in motion. She is your point of contact on this and will be in touch with your official orders as soon as everything is arranged.'

If Father was disconcerted that he was to work with me, he had the grace not to show it. He followed us to the door and said goodbye with every appearance of bonhomie.

'I think that went rather well,' said Edward as we walked back to the main house. 'Do you have all the contacts and forms you need to set that up while I am away tomorrow?'

'Yes, I think so,' I said. 'I'll get onto it first thing.' I threw a shy glance at him. 'Did you mean what you said about me rarely being wrong?'

He paused, shooting me a wide grin. 'I never say things I don't mean.'

I smiled back and we stood on the drive, a long, steady look passing between us for what felt like hours but could only have been seconds.

Suddenly he seemed to shake himself awake. 'We had better get on,' he said striding briskly over the gravel.

I fell into step, both grateful that the moment had passed and also sad at the same time. Why on earth did being around this man affect me so much? We walked back to the house in contemplative silence, each occupied with our own thoughts.

32

The next day, Edward was gone again. I was grateful to have the office to myself without his large distracting presence. Although it did give me too much time to think. I found it hard to settle and checked the time repeatedly. When I caught myself wondering for the third time when he would be back I knew I had a problem. I missed him.

June popped her head around the door, her face flushed, strands of hair escaping from under her cap.

'Goodness,' I said, delighted to have a distraction from my troublesome thoughts. 'What happened to you?'

'Tell me, Wren. If I ask for sanctuary from small children, does that make me a bad maternity nurse?'

I laughed and beckoned her in. 'The commander's not here today. No one will know if you hide out in here for five minutes.'

She dragged a chair over to my desk and slumped down on it. I passed her a couple of bobby pins from my desk drawer for her hair.

'Thank you,' she said. 'You're a lifesaver. Those Thomas twins are such a handful. Two years old and cute as buttons, with the destructive capabilities of a whole platoon of soldiers. Honestly, how their mother is going to manage them *and* the new baby once she leaves here is beyond me.'

I shuffled the papers on my desk. 'I'm just working on their evacuation details now. There's a billeting officer with a host family for them in Mousehole.' This was a part of the work for the maternity home that I'd grown to really appreciate. It might be a cover for my other activities, but, being involved in finding safe havens for vulnerable patients away from the bombs was important. I was genuinely doing good. It was a positive counterbalance to the time I spent focused on War Office communications, patrols, enemy transmissions and the threat of spies.

'Where's that?'

'Cornwall. Near Penzance. In fact, there are host families in the area for all four of the mothers who are ready to leave.'

'That's good,' said June, her hair now restored to order. 'It means they'll be company for each other. It can't be easy going to a whole new place so far away.'

I murmured agreement. Making sure the mothers had access to a support network was a vital part in the success of each placement. 'I've a list of what they are expected to pack, here. It's not much, though. There simply isn't room for loads of luggage. We'll supply some food for the journey and, of course, they have to remember their gas masks. I have some of the special units on order for the new babies.' I found the little suits, which totally encased a new-born, quite alarming, but they were a necessary evil. 'They should be with us in the next day or so.'

'When is the transport scheduled to leave?' asked June.

'Next Friday. A—'

An abrupt knock on the door made us both sit up straight.

Matron entered looking almost as harassed as June. 'There

you are, Nurse,' she declared. 'What are you doing in here? There's no time to be sat gossiping. You're needed in delivery.'

Before June could reply, I spoke. 'It's my fault, Matron. I am so sorry. I needed some information before I could process these evacuation orders.' I pointed to the papers on my desk.

Matron looked mystified. 'I thought we covered everything, yesterday.'

'I thought so too.' I shuffled the papers, squirming inside. The last thing I needed was to annoy Matron. Why had I felt the urge to defend June? I wasn't supposed to be drawing attention to myself. 'But I wanted to double-check a few things and I didn't like to disturb you when you are so busy.'

Matron's glance bounced from me to June and back, her lips compressed into a tight line. 'Well, next time, come to me. I would prefer it if you didn't bother my staff.'

'I won't. I promise.' I turned to June. 'Thank you for your help.'

'Chop, chop, Nurse,' said Matron. 'Else that poor baby will arrive without you.' She herded June from the room, shot me a look of extreme irritation and closed the door behind them both.

No sooner had I settled back to my typing than another knock sounded at the door and Major Stapleton walked in. I sprang to my feet in surprise and stood to attention, saluted her.

'I didn't know you were coming, Major.' Thank goodness she hadn't arrived ten minutes earlier and caught me gossiping.

'That is the point of the exercise,' she said, her tone dry. She gestured for me to relax. 'I drop in to visit all my operatives from time to time. I like to see them in action and check that all is as it should be. How are you settling in?'

'Good, thank you,' I said, not really believing her.

'Do you have what you need? Have you found everything where it was expected to be?'

She must be referring to the bunker and the other secret caches of equipment. 'Yes, everything is present and correct. And I have established a routine for monitoring the radio and patrolling as ordered.' This was all information that I had confirmed via radio message soon after my arrival. She must have another reason for coming.

'Excellent.' She paced over to the window. 'Tell me, what are your thoughts about the maternity home commander?'

I ducked my head to hide the stain spreading up my cheeks. She couldn't possibly know that I had kissed Edward, could she? Perhaps she did. Perhaps I had compromised myself. Could she be here to remove me from my post? Panic galloped through my mind. I wasn't ready to leave. In only a few weeks, I had gone from hating life at Ashworth to feeling like an integral part of things.

Before I could speak, she continued, 'I am not familiar with him.' She clasped her hands behind her back, her eyes on the stained glass. 'Does he strike you as trustworthy?'

It was best to say as little as possible, and stick to the truth. 'I don't know him well, ma'am. Although he is a friend of my brother's. I do believe he is trustworthy. Yes.'

She nodded and turned to face me. 'Good. And the other staff here?'

I thought of June, Matron and the general staff. 'They all seem as they should.'

'So, no areas of concern?'

'No. None.' Bemused, I wondered if I had missed something and then remembered. 'Oh, there was one thing. Although I'm not really sure if it is something or not.'

'What?'

I was reluctant to go on, in case she thought I was to blame, but the simple fact that it had happened still bothered me. 'I came back to the office the other day to find the door unlocked and a member of staff in here unattended. He said the door was open. Only I swear I locked it. And the commander wasn't here. No one else has a key.'

'Hmm,' she said, deep in thought. 'But you can't say for certain that it was locked?'

'I remember locking it, but...' I shrugged, helpless to explain further.

'And the member of staff, who was he?'

'One of the orderlies.'

'Was anything missing?'

I shook my head. 'No, definitely not. All confidential material was locked away.' I had checked thoroughly.

She frowned. 'You should have filed a report.'

'I'm sorry.' She was right. I should have. My only excuse was that I had been distracted by Edward but I could hardly tell her that. Bands of anxiety tightened around my chest until I could barely breathe. It was such an obvious failure to discharge my duties. She could replace me for this. It rammed home the point that letting June in to chat hadn't been a good move. I mustn't lose sight of the bigger picture. A degree of distance from those around me was essential so that I could see things in a clear, objective light.

She shook her head. 'Not to worry. Send me over his name and position and a full account of what happened. I'll get him checked out. Is there anything else I should know?'

'No, ma'am. Not that I can think of. Is there something specific you need information on?'

She shook her head. 'Not as such, no. Merely vague

rumblings. Enough for me to make a quick stop off here en route to Weymouth, to get a feel of the place.'

I wondered what constituted vague rumblings.

'Well,' she said, walking to the door, 'if you have nothing else to report, I will get back on the road. I have another couple of stops to make. Get in touch if you see or hear anything suspicious. No matter how small.' With that, she was gone.

I sat in stunned silence, both furious with myself for my lapse in judgement and relieved at my reprieve. The major's habit of knowing everything had always unnerved me. I was now part of her vast network of informers and I had learned that she never did or said anything without good reason. It was easy to conclude that she had made a point of reminding me of my real purpose at Ashworth. If I wanted to stay – and to my surprise, I did – I needed to keep things on a professional footing. Getting sucked into a friendship with June that could put me at odds with Matron was bad enough. Mooning over Edward was far, far worse. I couldn't indulge my growing feelings for him. And there absolutely could not be any more kissing.

I was here to do a job and I was going to do it properly.

33

The next couple of weeks whizzed by as I juggled the different aspects of my role at Ashworth. The transformation in Father, once he had settled into his new post with the Home Guard, was astonishing. Delighted to be back in uniform, he strode about, every inch the polished, efficient officer in charge. While it was a relief for me to know that his energies had a legitimate focus, I felt some sympathy for the recruits under his command.

I had established a series of dedicated patrol routes as soon as I had arrived at Ashworth. However, sticking to a regular schedule was proving difficult due to both the extent of my obligations in the office and the need to keep a surreptitious watch over people and events in and around the manor. Other than the single occasion of the mysteriously unlocked door, nothing else had occurred to arouse any level of suspicion. Workloads for everyone on site were intense, leaving little time for anything else. Nevertheless, one day, a couple of weeks after Father took over the Home Guard, I found myself with a little extra time on my hands. Edward was away, the telephones and radio were silent, and I had completed the stack of letters that needed typing far earlier than expected.

A complete patrol of the area was long overdue. Popping out for snatched runs here and there in the evenings simply wasn't enough. I needed time to check out all the local drop sites. Changing into the clothes issued at Hannington, I tied my hair back in a scarf and strapped on sturdy boots. I wrapped a hunk of bread, some carrots and a couple of apples into a muslin cloth and packed that with a flask of water into my day pack, and set off.

The weather was crisp and cold, making me thankful I'd had the foresight to grab Tommy's old greatcoat as I left. Pockets of mist lingered in dips and hollows across the forest. Spiderwebs stretched over bushes and low branches, their lacy filaments highlighted with delicate ice crystals. Rabbits and mice darted for cover as I approached. Pheasants rustled in the undergrowth just off the path, occasionally breaking for cover and throwing themselves into the air with their trademark mournful cackle.

Drumming hoofbeats alerted me to a herd of deer galloping away into the treeline. Watching them disappear from view, I mulled over the situation with Father. Edward had been so impressive in the way he had handled him. Respectful, whilst not taking any nonsense. It only made me admire him more. Keeping a professional distance between myself and June was relatively straightforward. But with Edward it was incredibly hard. My pulse jumped with happiness when he entered the room. It took a huge effort not to gaze dreamily at him as he dictated letters or answered the telephone. The number of times that I had replayed his words, *'Her strength and resilience are admirable'*, in my head was getting silly, yet I couldn't help myself no matter how hard I tried.

My patrol took me in a large arc. Starting from the main coastal headland to the east of Ashworth, where the edge of the forest looked out over Chewton Bunny towards Highcliffe Castle, I worked my way north to the village of Ambleford and then west. En route, I checked each drop site, making sure that I wasn't observed as I did so. There were sections of gates that came away, fallen tree trunks with concealed pockets under fake moss, a hollowed-out brick in the wall at the back of Ambleford churchyard and one on the village green near the memorial to those lost in the Great War. A similar hollowed brick arrangement was located in a wall near the hamlet of Ashworth.

Heading south later that afternoon, I followed a section of post-and-rail fencing in search of the final drop site on my list. The sound of a great northern diver reached my ears and the hairs on the back of my neck stood to attention. Pretending indifference, I glanced around. There. At the edge of the forest. A figure. It disappeared into the trees. The bird call sounded again. Keeping my movements casual, I wandered along the rail towards the forest and ducked into the trees, blinking as my eyes adjusted to the darkness.

There was a muted chuckle. 'Fancy seeing you here.'

'Lexi!' A rush of unexpected pleasure surprised me. 'How are you?' I glanced around. 'What are you doing here? I thought we weren't supposed to have any contact.'

'Oh, pshaw!' She made a dismissive gesture. 'I'm not really here. I'm just passing through. You mentioned an Ashworth Manor. The name came up in a dispatch recently. And I looked it up. Then I got sent down this way for something, and it seemed too good an opportunity to pass up. I figured there was no harm in seeing if you were here. Don't worry. I scouted out the area first. We're safe to talk for a bit.'

I pulled the apples from my bag and threw her one. 'What

do you mean you're just passing? Didn't you get assigned straight to a bunker unit after training?'

'No, I didn't.' She crossed her arms and skewered me with a stern look. 'Because *someone* couldn't keep schtum about my little issue with small spaces.'

I nearly choked as a piece of apple threatened to go down the wrong pipe. 'I'm sorry. I didn't mean to rat you out. I tried not to, but Major Stapleton already knew. She made it impossible for me not to say something.'

Lexi cackled with laughter. 'Your face. Don't look so guilty. You did me a favour.'

'I did?'

'Yup. I'm doing much more exciting stuff than operating some poxy bunker. I get sent all over the place. Plus, I get access to lots of top-level information. NOT that I can tell you anything, of course.'

'No, of course not.' I grinned, pleased to see that she was unchanged. 'Although, if you've access to information, do you know what happened to the others?'

She nodded.

'Are they all right?'

She hesitated, then nodded again.

I narrowed my eyes. 'Why don't I believe you?'

'They're fine,' she insisted. 'All except Connie.'

Sharp, icy claws clutched my heart. 'What happened to Connie?'

A dark look crept across her face. 'I don't know, not for sure.' Her obvious distress surprised me. I hadn't thought Lexi particularly close to any of our Hannington Hall companions. 'Last I heard, she went to France,' she said. 'Undercover.'

'Goodness. Although, I'm not surprised, what with her language skills. She's pretty exceptional.'

'Not exceptional enough, unfortunately. She went missing almost immediately.'

'Oh, no.' I covered my mouth with one hand. Not Connie. One of my first real friends. Her smile and sweet nature sprang to mind. Why had she agreed to be sent into occupied France? And what on earth had happened to her? I cursed this awful war. First Tommy and now my friend. Too many good people, people I loved, were being lost. 'Poor Connie,' I said. 'We'll have to hope and pray that she's safe somewhere.'

'Yes, we will.'

Lexi and I stared at each other in horrified silence.

Eventually, Lexi said, 'There's little else we can do. I'll keep my ear to the ground and see what I can find out. Meanwhile...' She put her hands on her hips and shot me a pointed look. 'I came to warn you to stay on your toes.'

'Why?'

'There's a rumour that something big is going down in this area. It's why I made this little detour, even though I'm not supposed to.'

'What sort of something?'

'Possible enemy incursion. There's a suggestion of U-boat movements offshore and potentially a double agent slipping them information.'

'A double agent? At Ashworth? Are you sure?' Was that why Major Stapleton had come calling?

She nodded. 'Important information is definitely falling into enemy hands. We believe that information is coming from Ashworth.'

I frowned. 'I've noticed a spike in enemy radio chatter in the evenings, but nothing specific. And I haven't seen or heard anything. Who do you suspect?'

Lexi crossed her arms. 'That's the problem. We don't know. Is there anyone new to the area?'

I let out an exasperated laugh. 'Pretty much everyone is new. Even Maria the land girl only arrived a few months back. I doubt it's her, though.'

'Why not?'

'Come on, Lex. Whoever it is needs access to sensitive information. Maria never comes inside.'

'As far as you know, she doesn't.' Lexi raised her eyebrows so high, they disappeared under her fringe and fixed me with a speaking look.

'Fine, I won't rule her out. Anyway, after she came, the manor was converted into a maternity home.' I frowned. 'I seriously doubt the pregnant mothers and their children are enemy agents.'

'What about the staff?'

My mind immediately jumped back to the day I found Roberts in the office unattended. 'I've already messaged Major Stapleton about one man. She is doing a background check on him.'

'Anyone else?'

I thought of Matron, June and the other nurses and shook my head. 'They all seem perfectly normal.'

'Don't dismiss anyone without proof.' Lexi leaned in. 'Even those you know personally.'

Thank goodness I had taken subtle steps to distance myself from June. She was so busy, it hadn't been difficult. 'Edward is the only one I know personally.'

'Edward? You mean your hunky captain?'

I rolled my eyes at her. 'He's the commander, and he's not my hunky anything.'

'Oh. He definitely is.' She wiggled her eyebrows at me. 'Lucky you, working with him.'

I shook my head in exasperation. 'There's nothing going on.'

'That's a shame. On a serious note, though, are you certain he can be trusted?'

'Lexi!'

'I mean it. I've seen his military record.'

'What?' I squeaked. 'How?'

'Don't get cross with me. It's my job to check people out. He spent quite a lot of time in a heavily occupied part of France.'

'He was injured.'

'Yes, he was. In a mission that was compromised. The enemy knew they were coming.'

'Are you suggesting that he betrayed his own division and then knowingly parachuted into a death trap?' White-hot outrage that she would even suggest such a thing burned in my chest. 'Lexi, come on.'

'Think about it. He was pretty much the only survivor.'

Surely that made him lucky, not guilty? No. I couldn't believe it. It wasn't possible. Not Edward. 'That's insane. He was shot, badly burned and broke his leg. He will never be the same again. How can you suggest that he's a traitor?' I would know if he was. But in the back of my mind, a small voice asked: *would I?*

She raised her hands in surrender. 'I'm not saying he is, for sure. I am just making the point that even *he* could be the leak. Which is why you have to be careful.'

'I don't believe it of him.' I shook my head. 'He told me he was hidden by a local until he was well enough to escape.'

'I know. That's what the record says. And that may be the truth. Believe me, Wren. I really hope it is. But you *have* to consider the bigger picture. The fact is that intelligence is leaking from your office. So, who else has access, besides you and Edward?'

I scratched my head, racking my brain. 'Matron often comes in, or she sends in one of the orderlies. There are four of them.'

'Who else?'

'Well, there's Father. Then there's June...'

'June?' Lexi raised an eyebrow.

'One of the nurses. She brings queries when Matron is tied up elsewhere.'

'What is she like.'

'June? Efficient. Kind. Nice. We sometimes eat lunch together.'

'And you're careful what you say to her?'

'Of course I am,' I said, crossing my fingers behind my back. I'd been a little bit lax, but I hadn't let anything slip. I was certain of it. That time June had sat in the office chatting with me there had been no confidential information out of the safe apart from patient details and she already knew those because of her job. And when we had lunch I made sure we stayed on safe, neutral topics. 'I'm always careful.'

'Calm down. I only asked.'

I threw up my hands. 'I can't see it, Lex. Apart from that one incident with Roberts, no one has been in the office without either Edward or I being present.'

'Could someone lurk outside and listen?'

I blew out my cheeks. 'I doubt it. Matron is pretty hot on keeping the hallway clear. The phone lines are checked regularly to make sure they're secure. And the office is always locked when we're not there. Edward and I have the only keys. There's only—' I broke off.

What if someone knew about the bunker? They could listen from the priest hole. I'd done it myself so I knew it was possible.

Only, no one other than myself and Major Stapleton's secret operations team were supposed to know it existed. Which meant that... What if someone inside special ops was the traitor? They could have leaked information about the bunker to a local double agent who was using it to spy on us. Could I even trust Lexi? I pressed my fingers to my temple, trying to stop my mind from spinning out of control. I told myself not to be so silly. Of course I could trust her. But, then again, what if she was trying to trick me into revealing information right now?

'What?' asked Lexi. 'There's only who?'

I shook my head. 'No one. It's nothing. I'm being silly.'

She gripped my shoulder. 'Please be careful, Wren. There's nothing more I can do to help you. I wish there was. If they find out I've come, I'll be for the high jump.'

I forced my lips to smile. 'Don't worry. I'll be fine and I'll keep my eyes peeled. Thanks for the heads up.' I squinted at the sun hanging low on the horizon. 'It'll be dark soon. You'd better go wherever it is you're going. I need to head back to Ashworth.' I threw my apple core away and gave her a swift hug.

She stiffened. 'Don't go getting all soppy on me.'

'I won't. Just promise me you'll look after yourself too, Lex.'

She pushed away, a wry smile lifting the corner of her mouth. 'Don't I always?' Seconds later, she was gone.

34

My thoughts tumbled over themselves in a whirlwind of suspicion and counter suspicion as I continued my route on towards the coast. I arrived at Ashworth Bay with all my preconceived certainties shattered like a heap of glass shards from a broken window. Tucking myself out of sight in the bushes on the cliff overlooking the beach, I sat down for a rest. I tugged the lapels of my coat closed against the chill evening air and watched night wrap the bay in a soft, protective mantle of darkness. The regular rhythm of the incoming tide soothed my frazzled nerves. Maybe it was emotional exhaustion, or the fact that my thoughts were full of Connie lost in France and potential traitors at Ashworth, but, to my shame, I didn't spot the small boat until it was nearly ashore.

A loud splash carried over the water. My head jerked up, my gaze zeroing in on two people-shaped silhouettes in a dinghy. One stood upright in the bow, facing the land, a small bag in hand. The other, sat in the rear, using an oar to negotiate a path for the shallow vessel over the scrap metal obstacles hidden under the surface. The sound of the keel scrunching into the sand as it ran aground released me from a curious torpor. I crept back from my bushy hideout and slipped into the trees to find a vantage point with a better view.

The person standing hopped ashore, giving the prow of the boat an almighty shove back out to sea. They lost their footing on the loose stones and stumbled, letting out a deep, guttural curse. It was definitely a man with a voice that low. He regained his balance, hurried along the shore to the headland on my left and started digging under the twists of razor wire, scooping armfuls of sand aside until he could wriggle underneath. Once past that obstacle, the confidence with which he negotiated the minefield told me he knew exactly where each explosive device was hidden. That was all the proof I needed that Lexi's warning was genuine. The safe route across the sand was not common knowledge and there was only one map. It was locked in the safe in the office. I'd drawn it myself at Edward's insistence, so that he could come here at night to swim safely. Damn it! I'd trusted him. Had he passed the information on?

I shrank back, holding my breath as the figure passed. Visibility wasn't brilliant, thanks to a low layer of cloud blocking out the moon, but there was enough to make out a tall, slim figure, with an upturned collar and a woollen hat pulled low over his brow. With silent, economical movements, he forged a path into the forest. I fell into step behind him, matching his stealth with my own, keeping him in my sights.

Where was he going?

Sometime later, he approached the smithy on the edge of Ambleford. The blacksmith's forge and the attached, thatched cottage sat between two small paddocks lining the road that ran through a shallow ford and on towards the village square. The enemy agent lingered in the trees, watching the property. I could only assume he was waiting to be certain that he wouldn't be seen. Once confident that the coast was clear, he crept forward, staying low, until he reached the stone wall at the edge of the cottage garden. I tiptoed closer too, ducking into a ditch further up the road, determined to see what he was doing.

The scrape of stone against stone told me he had removed a brick from the wall. He took something from his pocket, folded it, inserted it in the wall. There was more scraping as he pushed the brick back into place. It took a matter of moments. He retreated on silent feet.

I froze, torn with indecision. Did I go for the message, or follow him to see where he went next? I decided to do both. If I hurried, I could retrieve the message from the wall and then tail the stranger. Before I could stir, a movement tickled the corner of my eye. I froze. A second figure was approaching the wall. This one had a halting, uneven gait. Cold, heavy shackles wrapped themselves around my heart.

Edward crouched and removed the brick.

I had found my spy. The urge to heave nearly crippled me. Disbelief congealed into anger as hard as granite. I didn't watch any more. Edward was a problem I could deal with later. I used the ditch to slink far enough away not to alert him to my presence and then hurried after the first man as he made his way back through the forest to the coast. His companion was waiting in the small boat just offshore for him, and inched the craft in towards the beach to pick him up. Once they were both aboard, they rowed out to sea where the tower of a small submarine slowly broached the surface of the water.

I sank to the ground, my pulse dancing a rapid tattoo, my palms sweaty in spite of the chill. Lexi was right. She was right about it all. And I had been wrong. Very wrong. The U-boat, the possible enemy incursion and worse still, the double agent at Ashworth. It wasn't someone high up in special ops. Or Matron, or June. There was no one creeping up through the tunnel to the priest hole to listen. It was Edward.

A thought struck me. Was this why he had been so adamant I stay away from the bay in the evenings? Forget all that nonsense about keeping me safe. He must have known all this was going down and wanted to make sure I didn't stumble into it.

Fool that I was, I'd believed his false concern for my safety. I blinked back tears. Why on earth was I being so soft? It was better to know the truth even if it hurt. Edward didn't care about me. He just didn't want me to find out what he was up to.

Watching the submarine sink out of sight below the waves, a strange calm settled on my shoulders.

I needed to file a report.

The moon hid behind a thick blanket of cloud, meaning that my route back to Ashworth Manor was shrouded in the deepest darkness. As I crested the hill and started down towards the house, a chink of light flashed from inside the office. The minute I registered it, it was gone, as if someone had adjusted the blackout blind. Edward. He and I were the only two people with keys. It had to be him.

What was he doing?

Abandoning my goal to slip inside to my bedroom and send a coded message from my concealed radio, I changed tack and made for the bunker's escape hatch. There was no sign that it had been disturbed since my last visit. I hurried along the tunnel, adrenaline fizzing in my belly. Cutting straight through the bunker itself without stopping, I hastened into the stone passage beyond and tiptoed up the steps. Sending up a prayer of gratitude that the stone slab into the priest hole had well-oiled hinges and lifted in complete silence, I tiptoed along to the tiny hole in the wooden panelling and peered into the office.

Edward sat at his desk, a cup of tea before him, looking as if he hadn't a care in the world. He unfolded a map and seemed to be checking something written on a separate piece of paper. Then the paper disappeared from view. I heard a desk drawer opening and closing, and the faint chink of a key turning in a lock. He folded up the map and sat staring into space for several minutes before unlocking the safe and pulling out a bundle of documents.

An uneasy prickle crept up the back of my neck. He had access to so many confidential reports. Who knew what information he might be sending to the enemy? And why? Why would he do it?

He stayed at his desk for nearly an hour, flicking through reports.

I stayed in the priest hole, barely breathing for fear of alerting him to my presence. With every minute that passed my disappointment in him solidified into cold, hard anger.

The room settled into absolute silence around both of us. The stillness only broken by the slow trickle of hot tears creeping down my cheeks and soaking into my collar. Despite muscles cramping, begging for release, I maintained my position, determined not to give in before he did. At last, he switched off his desk lamp and left the room. The sound of his key turning in the door had barely died away before I eased the secret panel from the wall and climbed through. Pulling a couple of bobby pins from my hair, I picked the lock on his desk drawer. In no time at all, I read that piece of paper, taking note of three things.

A date.
A time.
A grid reference.

Two days from now.
Midnight.
Ashworth Bay.

A small part of me had hoped that I was reading the whole situation wrong. But the evidence was unmistakable. Edward was a spy. Whatever was going down, it was happening on Thursday night. I would be there and I'd make damned sure Edward didn't get away with his treachery.

Careful to leave everything as I'd found it, I retreated back into the wall and down to the bunker and the radio where I composed an urgent message for Major Stapleton. I detailed my sighting of the enemy agent at the beach, his route through the forest, the message left in the wall, his return to the bay and the submarine offshore. I reread my handiwork, biting my lip until it bled, before adding one final line.

Have reason to believe that Commander Edward Landers is compromised. Please advise.

Message sent, I sat in complete darkness feeling lonelier than I had ever felt before. Had my affections latched on to Edward because he was my last link to Tommy? If so, I was a fool. He wasn't what he seemed. That link didn't really exist and it broke my heart. Was it the loss of a connection with Tommy I grieved or with Edward himself? I couldn't be sure. Fighting back tears, I stared around the bunker. This was what was waiting for me should spies like Edward succeed in helping the enemy to invade. A life underground. Heavy, cold, damp air closed in, making it hard to breathe. I started to shake. Lurching to my feet, I paced up and down the short space between the desk and the bunk beds, rubbing my hands together. Everything would be all right. I could do this. It wasn't too late. There was no invasion. Not yet. Half an hour later, just before I lost the plot entirely, the radio sprang to life and a coded response came in.

Received and understood.
Do not confront.
Observe and report.

Could I do that? Could I keep quiet and simply watch Edward betray his country? It would be unbelievably hard, but orders were orders. It was my duty to do as I was told. The tears that had been gathering finally spilled over. I lurched from the desk to the bottom bunk, curled into a ball under the blankets and sobbed until finally, utterly exhausted, I fell into a fitful slumber.

35

I woke up in darkness, scrubbed at the dry salty tracks on my face, slipped from the bed to light the hurricane lamp and checked my watch. Almost nine in the morning. Time to get to work. I couldn't go up to the office from here. I'd have to take the escape route and double back to my room to clean up and change into my uniform. I cursed under my breath. How was I going to spend time with Edward without betraying my anger? I stumbled along the escape tunnel, giving myself a stern talking-to. I could do this. I'd be damned if I let the enemy succeed in whatever they had planned. I would protect Ashworth: the manor, the village, the forest. Whatever it took. But first, I had to button my lip and survive two days in the office with a spy. A traitor I had foolishly developed feelings for.

Back in my room, I splashed cold water over my face and dressed. Pulling my ATS uniform on felt like pulling on armour, and with each item of clothing, I worked on hardening my heart towards Edward. It didn't matter that he had the most beautiful eyes on the planet, or that his voice sent warm thrills through every cell in my body. I had a duty to my home and my country, and to Lexi who had risked so much to warn me.

As soon as I was ready, I headed to the office, determined to treat Edward with studied indifference. I would be calm, polite and professional. Everything would be fine.

* * *

'I'm a touch worried for the integrity of that typewriter,' said Edward, his words thick with amusement. 'You don't usually thump the keys so hard. Are you feeling all right?'

'I'm fine.' I ground my teeth together. How dare he talk about integrity?

He raised a questioning eyebrow, fixing me with those eyes. 'Are you sure?'

I squashed down the parts of me that wanted to believe I could be wrong. That he couldn't possibly be a traitor. 'I'm sure.'

'If you say so – only it's not like you to be mardy.'

My jaw clenched. I'd give him bloody mardy.

He got to his feet. 'I'm going to be out for the rest of the day at Bramshaw. And tomorrow, I'll be at RAF Sopley. Can I assume that you have everything you need to be getting on?'

I gave him a tight nod and concentrated on loading a fresh piece of paper and adjusting the typewriter ribbon.

He paused at the door as if he might say something else, before saying softly, 'Goodbye, then.'

The soft click of the door shutting behind him was almost my undoing. Hot tears scalded the backs of my eyes. I nearly rushed to follow him and demand he explain his actions. There must be a reason for his choice, surely? Blinking hard, I crushed the impulse. Whatever his reason, there was no excuse. The whole concept of treason was abhorrent. The very thought made me feel sick. Even so, a small part of me kept saying, *but this is Edward.*

I kept as busy as I could over the next two days, clearing all necessary paperwork in the office in record time. The rest of the time was easily filled by popping out to ask Matron if she had any additional jobs for me to do. She was inordinately grateful for the extra pair of hands and had me running from ward to ward writing letters for expectant mothers desperate to communicate with loved ones off fighting the war. This activity reminded me how important it was to hold on to what was right, and not give in to sentimentality. Regardless of my feelings for Edward, there were countless lives at stake. I had to hold firm.

36

All too soon, Thursday evening arrived. My orders were clear. I was to observe and report. I planned to arrive at the bay early and conceal myself where I would get a good view of events. I forced myself to eat, even though my throat was so tight I could barely swallow and the food sat in my belly like old shoe leather. Before leaving the dining room, I helped myself to extra bread and fruit for later, and retreated to the privacy of my room, where I dressed in warm camouflaging layers. I packed my knapsack with the food and a water bottle, and threw in some extra things to help keep me warm while I waited: gloves, scarf and a hat.

The revolver was cold and heavy in my hands. I cracked the back and loaded it, making sure the safety catch was on. With shaking fingers, I tucked it into a side pocket and slung the bag over my shoulder.

Out in the forest, the night was grey. Everything seemed agitated. Banks of thick cloud scudded across the sky, periodically blacking out the moon. Branches waved wildly overhead. A cold wind pushed at my back as if urging me to hurry. Rustling leaves whispered encouragement. Staying off the main path brought a little respite from the weather. I approached the bay through a section of trees where the undergrowth was dense and a thick leaf litter cushioned my footsteps. My plan was to hide in an old oak tree where Tommy and I had played as children. The trunk had a huge split that formed a hollow large enough to sit inside. It made a perfect secret hideout. Overlooking the bay, it offered both shelter from the elements and an ideal spot from which to keep watch. The tree was just as I remembered, although the space more cramped. Fortunately, bushes had grown up around the base, creating additional screening, and I was able to tuck myself out of sight. Pulling on my hat and gloves, I settled down to watch and wait.

As is always the way in the forest, once you stop moving and simply sit and breathe, busy woodland creatures start to bustle around you. Hedgehogs and mice scuffled through the undergrowth, bats danced overhead and owls called. Time passed. I started to kid myself that this was all a misunderstanding. Either I was overreacting or the world had gone mad. There I was, armed with a revolver, waiting for the man I loved to commit a crime.

The man I loved.

There, I'd admitted it. I loved him. Why else would I be so heartbroken?

My feet went numb. I wriggled my toes and rotated my ankles. It was no good. I had to move around. I checked my watch: nearly midnight. There was no sign of anything happening. I got to my feet, trying to stay low. Hot pins and needles stabbed at my legs as the blood started to flow again, making me want to gasp in pain. Before I could utter a sound, a twig snapped.

That wasn't wildlife.

I crouched back down, ignoring the screaming from my muscles, and scanned the treeline and beach.

Nothing.

I turned my eyes out to sea.

There.

Half a mile offshore, small waves rippled white against a shadow. A shadow that grew and grew. The turret of a submarine slowly inched up from the water.

My pulse drummed in my ears. I tugged off my hat, scarf and gloves. The rush of cool night air to my scalp helped shake off the residual sluggishness from sitting still and waiting. I slid the revolver from the hidden compartment in my knapsack, the black metal glinting menacingly.

As before, a small boat inched its way from the submarine to the shoreline. The same two figures were on board. Small whispering waves ushered the boat onto the beach. The tall one I had followed before leapt out and hauled the bow further onto the sand. Then he started pacing up and down, his footsteps scrunching in the sand. There was a spark as he lit a cigarette, the match illuminating his face for an instant, then he resumed his pacing. The rower stayed in the boat.

Forcing my breath to stay slow and steady, I examined the beach and treeline again.

Who were they waiting for? Edward?

All was still. There was nothing... except... Call it instinct, but something tugged at my subconscious. There was a faint glimmer from the rocks further along the bay to my left. It was barely there at all. Yet... someone else was watching. I was sure of it. There it was again. Moonlight on binocular glass. Huh! Such a rookie mistake. I squinted into the darkness, making out a head and shoulders as they ducked down behind the rocks.

Before I could discern any more details, a low whistle sounded from the forest.

A cloaked and hooded figure carrying a large bundle emerged from the trees and marched with confidence along the safe route through the beach mines. The shadow on the sand threw his cigarette away and hurried across to the razor wire and helped dig a tunnel underneath until the new arrival could pass the bundle through and slip under to join him. A break in the clouds allowed a shaft of moonlight to illuminate both figures on the beach. The new arrival was shorter and stockier. Something about them was familiar but I couldn't quite put my finger on it. This was someone I knew. I shuffled forwards, straining to see, just as another bank of clouds raced in front of the moon and reduced everything back to murky shades of grey once more. Both figures on the beach climbed into the boat. It all happened so quickly.

My instinct was to run down and stop them somehow. Fortunately, sanity prevailed. There were three of them. Plus, the second watcher. Whoever that was. Revolver or no revolver, I was outnumbered. In any case, my orders were to observe and report, not engage. It was hard to watch the boat head steadily back towards the submarine. I held my ground.

The second watcher didn't move until the boat was nearly at the sub. Then, a tall shadow detached itself from the rocks and crept down the far headland onto the beach. I'd know those shoulders and that uneven gait anywhere.

Edward. What was he doing? Had he been acting as a lookout to make sure no one pursued them? And why approach the beach now?

I watched in consternation as he shrugged off his clothes and slipped into the water, striking out in the direction of the U-boat. It looked like he had some sort of bag slung over his shoulders. Were there more state secrets in it? Had they forgotten him? It didn't make sense.

Acting on impulse, I followed. Forget orders. Whatever he was up to, I wanted answers. I hurried down to the water, dumped my outer layers on the sand and dashed into the sea. With a strong overarm stroke, I gained on him easily and dived under the water to snatch at his legs, dragging him under. He kicked out, spun, and threw both arms around me, taking us both down into a barrel roll. Desperate for air, I made a rigid arrow of my fingers and jabbed the tip into his throat with as much force as I could, like the instructor at Hannington had shown me. The unexpected blow caused his grip to slacken. Wriggling free, I shot upwards.

We surfaced, coughing.

Dashing water from his eyes he stared at me in disbelief, his voice a whispered hiss. 'Wren? What the hell are you doing here?'

'I could ask you the same thing.'

He cursed. 'I told you to stay away from the beach at night.'

'Like I was going to do what you told me, you bastard.'

'Shh! Keep your voice down.' I followed his gaze as it darted towards the U-boat tower. The three in the boat were busy climbing aboard and hadn't noticed us. Edward grabbed my wrist, tugging me closer.

I shook him off, slipping out of reach. 'I saw you pick up that hidden message.'

'Were you following me?'

'No. I was following one of them.' I stabbed a finger towards the submarine. '*He* dropped the message off. *You* picked it up. The date, time and location for here.'

He shook his head. 'I didn't pick it up.'

'Yes, you did. I saw you.' He was lying. He had to be.

'No, you saw me read it. I've been keeping an eye on that drop site for days. I memorised the message and put it back. Then, I watched to see who *did* pick it up. Only they didn't come until the next morning.'

I wasn't sure what to believe. 'And who were they?'

'I'm not sure. They were heavily cloaked. I followed them back to Ashworth but lost them as soon as they went inside.'

'Lost them how?' I asked.

'A hospital transport had just arrived and there were new patients with small children everywhere. The sheer number of people milling around in the front hall made keeping track impossible.'

It was too convenient. 'I don't believe you.'

'Why would I lie?' he asked.

'To cover your tracks.'

He growled. 'For heaven's sake. Did you not see a someone go with those two on that boat out to an enemy submarine? *That's* our traitor, not me.'

I wanted to believe him. The figure I'd seen bothered me. Who was it?

A clanking sound came from the sub. While we were arguing in the water, everyone had gone below decks. The hatch was closing.

'They're getting ready to move.' Edward cursed under his breath. 'They'll dive soon. Damn it, Wren, can we do this later? I have to go.'

'Where?'

'Out there.' He struck out towards the sub, calling over his shoulder. 'To stop them.'

Two strong strokes and I drew level with him. 'How are you planning to do that? There's no way to break into a submarine from the outside. Unless they know you're coming and are waiting for you to let you on board.'

'For heaven's sake, I am not a traitor. There's a limpet mine in my backpack. I'll set it on the hull. If I can get there before they get underway, that is. A big enough explosion below the waterline should disable them. They'll be forced to abandon ship.'

I gasped. 'Will that actually work?'

'I hope so. It's the only plan I have. Stay back, Wren. I don't want you getting hurt.'

'I'm still not convinced about you,' I said. 'If you're going to do this thing then you'll do it with me along for the ride.'

'But—'

'No. Shut up and swim.' I set off at speed. He fell in behind me. I adjusted my speed to keep him with me, aware that his weak arm and leg hampered the efficiency of his stroke There were definite signs of movement from the submarine.

Eventually, Edward faltered, his breathing laboured. 'Damn it. This bloody arm of mine.'

I slowed and trod water beside him. 'I can make it. Give me the mine.'

'No, Wren. I can't let you. It's too dangerous.'

'Dangerous for me but not for you? Stop playing the hero.' I grabbed at the backpack, trying to wrestle it from his shoulders. 'I can do it.'

He shook me off. 'No. It's too late, you'll get caught in the blast.'

'Not if I go now. Unless you really are a traitor and you're stalling to give them time to get away.'

'I'm not.'

'Prove it,' I insisted. 'Give. Me. The. Mine. *Now*. While there's still a chance.'

'Fine.' He slipped his arms from the straps. 'Do you know how to arm it?'

'Yes.' I tugged the pack onto my own back. 'Coding wasn't the only thing I learned at Hannington. Watch and I just might surprise you.'

He grabbed my chin, forcing me to look at him. 'You never stop surprising me, Wren. Just set it and get the hell out, yes? Trust me. I've got everything else covered.'

Flashing him a grin, I dived under the water, turned and kicked with all my might to pick up speed. The pack on my back added extra drag. I compensated, setting a steady, efficient rhythm that ate up the distance and soon brought me alongside my target.

The engines thrummed and the sub started to move. I grabbed a length of chain attached to the hull. Water buffeted me, slamming me against the metal side, trying to tug my hold free. I clung on for dear life. My fingers, numb with cold, locked in place. As long as they didn't dive, I could still do this.

Turning my back towards the force of the water, I sheltered the bag in front of me and, with my free hand, pulled the mine out. Attaching it to the hull below the waterline should be easy enough thanks to the powerful magnet inside it. Setting the fuse was a little trickier. It was a short one. Edward clearly hadn't intended on the sub getting very far before it was disabled. It wouldn't give me much time to get out of range of the blast.

There was nothing I could do, except set things in motion and hope for the best. With the mine armed and locked onto the hull, I let go of the chain and pushed away, allowing the water to whisk me along parallel to the length of the moving sub. Once I was clear of the engines, the rudder and any backwash, I wasted no time heading back towards the bay. I battled the churning water with my best front crawl, desperate to put as much distance between myself and the mine before it blew. In the distance, a blurry outline of Edward swam towards me, urging me to hurry.

Seconds later, the explosion came.

Bizarrely, I felt it more than I heard it, thanks to a series of immense percussion waves rolling through the water. They created a back eddy that dragged me under. Sound disappeared, replaced by a thickness in my head and pressure on my chest. Disorientated, I struggled against a roiling mass of sea and bubbles as I fought for air, my limbs rapidly weakening, not even certain which way was up.

Just as I was about to give in, strong hands closed around my middle, dragging me towards the surface.

'I've got you.' Edward's voice cut through the pain in my head and the ringing in my ears. I coughed and spluttered, my eyes and throat raw from the salt water. Unable to process anything, I focused on his voice, a calm and steady beacon carving through the chaos and confusion. 'You're safe, Wren. I've got you.'

Dashing water from my face with a shaky hand in a futile attempt to clear my vision, I twisted around trying to look out to sea. 'Did it work?'

'Yes!' Edward laughed. 'It worked. You bloody did it, Wren. You disabled an enemy submarine, all by yourself.'

'I can't see properly. Tell me what's happening.'

He pulled me against his chest, wrapping his arms around me. 'The sub has come to a stop and surfaced fully. They're abandoning ship.'

Alarm shot through me. 'Abandoning ship? Are they coming this way? What do we do? My revolver is back on shore.'

'You have a gun?' he said. 'Wait. Never mind. We'll talk about that another day. For now, calm down. Our part here is done. I told you I had everything else in hand. There's a navy ship closing in. They were lurking out of sight behind the island. They'll scoop up most of the lifeboats and impound the sub. Any personnel who make it to shore will find your father and the Home Guard waiting for them. And with any luck we'll be able to unmask our traitor, whoever they are.'

'The navy? Father? How…?'

'What do you think I've been doing for the last two days? I've been trying to cut through all the red tape needed to co-ordinate this little ambush.'

The world was slowly coming back into focus. I stared into his handsome face. 'So, you're not a traitor?'

'I am not. No.' He smoothed a piece of hair from my forehead. 'And I know from your actions today, if nothing else, that neither are you.'

'Me?' I pushed away from him. Outrage singing through me. 'Of course I'm not. How could you think such a thing?'

He chuckled. 'Probably the same reason you suspected me, I expect. I received intel that information that could only have come from Ashworth was falling into enemy hands. But I had no details about how it was happening. Only that it started at around the time you arrived.'

'And you thought I…? Edward! How could you?'

'I had no way of knowing what had happened at Hannington after I left, did I? All I knew for certain is that you were posted back to Ashworth and you weren't happy about it.'

'Neither would you have been,' I grumbled.

'Come on,' he said. 'Let's get back to shore.'

With limbs like soggy cotton wool, I swam to the shore with Edward staying nearby to support me when I struggled. After crawling up the beach, I collapsed on the sand, my body juddering so hard that my teeth rattled. My bones seemed to be trying shake themselves loose from my skin.

'Here.' He scooped my things up from where I'd abandoned them. 'Quick, get dressed and try to keep moving. Else you'll freeze.' He led me off the beach and into the shelter of the trees, before giving me a quick hug. 'Stay here. I'll be back in a minute.'

Bereft at his leaving, I tried to follow, but my legs refused to co-operate.

Father's gruff voice called from further along the clifftop. 'Commander Landers. We picked up a dozen of them.'

I slipped behind the wide trunk of an oak tree out of sight. The last thing I needed was a scolding for unladylike behaviour.

I heard Edward's reply. 'Good work. Secure them back at the barracks, please. Then you can stand your men down. Remember, we need absolute secrecy about what happened here tonight. Come to the office at ten tomorrow and we'll debrief.'

'Yes, sir.' Father's commands to his troops faded as he moved away.

Edward returned. 'We should head back, Wren. You're exhausted.'

'I'm fine.' I swayed, almost toppling over.

'Indeed, you are.' He slung a bracing arm around my shoulders. 'We both need to get warm. The quickest way to do that is to move. Come on.'

Marching back through the forest certainly got my blood pumping, yet the bone-deep chill persisted. My legs had a nerveless rubbery feel to them as if they weren't properly attached to the rest of me. If it weren't for Edward steering me through the back door and along the passage to my bedroom, I'm not sure I would have made it. Fortunately, there was no one around to see us. The place was deserted, with everyone tucked up in bed, oblivious to the drama taking place down at the coast.

'Get into some dry things as quick as you can,' he whispered.

'You should do the same,' I whispered back. 'Borrow something of Tommy's.' I pointed to the chest of my brother's things just inside the door. 'You're about the same size. He won't mind.'

A smile lit up his face. He rummaged through the chest, selecting a soft shirt, a thick jumper and some warm trousers. 'Thanks. It's too late to go back to my lodgings in Ambleford, tonight. If I turn up there, now, it will simply cause a fuss. I'll go and change down in the office. I can sleep on the floor down there.'

I tried to reply, but a yawn took over, making it impossible to get words out.

He nudged me towards the bed. 'Go to bed, sweetheart. You're practically dead on your feet.' He lifted my hand to his lips and pressed a kiss to it. A warm sensation spread through my belly in spite of my tiredness. Before I could reach for him, he was gone. The door swung closed, leaving me alone.

A wave of bleak desolation engulfed me at the enormity of what I had done. I'd set a mine on the side of a ship full of people. I could have been responsible for so many deaths. They might be the enemy, but they were still people. It was too much. Tears poured down my cheeks as I stripped off my soggy things and towelled myself down. Dragging on dry pyjamas and a thick belted robe, still sobbing, I crawled into bed, flopped down onto my back and stared up at the ceiling as scalding tracks of salty water trickled across my temples into my hair. Filled with a sense of loss too enormous to bear, I pulled the blankets up to my chin. The world began to go fuzzy around the edges. A noise from the door briefly interrupted my descent into sleep. I felt the bedclothes at the foot of the bed lift. Warmth arrived in the form of a hot water bottle wrapped in a scrap of soft fabric shoved next to my feet.

The side of the bed sagged.

'You were very brave tonight,' Edward murmured. 'The only reason the operation was a success, was because of you. You're amazing, Wren. I hope you know that.' He stroked the side of my face with a gentle hand, stopping when he encountered the damp tear tracks. He cursed, and lowered his forehead to touch mine. 'I am sorry I couldn't protect you from this.'

I draped a tired arm around his neck, murmuring, 'I don't need you to protect me.'

His shoulders shook with silent laughter. 'You don't give up, do you?'

'Never.' The defiance I was aiming for was spoiled by my teeth chattering.

'Go to sleep. You'll feel better when you've rested.' He pressed a light kiss to my lips.

The weight on the bed lifted. Sensing that he was about to leave, I grabbed his sleeve. 'Don't go.'

'Wren?'

'Stay... with... me.' This last was uttered on a sigh, as I grappled with exhaustion. 'Please stay.'

The bed dipped again. There was a momentary silence and then the rustle of fabric.

'Come here, then.' He slid an arm under my neck, turned me onto my side so that my back rested against his chest. He was warm and solid and, all of a sudden, I felt safe. Wrapped in his arms, I slowly stopped shaking and began to relax.

Within seconds, we were both fast asleep.

37

The next morning, he was gone. All signs that Edward had ever been in my room, in my bed, had been erased. Had I dreamt it all?

I sat up and rubbed my eyes, kicking myself for missing the opportunity to kiss him, to run my hands all over his body and get to know him better. Then, quite unfairly, I cursed him for being a gentleman and not taking advantage of the situation. Glancing at my watch, I was horrified to see it was nearly nine. I'd not slept so deeply for ages. I launched myself out of bed and washed and dressed, and then scurried along to the office, pinning my hair into a tight knot at the nape of my neck as I went, eager to see him.

Edward looked up from his desk as I walked in. 'Good morning. How are you feeling? Have you eaten?'

I shook my head, my eyes drinking him in. Before I could say anything, he gave a brisk nod and carried on speaking. 'Neither have I. I've asked the kitchens to send something in. Mind you, everything seems to be a little chaotic this morning. The nursing staff seem somewhat out of sorts too.' A knock sounded at the door and a harassed-looking orderly hurried in with a tray of tea and toast, deposited it and left. When we were alone, Edward gestured to the food. 'Help yourself.'

I retreated to my desk, a cup of tea in one hand, a slice of toast in the other, aware that he was watching me closely. I wondered why he seemed so stiff, almost formal. Was he embarrassed about staying in my room last night?

'What exactly is your real role here, Wren?' he said.

Ah! So that was the problem. I chewed my bite of toast for an unnecessarily long period of time; not sure how to answer.

'You're not just a military secretary, are you?' His question was soft but loaded.

I took a sip of tea, focusing my gaze on my desk. I couldn't tell him the truth, yet, I'd be damned if I'd lie to him. Not replying was my only option.

'You didn't flunk out of whatever training was going on at Hannington Hall, did you?'

I took another bite of toast and kept chewing.

'I thought as much,' he said. Silence fell, broken only by the creak of his chair and a whisper of fabric as he sat back and crossed his arms. 'I am well aware that there are units operating at different levels of secrecy in the area. I am also aware that I have not been briefed on the identity of personnel in those units, or their exact purpose, for very good reasons. I am going to assume that you are affiliated with one of them. I just need to know you are on the same side that I am. That we are both putting Britain first in this war.'

How could he even think anything else?

He padded over to my desk, placed a hand under my chin and gently but firmly forced me to look at him. 'In the absence of any other details, Wren, can you at least confirm that? Otherwise I don't see how we can continue to work together.'

The thought of not working with him made me ache deep inside, yet I could not speak.

'Can you understand my position, Wren? I have to assume you are reporting everything that happens in here to your superiors, whoever they are. Do you see that?'

I gave the faintest of nods.

'So, can I trust you?'

Another nod. Barely any movement.

'Is that all you're willing to say?'

'Technically, I haven't said anything,' I murmured.

A small smile teased his lips. 'No, you haven't. Nothing at all.' He sighed. 'I'm going to have to trust you. Aren't I?'

I shrugged.

'Fine.' He stepped back. 'In which case, let's get to work. Firstly, we need to debrief your father. Then, we must go to the barracks to check on the prisoners.'

That was unexpected. 'Why?'

'Don't you want to know who our traitor is? They were on board that sub. It was impounded and all personnel detained either at sea or the minute they made it to land. Therefore, we should have them in custody. If we know who they are, maybe we can work out how they were getting their intel.'

'Good point. Although I already have my suspicions as to who it is.'

Edward frowned. 'Who?'

'I caught one of the orderlies in here unattended about ten days ago.'

'Who?'

'I think his name is Roberts but I can't be sure. He's always very short-tempered and gruff with everyone.'

'Why didn't you tell me?'

I raised both hands palm up. 'As far as I could tell, nothing had been disturbed. But the door had been unlocked, even though I know I left everything secure. You are the only other person with a key. I wasn't sure if—' I broke off at his thunderous expression.

'You thought I had let him in?'

'It was a possibility.'

He tutted. 'You suspected me and I suspected you, which took our focus off the real culprit.'

'Yes,' I said.

'Do you have any other suspects?'

I shook my head. 'None. Matron is always sending people in with messages, and coming in herself, but no one sets off any alarm bells.'

'One of the nurses has come in a few times for no obvious reason, then made an excuse and left again,' he said.

'Which one?'

'The small, blonde, chatty one.'

'You mean June?' I said.

'If you say so.'

If the traitor was June, I would be very surprised. Shocked even. She had always seemed so open and honest, to me. Our conversations light and breezy. She had made no attempt to inveigle information from me. Could I have misjudged her? Absolutely, I could. After all, I had doubted Edward and been proven wrong. 'I don't remember her doing that.'

'You weren't there at the time,' he said. 'She merely apologised for disturbing me and then left. Which struck me as odd.'

'She and I have eaten lunch together in the past. Maybe she came looking for me and left when she realised I wasn't here.'

He pursed his lips. 'It's possible, I suppose. Well, we'll find out if you're right about this Roberts chap when we get to the barracks.'

'Yes.' I mentally crossed my fingers, hoping it was him and not June.

'And we also need to send in a report about all this to the higher-ups. Or, at least, I do.' He looked at me closely. 'And I expect you do too.'

I merely reached for more toast, neither confirming nor denying his unsubtle dig for information.

A heavy knock sounded and the door opened. Father, in all the glory of his Home Guard uniform, burst in. He saluted Edward, his brows beetling together briefly at the sight of me. 'Reporting for debrief as requested, sir.'

'Good man. Sit down.' Edward gestured to the chair directly in front of his desk before moving to take his own seat. 'Can you tell me, in your own words, how last night's exercise went down from the perspective of the Home Guard, please.'

'Now?' Father darted a glance at me.

'Yes. Now. For the record.'

Father shifted on his chair. 'I thought this was supposed to be hush-hush.'

'Everyone in this room has clearance at the highest level,' Edward replied.

I kept my expression neutral and pulled out a pad and pencil.

Father hesitated.

'Do you have a problem with that?' Edward's tone held a note of warning. 'Come, come. We have a lot of ground to cover.'

Father talked.

I took notes in shorthand. As Father's account unfolded, I began to appreciate all the things that Edward had put in place to set up the sting operation to trap the sub. All things that he'd had to do without involving me, because he couldn't be certain that I wasn't a rogue agent. And if it wasn't either of us, who could it be? Was Edward right about it being someone connected with the maternity home? It made sense. The presence of a nurse or orderly would be unremarkable. Which set my mind off down a dark rabbit hole of suspicion. The traitor had to be someone with access to both Ashworth and Ambleford. Most of the staff lived on site. They often went to the village in their down time. If they could discover confidential material from this office, they could easily pass that information on. But who was it? And how were they doing it?

Father's agitated tone caused me to tune back in to his words. 'I saw you being tackled in the water, Captain. But I couldn't make out who it was. Quite a small chap. Moved like lightning. I couldn't get a clear shot.'

Edward gave a sharp laugh. 'It's as well you didn't shoot. They were on our side. Although I wasn't certain of that, at first.'

'Who was it then?'

Edward's eyes darted to me.

I gave my head a slight shake.

Edward smothered a smile. 'An undercover agent. An extremely brave one. Without whose help yesterday would have ended very differently.'

Father gave his chin a thoughtful stroke. 'Undercover, you say?'

'Yes.'

Father huffed in satisfaction. 'By Jove. Sounds like we owe whoever he is a huge debt of gratitude.'

'We do,' agreed Edward. 'And I plan to say so in my dispatches.'

Just then the telephone rang. I hurried to answer it. By the time I had finished with the caller, Father was gone. Edward got to his feet. 'Was that news on our prisoners?'

'Yes. They're being held at the POW Camp at Setley Plain.

You're expected at fourteen hundred hours this afternoon. They are sending a car.'

'You should come too,' he said. 'Which means we had better crack on with today's dispatches so that they're done before we leave.'

38

We arrived at Setley Plain, just south of Brockenhurst, at two o'clock exactly. Our driver pulled up at a heavily guarded gate set in acres of barbed wire. Our identity papers were shown to the officer on duty, who, after a thorough examination of the documents, finally waved the car through. I gazed out of the window at a series of Nissen huts, their characteristic semicircular steel structures very similar to those we had slept in at Hannington, merely bigger. Eventually we parked outside a large brick building and were ushered inside, where Commander Whitmore stood waiting for us.

He greeted Edward and ignored me. 'It sounds like you had quite a lot of excitement at Ashworth last night.'

'Nothing we couldn't handle.' Edward gave a polite smile. 'Thank you for taking charge of our prisoners.'

'Not at all. That's what we're here for.'

'What will happen to them?' I asked.

Commander Whitmore blinked as if he'd not even realised I was there. 'Any high-risk prisoners will be shipped over to the

Isle of Wight, or even up north where detention facilities are more robust than those here.'

'What constitutes high risk?' I asked.

'Anyone daft enough to try to escape,' he said, his tone implying that I should know better than to waste his time with silly questions.

'Don't they *all* try to do that?' asked Edward, shooting me a brief, reassuring glance.

'Not as many as you'd think.' The commander jerked his head towards the window. Several prisoners of war were walking past outside. 'Most of this lot are happy to sit the rest of the war out, which makes keeping track of them very easy.'

'I see,' said Edward. 'And how do the detainees from last night classify?'

The commander scratched his head. 'That is yet to be determined. We're still processing them.'

'We're interested in one in particular,' said Edward.

'I suspected as much,' said the commander, gesturing along the corridor. 'She's through here.'

'She?' My heart sank. Not June. Please, let it not be June.

'Yes. The only woman on the ship,' said Commander Whitmore, leading us along a corridor. 'She had no papers on her and is refusing to say who she is.' He ushered us towards a door with a guard posted outside. The guard unlocked the door and stood back to let us inside. The room was sparsely furnished with a table and two chairs and little else. A woman stood at the window, staring outside. With her back to us and bright sunshine pouring through the glass, throwing her into shadow, it was difficult to see who she was. I edged closer, my heart in my mouth.

She turned.

I gasped. 'Matron.'

This wasn't a version of Matron I'd seen before. Her eyes were hard. Her brisk but caring demeanour gone. She looked at me, unblinking, saying nothing.

'Why?' I asked, the single word carrying intense shock.

She sauntered over to one of the chairs and sat. 'Why what?'

'Why have you betrayed your country?' asked Edward.

She scowled. 'I'm not saying anything.'

'She doesn't need to,' said Commander Whitmore. 'Her boyfriend has said plenty.'

Matron's eyes widened fractionally, which told me this was news to her.

'Boyfriend?' asked Edward.

'An enemy submariner,' said Commander Whitmore. 'Apparently, they met studying abroad before the war. They've been passing information to each other for several months now. It's only a matter of time before we find out everything. The police interrogator is on his way.' The steel in the commander's voice coupled with the defiance in Matron's eyes made me feel almost sorry for her. Police interrogators weren't gentle with traitors. I didn't envy her the coming days if she remained resolute in her silence.

'Did he pressure you?' I asked. Perhaps there was a plausible reason for her actions. Something I could understand. Not that it made everything all right. 'Was he blackmailing you?' I drew out the chair next to her and sat. 'Matron, this is very serious. Do you understand what will happen to you, if you are found guilty of treason?'

A muscle worked in her jaw, the only sign that she was listening.

'You'll go to prison. You could even hang.' I dropped my voice, making it low and soft. 'Is he worth it?'

She blinked rapidly and turned her head away.

'Please, Matron,' I said, trying to fit the kind woman I knew with the hard, distant figure before me. She had seemed to care about each and every patient at the maternity home. I had watched her soothe fractious new-borns and speak to their frightened mothers with kindness. It was hard to believe that she had knowingly betrayed us all. Why on earth had she done this awful thing? 'You have a chance to make this right.'

'How?' she asked.

'Co-operate with the authorities,' I urged. 'Tell them what you know. It could save your life.'

She turned her head away. Silence fell, thick and heavy.

I sighed and got to my feet, sadness weighing me down. This was all such a waste. 'I think we've seen enough.'

'We need to know how she obtained the information she shared,' said Edward.

'I'm not telling you anything,' sneered Matron.

'There's no need,' I said. The answer had come to me as I'd sat looking into her eyes. It was obvious. I was a fool for not thinking of it before. 'I know how she did it.'

'How?' demanded Commander Whitmore.

I ignored him and turned to Edward. 'Let's go.'

Edward shot me a searching look but didn't argue.

39

Ten minutes later, sat side by side in the back of the military car on the way back to Ashworth, with the silent driver focusing on the road ahead, Edward's hand edged across the seat towards mine.

I moved my hand a fraction towards his.

His large, warm fingers interlaced with mine.

We stayed like that for the entire journey back. Quiet but connected. Only breaking contact as the car rolled up the Ashworth driveway.

'So, are you going to tell me how she did it?'

'I'll show you.' I led the way to the staff quarters and along the corridor to Matron's room. Once inside, I started searching. I checked inside her chest of drawers, under the mattress, the bottom of the wardrobe and ran my hands along the wooden panelling, searching for any movement.

'What are we looking for?' asked Edward, mild amusement colouring his words.

I sat on the bed and scanned the room, searching my memory for all the ways the special ops used to hide things.

Going back over to the chest of drawers, I pulled each one out and turned it over, hoping to find something taped to the bottom. Then I checked the back of the unit.

'Wren?' Edward was starting to sound concerned.

'Give me a second,' I said. 'It's here somewhere.' My eyes fell on the curtain pole. Dragging a chair over, I climbed up, and unscrewed the finial on the end. 'Aha! Here.' A small compartment had been drilled into the pole.

'Here what?'

I grinned at him. 'The only way anyone can access the office without our knowledge is when neither you nor I are there, right?'

'Yes, except the door is always locked when we're not there.'

'Exactly, so she had to have a key.' I dug my finger into the secret compartment and pulled out a key and handed it to him.

He compared it to his. 'A copy. But when and how?'

'The day I arrived, she handed me my key.'

Edward slapped his forehead. 'Of course she did. *I* even gave it to her to pass on to you. I'd forgotten. How stupid of me.'

'Not stupid,' I said, hopping down from the chair. 'I only worked it out when I saw her today. Once I knew she was the traitor, it was obvious.'

He tugged me into his arms. 'I'm very glad you're on the same side as me.'

'Are you?' I moved closer. 'And why is that?'

'Because you're brilliant, of course.'

I couldn't help returning his wide grin. 'I am glad you think so.'

'I do. I definitely do.' He lowered his lips to mine and kissed me. The room, Ashworth, traitors and even the war disappeared in an instant, replaced by warm lips, sweet breath, a spicy male scent and firm but gentle arms holding me close. I felt as if I were the most precious person in the world. He was an excellent kisser and as wave after wave of delicious tingles rippled through me, I decided I didn't ever want him to stop. Eventually, however, we had to break off for air. He touched his forehead to mine and gazed into my eyes. I could have stayed like that forever.

'I have been fighting the urge to do that for so long,' he said.

'Why?'

He pulled away, his expression rueful. 'I'm your senior officer.'

I refused to let go. 'Are you my senior officer, though? Can you be sure?'

'Yes, I... oh,' His expression clouded. 'No, I'm not, am I? I'm just your cover story.'

'Which means you can kiss me again, doesn't it?' I tugged at his lapel and glanced over my shoulder. 'We just need to be careful no one sees us.'

'No.' He covered my hand with one of his and shook his head. 'I really can't.'

Alarm shot through me at his serious tone. 'Why not?'

'I think I am in danger of falling in love with you.' His words hit me with the force of a runaway boulder, filling me with a happiness I daren't acknowledge given the grim expression on his face.

'Why is that a problem?' I asked.

'Because you are keeping secrets from me.'

'I see.' I withdrew my hand, fighting to not show my disappointment. 'You still don't trust me.'

'It's not that.'

I stepped back. 'Then what is it?'

'I've never felt like this about anyone before. It's not something I ever expected.'

The earnest intensity in his eyes was mesmerising. I swayed towards him, unable to find words to reply. The thought that anyone could feel such emotions for me was beyond anything I had ever dreamed of. But this was Edward, and his words described my own thoughts about him to perfection. If only time could stand still and keep us in that moment forever.

'But, if we were to explore what this might be, then I think that needs honesty. Don't you?'

'I've never really thought about it,' I murmured. I'd never believed anyone would ever love me. But that was before meeting *him*. That was when I thought all men would be like my father, dictatorial and restrictive.

'I have.' He gave a small smile. 'And I think truth is the cornerstone of any successful relationship.'

My chest felt so tight, as if my heart were a caged bird. I could barely breathe. 'What are you asking me to do? Confess all my dark secrets?'

He grimaced. 'No. I'd be no better than Matron's suitor, putting pressure on her to betray her country, if I did that. I'll be damned if I put you in such a difficult position.' He placed a gentle hand on my shoulder, his eyes locked on to mine. 'There are things you can't tell me. I accept that. But, when this is all over, then we can be completely honest with each other. And that would be a solid foundation on which to build a life together.'

I dropped my gaze. Even after the war, I wouldn't be able to share my secrets. Thanks to the Official Secrets Act I would never be able to be completely honest with him, despite the fact that I wanted nothing more than to tell him everything.

'Your silence tells me you disagree,' he said.

'It's not that.' I looked up, hoping he could see my heart in my eyes. 'It's just... complicated.'

'I see.' He dipped his head. 'Then, let us leave things as they are, for both our sakes.' He turned and left, and all the air in the room left with him.

I sank onto the bed, my head in my hands. Why did everything have to be so difficult?

40

I walked around in a cloud of confusion for the next couple of weeks, torn between admiration for, and annoyance at, Edward's sense of integrity. I swung from desperately wanting to be with him to wondering whether I wanted a relationship with him at all. For much of my life, the thought of giving a man any influence had made me feel sick. Edward was different. It was rare to find a man prepared to allow a woman the space to make her own choices. A man who didn't automatically assume that a woman couldn't possibly know what she was talking about. A man who needed to be in control of everything around him. Edward hadn't simply brushed my wishes aside in favour of what *he* wanted. He knew there was more going on than I was allowed to speak about and he wasn't pushing. That, in my experience, was a minor miracle.

The idea of a relationship with a man, if Edward was the man, didn't make me feel trapped and unable to breathe. It actually might be possible to build something meaningful with him, something that worked for both of us. I could only hope that after the war, when tensions were not so fraught, the secrets

I held would fade into obscurity and become something we needn't think of.

In complete contrast to the direction of my thoughts, it was as if Edward had flipped a switch inside himself. One that closed me out. He didn't mention our conversation again. He retreated into polite professionalism, leaving not the smallest trace of what had passed between us in his manner. He worked away from Ashworth more and more. While I continued processing messages and typing reports. Outside office hours, I never saw him.

Life carried on as it had before, only emptier. I took my cue from him, focusing on practicalities rather than emotions during the day. It was only in the evenings when I was patrolling and checking drop sites that I allowed myself to probe how I felt. I missed him. I definitely wanted him to kiss me again. I wanted to explore everything that might come from that too. The more I thought about the rest of my life, the more I knew that I wanted to be with Edward forever.

Late one Saturday afternoon, as I crouched to check a concealed section of gatepost, the call of a great northern diver came from behind. I spun around. A familiar figure stood a few yards away watching.

'Tut-tut. No points for observation there.' Lexi shook her head. 'You're getting slow in your old age. You're lucky *I'm* not an enemy agent.'

'True.' I laughed, getting to my feet and strolling over to stare at the contraption at her side. 'Is that a motorbike?'

She grinned and stood back so I could see it properly. 'It is. It's called a Welbike. It's the smallest one they've ever made. Can you believe it folds up? Look.' She indicated several points on the frame that could be adjusted. 'You should see it go, though.

It's pretty fast. Well, when there's enough fuel, of course. They send me all over the place. I love it.'

'I bet you do.' I shook my head. Typical Lexi. 'So, you just happened to be passing. *Again*. Right?'

'Yup. I can't stay away from you, Wren. Well done for rooting out your traitor.'

'Thanks. Only, it doesn't feel as good as I thought it would.' I sighed. 'Anyway, how do you know about it?'

Lexi wiggled her eyebrows. 'Lots of reports come across my desk.'

'What exactly do you do?' I asked before shaking my head in exasperation. 'Forget I asked. I know you can't tell me.'

Lexi pulled out a tobacco tin and rolled a cigarette. 'So, you never suspected Matron then?'

'No,' I said. 'But I should have. It was obvious when I thought about it.'

'Don't beat yourself up about it. You got her in the end.'

'But I feel sorry for her too.' I sighed. 'I must be going soft...'

Lexi leaned against a tree trunk and lit her roll-up. 'Nothing is ever as cut and dried as we think it will be. Poor cow got suckered in by a man. Who of us haven't experienced that at some time or another?' She blew out a stream of smoke.

I waved it away from my face and moved upwind. 'You didn't used to smoke, Lex.'

'Things change.' She pulled a face. 'It helps me stay calm.'

I peered at the huge dark circles under her eyes. 'Are you all right?'

'I'm always all right, me.' Her words lacked their usual defiance.

Apart from her fear of small spaces, I had always thought Lexi had nerves of steel, but I could see traces of vulnerability that weren't there before. Her usual spark and defiance were muted. The pallor of her skin spoke of bone-deep exhaustion. The hand holding the cigarette to her lips trembled. Stark evidence of how draining it was to keep going under wartime conditions. Sometimes I wondered if it would ever end. And if it did end, would there be anything left? Would all the suffering and death be worth it? I could only hope so.

'What's going on, Lex?'

She shook her head. 'Nothing. Or nothing I can share.'

And that was the problem. We were all in this huge battle together, striving towards a common goal, and yet we all carried a personal weight that couldn't be shared. The very nature of special ops work meant not trusting anyone and yet as human beings we need connection. It hurt to see my friend so sad and alone.

'You know I'm here for you, don't you?' I said.

'Yup.' She flicked ash on the ground, a muscle twitching in her jaw. 'I know. Thanks.'

I glanced around. 'Why exactly *are* you here? Not that it's not always great to see you.'

She took a long drag, exhaling slowly. 'We've been picking up a faint radio message. Morse code. It's been repeated every night for two weeks.'

How odd. 'What does it say?'

'That's the problem. The Morse code bit we understand, of course, but the message itself is gibberish. It's not in any language we understand.'

'Is it double coded?'

'Probably. For all we know it's triple coded. We've had our best people on it, and they can't break it.'

I flashed her a disbelieving side-eye. 'Are you bringing it to me because you think I'm better than your best people?'

'Don't flatter yourself. You're not that good.'

I laughed.

She waved a dismissive hand. 'Having said that, I do think you might be able to translate it.'

'Why?'

'Here.' She passed me a slip of paper. 'Tell me I'm not seeing things.'

The minute I saw the string of letters my breath caught. 'Oh my!' I ran my index finger over the beginning. WAWAWA. And at the end, TATATA. 'It's Tommy.' He was alive. Or, at least he was when he sent this. I felt sick as delight warred with terror. My thoughts exploded in a hundred different directions at once. Where was he? How was he? Was he in danger? What could I do? My heart thumped and my hands shook, making it almost impossible to read the rest of the message.

'I knew it,' said Lexi, a triumphant grin spreading across her face. 'Only the next bit doesn't make sense. There's a JA. You said that was for Jane Austen, but then he puts SOS. *That's* not one of her novels. Unless he made a mistake and means SAS. You know, *Sense and Sensibility*. I tried that. It didn't work.'

I smiled, my heart skipping. 'SOS tells me to use the emergency key in my head.'

'Which is what?'

'It's one of our secret languages. The ones we made up as children.'

She rolled her eyes. 'I might have guessed. No wonder we couldn't break it. What does he say?'

'Hang on. It's been a while since I've done this. Let me work out which one he's using.' I devoured the message with my eyes, my mind galloping ahead, converting letters and symbols, and tried not to react emotionally to what I was reading. 'He is asking for help. He's injured. He's hiding out on the French coast, due south of here.'

'Shit.' Lexi grunted. 'The vast majority of northern and western France is occupied. The coastal regions south of here are the most heavily patrolled.' She bit her lip. 'It's strange, though. He can't be with the French Resistance, or we'd have heard through more official channels. Even so, he clearly has regular access to a radio.'

I thought back to the day I had said goodbye to him all those months ago. When I had mentioned that I'd like to work in radio communications, he'd made a jokey comment about liking the thought that I might be listening out for messages. And here he was sending me one, with no idea if I was receiving it. By some miracle, thanks to Lexi and a passing chat in a dank underground bunker, I held his words in my hands, and possibly his life.

'Is there some way to bring him home?' I asked.

Lexi shook her head. 'Not officially. No. Not right now. There are a few... shall we say, *delicate* projects in the pipeline that need to take priority.'

'Meaning he's stuck.'

'Unfortunately, yes.'

Thick oily dread oozed through my core. 'How long do you think he can last?'

'There's no way to tell.' She cursed. 'Are you absolutely sure it's him?'

I reread the message. 'Yes. It's him.'

She ground her cigarette out underfoot before dusting off the spent butt and popping it in her pocket. 'Why don't you listen out for him tonight? Assuming he is able to transmit again. I put the time and wavelength the messages usually appear at on the bottom, there. It's nearly six now. If you hurry, you could catch tonight's. You could reply. Ask for more details.

Anything that will mark it as genuine. Make doubly, triply, sure it's him. Then...'

'Then?'

She shrugged. 'That's up to you.'

'You are surely not suggesting I do something about rescuing him?'

She shrugged again. 'I've heard what you can do to enemy submarines. I wouldn't put anything past you.'

'Perhaps I should ask Edward what he thinks. He and Tommy have been friends for years.'

She grimaced. 'How good a friend is he, though? Will he put your brother over official orders? He could face a court martial if he's caught?'

My heart plummeted. I'd not thought about the risks to him. How selfish of me. 'You're right. I can't ask him. It wouldn't be fair.'

'Whereas, *you* are already operating under the radar. You might get away with it.'

'You mean I should go and get him myself?'

'You did mention you had a boat.'

'My father does,' I corrected, my voice weak at the thought of crossing the Channel alone, even though I knew I would do it. For Tommy.

Lexi sighed. 'I don't know what I'm suggesting really. I just know it's... well, it's family, isn't it? If I had a brother I'd do whatever it takes. But it's not fair of me to put that on you. I'm sorry.'

'Don't be.' I shook my head. 'You're right.'

She rubbed a hand across her face. 'Maybe you *should* ask your captain.'

'No. I can't do that to him. But I will think of something.' Resolve settled around my shoulders. Tommy needed me. I'd go. No question.

She wriggled her eyebrows at me. 'You're not denying that he's your captain, then? Interesting.'

A warm flush stained my cheeks. I couldn't meet her eyes. 'Yes, well...'

'Ha! Told you.' Her laughter died away as fast as it had arrived. 'Look. I have to go. I shouldn't even be here.'

'Why did you come? I mean, you're taking quite a risk and...' I blinked several times to stem a hot prickle behind my eyes.

'You stood up for me before, when you didn't have to.' She shrugged. 'When I realised this might be from your brother, I couldn't just sit on it.'

'Thank you. I owe you one.'

'No. You don't. It's what friends do for each other.' She pulled me into a tight hug. 'Whatever you decide to do, I wish you all the luck in the world. Stay safe, yeah?'

41

I hurried back to Ashworth, my mind a mass of churning thoughts all ducking and diving around each other like the bats that danced overhead as I marched along the forest path. The best thing to do was to go straight down to the bunker and spend the evening listening to radio chatter. That plan ground to an unexpected halt when I arrived at the office to find the door unlocked and Edward at his desk.

'Oh,' I said. 'I thought you had gone for the evening.'

'I had. Then, I remembered I needed to finish this report for tomorrow.' He frowned. 'What's wrong? You're looking flustered.'

Flustered didn't cover it. I couldn't think straight. My insides had turned into a quivering mass of nerves all firing contradictory instructions to each other about what I should do. I *needed* to get down to the bunker. The radio down there was more powerful than the one in my room. It stood a better chance of picking up a communication from Tommy. 'Nothing's wrong.' I cast around for a reason for my own presence. 'I thought I had left a personal letter here.' I made a pretence of rummaging through my desk drawer. 'How silly. It must be in my room. I'll go and check. Goodnight.' I scurried out, aware of Edward's curious gaze following me.

There was no time to worry about him. My heart thumped wildly as I dashed back outside and into the forest to the escape hatch. I raced along the escape tunnel to the bunker and switched on the radio. With shaking fingers, I turned the dial in search of that faint signal, convinced I was too late. There was nothing apart from static. The hiss of open airwaves filled the headphones.

Suddenly.

There.

That was it. The same message. Repeated twice.

Tommy.

How could I be sure? I racked my brain. I had to reply. What would only he and I know? I scribbled on a piece of paper, pulling rusty code from my head, translating it into dots and dashes. Then, when I was certain, I started transmission.

```
TATATA — NAME THAT CROW — WAWAWA
```

Seconds ticked by in silence. I held my breath. Then, came the reply.

```
WAWAWA — MARCUS — TATATA
```

I gave a short laugh as old memories crowded in. A crow had fallen down the chimney into our playroom when we were children. The maid had gone into a panic, shooing it out of the window. We'd found the whole thing hilarious and joked about it later, in secret. Tommy had insisted the crow was a long-lost friend and given him a name: Marcus.

What else could I ask?

```
TATATA — WHERE DID THE FROG GO? — WAWAWA

WAWAWA — FREDA THE FROG WENT TO SEE THE
SEA — TATATA
```

Only Tommy would know that we had rescued a frog from Father's dog and released it back to Ashworth stream, pretending that it was going on holiday to the seaside. Silly childhood things that no one could make up. The secret code, in conjunction with those two correct answers: Marcus and Freda. It was definitely my brother. I tapped out another message.

```
TATATA — TELL ME WHAT YOU NEED — WAWAWA
```

His next transmission was a long one. I scribbled as much information down as I could. Eventually, I sent back a final reply.

```
TATATA — SIT TIGHT. WILL BE IN TOUCH —
WAWAWA
```

Once he signed off, I sat and stared at my notes for ages, a plan forming in the back of my mind. It was outrageous, but it just might work. The question was, could I pull it off? There was no doubt in my mind, I had to try. In order to do that, there was something I needed, and there was only one place to get it. I pulled my headset off and checked my watch. Ten o'clock. Perfect. I powered the radio down, grabbed a torch from one of the packs on the shelving unit and started back down the escape tunnel. There was no time to lose.

* * *

Emerging from the hatch, I paused in the darkness and listened to the forest. The air was crisp, a light breeze rustled branches overhead and owls called to each other. Nothing unusual. Once my eyes had adjusted to the darkness, I hastened along a path that skirted the manor and led to the gatehouse. With luck, Father would already be in bed. The last thing I wanted was an altercation with him.

Creeping along the hedge marking the perimeter of the gatehouse garden, I slunk across the lawn towards a set of French windows. As expected, these had been secured for the night. I examined the lock and pulled a couple of bobby pins from my hair. A twig snapped behind me. I whirled around, raising my fists.

The gate swung, the hinge squeaking in protest.

'Who's there?' I whispered, my heartbeat drumming in my ears. 'Show yourself.'

A dark shadow detached itself from the hedge. Edward.

'What are you doing here?' I hissed.

'I rather think that's my line,' he muttered. 'What the hell are you up to? And don't tell me you've suddenly been overcome with familial duty and decided to pay a quick visit to your dear old dad to say nighty-night, because I won't believe you.'

'Fine, I won't then.' I crouched down to finish picking the lock.

He leaned against the wall and gave a low whistle. 'You're full of surprises, aren't you?'

'Only when people underestimate me.' Turning the handle,

I stepped into the room with Edward hard on my heels. 'How long have you been following me?'

'Ever since you left the office.'

Prickles ran over my scalp and down my back. 'Are you serious?'

'Yes.' His tone was very matter-of-fact. 'If you're wondering whether I saw you disappear underground? The answer is yes. But, don't worry, I didn't follow you. I figured it was connected to all the stuff you can't tell me about.'

'What did you do?' I whispered.

'I waited for you to come back out so I could tail you. And here we are. Breaking into your father's home in the dead of night. Why *are* we breaking into your father's home in the dead of night?'

Letting out a long sigh of frustration, I closed the door and yanked the blackout curtains back into place. Flicking on my torch, I crossed the room to peer into the hall.

In seconds he was behind me, his breath warming the back of my neck as he murmured, 'What are we looking for?'

'Shh!' I glared at him. '*We* aren't doing anything.'

'Yes, we are. Look.' He pointed. 'You. Me. That makes we.' His eyes danced, inviting me to share the joke.

'Go away.'

'Not a chance. You wouldn't believe how hard it has been to stay away from you this last week, Wren.'

I growled under my breath. 'And you've chosen right now to change tack?'

'I have.' He sounded very pleased with himself. 'I'm here for *all* of... uh, well... whatever this is.'

'Fine,' I snapped. 'Just for goodness' sake be quiet. The last thing I need is Father waking up.'

'It's too late for that, my girl,' Father's voice boomed from somewhere nearby.

Oh great!

Footsteps sounded in the hall and the shadows shifted as Father appeared holding a paraffin lamp aloft. He glared from Edward to me and back to Edward again. 'Commander?' Disapproval spilled from his eyes. His words were clipped and deliberate. 'What's going on?'

Edward stepped forward. 'I'm afraid you'll have to ask your daughter that. This is her mission. I'm just along for the ride.'

Father glowered. 'Mission? What on earth are you talking about?'

I prayed for the ground to swallow me up. When it refused, I fixed my father with a steady gaze. For Tommy's sake, I had to do this. 'I need to see a marine chart for the English Channel, Father. Preferably one that covers the French coast due south of here.'

Father's eyes nearly popped out of his head. 'Why?'

'Because Tommy is in hiding at Landemer. He's injured.'

Father paled. 'How do you know?'

'I can't say.'

'What do you mean, you can't say?' he demanded. 'That's my son you're talking about.'

Edward cleared his throat. 'I think... what she means is that it's best if you don't know, sir.'

'Don't be ridiculous.' Father turned on him. 'Why are you giving this nonsense of hers any credibility?'

Edward drew himself up to his full height, all hint of amusement gone. 'The other day, you asked me who the brave officer was who planted the mine on that enemy submarine.'

'What has that got to do with it?' blustered Father.

Edward gestured to me. 'You are looking at her.'

'Wren?' Father's eyes darted from Edward to me and back again. 'No. I don't believe you.'

'That is your prerogative.' Edward's tone was deceptively mild. 'But it doesn't make what I said any less true.'

Father examined me as if he'd never seen me before. 'You swam all that way? Carrying a mine?'

I nodded.

'Damn me, my girl. That was brave. Yes. Very brave.'

'Your daughter is one of the bravest and strongest people I know,' said Edward. 'I would follow her into battle any day.'

Father tugged a handkerchief from his pocket and mopped his brow, all the while peering at me with curiosity. 'My, my. And... er... you say you've had word about Tommy?'

'I've had a radio exchange with him this very evening.'

'How...?' He tucked his handkerchief away. 'Ah... you can't say.'

'I *won't* say, Father. I'm sorry. Please trust me? It's definitely him.'

'My boy.' He swayed on his feet, suddenly seeming old and frail. Then he stiffened. 'This is good news. If we know where he is, the War Office can arrange a rescue.'

I shook my head. 'There are no plans to do that. In fact, quite the opposite. We need to move before they stop us.'

'Why ever would they do that?'

'It might endanger another delicate mission in the area,' I said.

'I see.' Father frowned. 'Landemer, you said. And you want a marine chart. What is your plan?'

'To slip across the Channel, under the cover of darkness, and bring him home.' I braced myself to be told not to be so ridiculous, but Father didn't say a word. He just stood stock-still staring at me.

Edward gave a short humourless laugh. 'That's quite an undertaking.'

'I haven't worked out all the details yet,' I admitted. 'That's why I need the map. It might be impossible.'

'It's not impossible,' said Father. 'Difficult, yes, and probably unwise. But not impossible. Come on. Let's take a look.' He marched down the hall to a small office. I scurried in his wake with Edward behind me. We both watched as Father rummaged through a pile of rolled maps on a shelf under the window. 'Hmm, which chart do we need. Ah! This one,' he muttered, pulling one out and unrolling it on his desk. He glanced up. 'I assume you're planning to take *The Lady*?'

I nodded. 'Yes. If I can find enough fuel. I figured she could get me close enough to the French coast to anchor offshore. Then, if I have the tender in tow, I could use it to row ashore and pick him up.'

'Towing the tender will slow you down *and* use more fuel, we'll have to account for that in our calculations.' Father ran a finger across the chart. 'Let's see. Landemer. It's close to Cherbourg. Hmm. That part of the coast is heavily armed. It's a miracle he's not been captured.'

'I know,' I said. 'That's another reason we should move as soon as we can.'

Father stroked his chin, deep in thought. 'It's risky. There are gun batteries everywhere. You're right though. A small rowing boat at night might pass unnoticed. Can you confirm a specific location with him? Somewhere he can slip past patrols. And we'll need a precise time for the pick-up, or at least a rough window. Then, I can account for the tides and work out when we need to leave here to get there.'

'We?' I wasn't sure why he kept using that word.

'I don't care how brave you are, my girl. You'll need a proper navigator. Preferably someone who has sailed those waters before. I know that crossing like the back of my hand. It'll increase your chances of success if you take me with you.'

'He's right,' said Edward. 'The three of us working together stand a much better chance.'

I put my hands on my hips. 'When did this become the three of us?'

'He's my friend, Wren,' said Edward. 'I have to help him.'

I shook my head. 'If the enemy catch us, there'll be no way back.'

'I know.' Grave lines scored either side of Edward's mouth. 'Remember. I've been trapped behind enemy lines before. If someone hadn't stuck their neck out for me, I wouldn't have survived, let alone escaped.'

'It's more complicated than that.' I needed to know he understood. 'The enemy are only part of the problem. This goes directly against War Office orders. If our own side get wind of this, they'll court martial us.'

'Let them try,' scoffed Father. 'I'll have a few things to say to them if they do. You mark my words.' For the first time ever, the sound of his outraged bluster warmed my heart.

Edward straightened. 'I'll risk court martial for Tommy. He'd do the same for me. And anyway, you need me, Wren.'

He wasn't wrong. The thought of Edward at my side gave me strength, even though I wasn't ready to admit that fact to him. 'Why do I need you? What can you offer this mission?'

He grinned. 'For starters, I can requisition fuel.'

'Can you divert the local patrols away from the coast for a day or so?' asked Father. 'I need to pull *The Lady* from storage.'

'Where is she?' asked Edward.

'In a boathouse over at Christchurch Harbour,' replied Father. 'I had her tucked away at the start of the war.'

'I'm rather surprised she wasn't requisitioned by the navy,' said Edward.

'If her engine wasn't unreliable, she probably would have been,' said Father. 'It's such a shame that it seized completely, just at the wrong time.'

'What?' I said with horror. 'Father, that's terrible news. This whole plan hinges on that engine working.'

He gave me a fleeting wink. 'Don't worry. It will be fine.'

Edward raised an eyebrow. 'I heard that a lot of vessels were sabotaged to avoid requisitioning.'

'Dear me! How very unpatriotic,' said Father. 'That would be a terrible thing to do.'

I looked at him closely. I had heard him outraged often enough. This time, it didn't ring true.

'Understandable, though,' continued Edward. 'After all, there is no telling what state a requisitioned ship will come back in. That's if it's returned at all.'

'Indeed,' replied Father. 'Anyway, I'll bring *The Lady* round to the bay to get her ready. She has a white hull, which will stand out like a beacon at night. We'll have to darken it and add some camouflage to the decking.'

'Good idea,' I said. 'If we're going to avoid enemy detection, we'll have to moor her a long way off the French coast as it is. If she's darker, it will be a huge help.'

'Your dad can stay on board while we row in to get Tommy,' said Edward.

I frowned. 'It won't take two of us to do that.'

'I disagree,' said Edward.

'I do too,' said Father.

'Fine, we'll both go. But you both have to remember that this is *my* mission.' I stared from one to the other, my mind racing through possibilities. 'If I let you come, you have to agree to take your orders from me.'

Edward grinned, raising both hands in mock surrender. 'I wouldn't have it any other way.'

A few seconds of silence passed. Father chewed on his lip thoughtfully, before jerking his chin down once. 'I agree.'

I smiled. 'Then, let's bring Tommy home.'

42

Organisation for the trip was far more complicated and took much longer than I had expected. It wasn't a case of simply springing the boat from the boathouse undetected, filling the tank with fuel and heading off. There was the weather to contend with, not to mention tides and currents to consider, and supplies to be ordered.

I messaged Tommy to confirm a time and location, keeping the communication brief. Every second on the airwaves increased his risk of capture. My nerves shredded themselves with every delay. The longer this took, the greater the chance of failure. Finally, we were ready. Everything was in place to set off. Landemer was sixty-seven nautical miles due south. Father estimated that – winds, tides, currents and enemy ships willing – the trip should take us approximately twelve to fifteen hours. I sent a brief message to Tommy the night before we left. There was no reply, which left me shredding my nails with worry.

* * *

Father's attempts to camouflage his beautiful ship were very successful. A small motor cruiser built of teak, *The Lady's* usual glossy white-paint finish had disappeared under a muddy blue-grey that seemed to sink into the murky waters around her. The tender was a similarly drab hue. Yards of dark netting draped around the edge of the main deck and across the cabin top broke up the sharp, sleek lines and hid any shiny metal rails and portholes. The overall effect aged her, making her easy to overlook.

Dressed in worn, brown corduroy trousers, drab thick-knit jumpers under oilskin jackets, with boots and dark woolly hats, I hoped that Edward, Father and I looked equally unremarkable. 'She's perfect, Father,' I said, and climbed aboard. 'Thank you.'

He grunted. 'Needs must.' It would have caused him great pain to make his pride and joy look like a tatty old fishing vessel. He made short work of firing up the engine and called for Edward to cast off from the buoy. While Edward climbed over the cabin roof to comply, Father and I were left alone in the cockpit. He fixed me with a stern look that instantly made me apprehensive. Was I going to regret involving him?

'What's the problem, Father?' I asked.

'I underestimated you, my girl.'

'Oh.' That was the last thing I had ever expected him to say.

'You're stronger than I thought,' he continued, 'and very brave. Setting off to rescue your brother like this, without pausing to think about your own safety.'

'I haven't rescued him yet.'

'That isn't the point.' A touch of his usual irritation crept back into his voice. 'Not many young ladies would attempt something like this.'

I didn't know what to say.

Fortunately, Edward arrived back in the cockpit, dusting his hands off. He glanced from Father to me. 'What do we do now?'

Father raised an eyebrow. 'Yes, Wren? You're in charge. What are your orders?'

I blinked momentarily, gathering my wits, and then grinned. 'Take her out, Captain.'

'Aye, aye.' Father saluted and put *The Lady* into gear. 'Next stop, France.'

* * *

The crossing was relatively easy, thanks to the mild conditions. Early August was undoubtedly the best time of year to be attempting a Channel crossing in a small craft and the weather was on our side with a gentle breeze and calm water. Our stealthy approach to the French Coast was assisted by a handy sea mist that rolled over us in the late afternoon like a thick blanket of cotton wool and only dissipated once it was fully dark.

'This is as close in as I dare take her,' muttered Father.

'I agree. There will be patrols further in and we can't risk *The Lady* being impounded.' I turned to Edward. 'Can you cast out the sea anchor, please.'

He hurried to comply. The thrum of the engine died away, leaving an eerie silence broken only by the minor slap-slap of small waves against the hull as *The Lady* responded to the controlling tug of the anchor and settled in the water. We turned our eyes towards the shadowy coastline.

'You've got a fair old distance to row,' said Father. 'At least the mist has lifted a bit and the water is calm, which will make things easier. There's not much wind either.'

He was right. Choppy water and a howling gale would make

achieving our objective much harder. I tried to be grateful for small mercies.

'Tommy is meeting us halfway,' I said. 'Whoever is sheltering him has agreed to row him out. We just have to hope they are able to do so without being seen.'

Edward peered into the gloom. 'How are we going to find him in the dark when we're also trying not to be seen?'

'We'll aim for the northern headland.' I pointed at a darker section of shadow. 'Then, it's over to torchlight and Morse code.'

'How's that going to work?' he asked.

'Every ten minutes from midnight, I'll send a brief message by flashing the torch. Hopefully, quickly enough not to attract enemy attention. With luck, he'll reply. Then we move towards each other's lights until we meet.'

Edward untied the painter and drew the tender alongside *The Lady*. 'Do we have a backup plan?'

'No.' My response dropped into silence.

I suppressed a rising tide of anxiety. I couldn't give in to it, because it wasn't just me on the line here. Or Tommy. I glanced across at Father and then Edward, marvelling at how brave they were to trust me and back me up. I didn't dare examine the enormity of what I had put into play here too closely. If I did, I might lose my nerve and we would all be lost. The only thing to do was keep going and hope for the best.

Father helped to steady the tender as Edward and I scrambled aboard.

'You're in charge of direction,' said Edward, setting the rowlocks into place. 'I'll row.'

'Wait a minute,' said Father. 'How are you going to find your way back here?'

Pulling a compass from my pocket I took several bearings. 'There's a torch in the back locker. Wait until half past midnight.

Then, shine it towards the coast, just a short burst of three flashes. Do that every fifteen minutes. We'll use it as a guide when we're on our way back. There's still fog hugging the beach, so I'm hoping your light won't be seen from the shore. But, if there's any sign of enemy ships nearby, stop and go dark. Move further away from the coast if you have to and wait until it's safe to move back in and start again.'

'Wren... I...' Father snapped his mouth shut, as if afraid to let the words out.

'What is it?'

'Nothing,' he muttered. 'Just keep safe. Please.'

A lump appeared in my throat at the tender expression in his eyes. He'd never seemed so approachable before. I had the unexpected urge to spend time with him and get to know him better. I stiffened my spine and told myself to stay on track. First, we had to rescue Tommy.

'I will, Father. You too,' I said, thinking my plan had better jolly well work. If it didn't we risked capture, torture as spies and execution. And it would be my fault.

He saluted. '*The Lady* and I will be here when you get back.'

'Ready?' Edward set the end of an oar against the hull of the bigger ship and gently pushed off. A few minutes later Father and *The Lady* disappeared into the darkness.

We rowed in silence for ages, whispering briefly to correct our course.

Suddenly, Edward stopped. 'Can you hear that?'

I listened. A faint humming noise was getting louder.

'That's not Tommy,' I murmured, prickles of alarm crawling up my back. 'He said he'd be rowing, not using an engine.'

Edward shipped his oars and crouched down in the belly of the tender, whispering, 'Whoever they are, they're coming this way.'

The vague shape of a tug boat slowly materialised from the gloom. Voices carried across the water. An enemy patrol, heading straight for us. Any minute and we'd be spotted. I leaned closer to Edward, putting my mouth as close to his ear as I could. 'We'll have to go over the side and tread water until they've gone.'

He frowned as he processed what I'd said, and then nodded. Tugging off his jumper, and shucking his boots and trousers, he rolled them all inside his oilskin to form a tight ball and shoved them under his seat out of sight. I stuffed the torch and compass in my pocket and did the same. One by one, we slipped over the back of the tender and into the icy water, careful not to splash, using the body of the boat to block the sight of us from the approaching launch. At the last minute, Edward reached back up to grab one of the oars and eased it into the water alongside him, forcing it under the surface out of sight.

There was a shout, and then a series of indecipherable comments. Lurking in the shadow of the tender, slowly circling my arms and legs, I sank down in the water, tipping my head back until only my eyes, ears, mouth and nose remained on the surface. In the very corner of my vision, I could see Edward doing the same.

The engine of the enemy patrol boat stopped. A powerful light swept over the tender and the water around it, coming within inches of falling on us. I felt a tickle in my nose. *Please don't sneeze. Please don't sneeze.* I squeezed my eyes shut, concentrated on my breathing and listened to the conversation taking place on board.

'What do you think?' asked a voice in German.

A dismissive grunt followed. 'It's empty. Whoever was on board must have had an accident.'

'Should we take it in tow?' The first voice sounded tired.

I held my breath, focusing intently to follow what they were saying and wishing I had Connie's fluency with languages.

Another grunt. 'It'll slow us down. We've little enough fuel as it is.'

'That's true.'

'But what if—' That was a third voice. Younger, more eager.

'There's only one oar.' The grunter sounded increasingly irritated. 'And it's no use to anyone way out here. We'll pick it up in the morning, *if* the currents haven't dealt with it for us by then. Come on. Let's go.'

The engine started again and the launch moved off. As the thrumming of the propeller died away, I felt Edward's hand brush against mine in the water. My legs were so tired they felt like lead weights. Somehow, I found the energy to kick harder and raised my head from the water. I peered cautiously around the tender.

'They've gone,' I murmured. 'Well done for removing the oar like that. They might not have left the boat behind otherwise.'

Edward had been holding the oar underneath the boat, using the weight of the tender to keep the length of the wood underwater. He tugged it out and it bobbed up to the surface. Heavy and unwieldy, it took two of us working together to slide it back onto the boat without making any obvious noise.

'How do we get back on board without capsizing the ruddy thing?' muttered Edward.

'Over the stern. I'll steady the bow while you climb in, then you can help balance things while I do the same.'

'You should go first.'

I grinned into the darkness. 'Don't go getting all chivalrous on me. Just do as you're told.'

'Aye, aye, Captain.'

We moved into position. There was a whoosh of water. The boat lurched and bobbed furiously. 'I'm in,' he said. 'Your turn.'

I grasped the gunwale at the back of the boat and pulled. My arms quivered with all the strength of a half-set jelly. Whether this was due to adrenaline, shock or cold, I couldn't tell. It was almost impossible to heave myself up. Edward reached over the stern and grabbed me by the back of my shirt. 'I'm going to push you under the water a bit and then, when I let go you should bob back up. We can use that momentum. If you give an almighty kick and pull up hard at the same time, and if I yank too, you'll be in. Ready? One, two, three.'

Seconds later I dropped into the belly of the tender, helpless and gasping like a landed fish. Edward grabbed a tarpaulin and wrapped it around me, rubbing my arms and shoulders. Pins and needles prickled all over. Half pleasure, half pain. Whether it was from the friction or merely contact with *him*, I couldn't tell.

'Come on,' he said. 'Strip off that wet shirt and get your dry stuff back on. You'll soon feel better. I'll turn my back.'

Supressing the urge to beg him to put his arms around me, I did as I was told. By the time I was fumbling to do up my coat buttons, my teeth had at least stopped chattering enough for me to talk. 'What time is it?'

He checked his watch, then shook his wrist, lifting the dial to his ear. 'Damn, it's stopped. Not that it's any wonder, given the dunking it just got.' He squinted at it. 'It looks like we went into the water at five minutes to midnight.'

'That was ages ago. We were supposed to start signalling at midnight.' My voice quailed as I realised what this meant. 'What if we've missed Tommy?'

Edward put a steadying hand on my arm. 'The only thing we

can do is start signalling now. We'll just have to pray that enemy patrol boat is far enough away.'

It was the only choice we had. I tugged my hat on and dug the compass and torch out of my coat pocket. 'Here goes. Keep your eyes peeled.' I checked the direction, then shone the torch out into the darkness, blasting out a short burst of Morse code. TATATA.

We stared into the darkness as time passed with no response.

Counting the seconds under my breath as best I could, I waited for what I thought was ten minutes. Then I sent another burst. In my head, one single refrain kept repeating itself: *please, Tommy, please be there.*

No response. Approximately ten minutes later, I signalled again. And again. My heart sank further into my boots with each unanswered message.

'What if he's been captured?' I whispered.

'Don't think like that. We can't give up. If there's anyone with the brains to outwit the enemy, it's Tommy Ashworth.' Edward was trying to be reassuring, but I could hear a sliver of doubt in his tone.

'We are going to have to start back soon, if we're to get out of enemy waters before the sun comes up,' I said. I didn't want to give up on my brother, but I had a responsibility to Edward and Father. They were both here, in danger, because of my crazy idea. We'd had one close call already. How far should I push this?

He placed a gentle hand on my shoulder. 'Let's give it another half an hour.'

43

Another half an hour brought no joy. Blinded by hot tears, I sent our final message out into the night and closed my eyes in prayer. *Please, please, please.*

'There,' said Edward, pointing.

I held my breath, opening my eyes so wide I thought my eyeballs might pop out. Yes. There. A light. Flashing back at us.

Edward grabbed for the oars.

'Wait,' I said. 'We need to be sure it's him.'

I rattled off another message. TATATAWHOGOESTHEREWAWAWA

There was only a brief pause before the answer flashed back.

'What did he say?' asked Edward.

I laughed. 'He said MARCUS IS LOOKING FOR FREDA.'

Edward raised one eyebrow. 'That means something to you, does it?'

'Yes. It's definitely him.' I took a quick compass bearing. 'Let's go.'

With Edward on the oars and me directing – my eyes

bouncing from the compass to the darkness – it wasn't long before the shape of a small rowing boat emerged from the gloom. There were two figures on board.

'Serenity Ashworth,' a hushed male voice called. 'Fancy seeing you here.'

My heart skipped with delight. 'Thomas Ashworth. You're late.'

'But worth waiting for,' he said.

Edward gave a low chuckle. 'Your time on the run clearly hasn't diminished your immense ego, Tom.'

'Ed? Heavens above! What are you doing here?'

'Digging you out of yet another scrape, my friend.'

The smaller of the two figures manoeuvred their boat alongside ours, shipping the oars with expert precision at the last minute. I grabbed the gunwale to stop the two tenders bashing each other and stared into the gaunt but very much alive face of my twin. Grubby and bearded, with dark smudges of exhaustion under his eyes and one arm strapped across his chest, he had clearly been through a tough time.

'It's good to see you,' I said.

'Not as good as it is to see you,' he replied.

I turned to look at his companion for the first time. 'Thank you for keeping him safe.'

Wrapped up in a thick coat with the collar turned up and a large knitted hat pulled down low, it was almost impossible to see the person inside.

'Anything for a friend,' came the reply.

That was a voice I recognised. 'Connie?!'

She tugged her collar down and flashed me a quick grin. 'One and the same.'

'What... How...?' My jaw flapped with a thousand unasked questions as I drank in the sight of my friend. I'd worried so much about her and here she was, alive and well. The relief was immeasurable.

'Don't ask, my lovely.' She winked. 'You know I can't say.'

'Yes, of course.' My mind started whirling with the logistics of an extra person. It would be tight, but we could do it. 'Are you coming back with us?'

She shook her head. 'I'd love nothing more, but I can't. There's too much at stake here.'

Tommy's gaze locked with Connie's as if willing her to change her mind. 'Please come with us.'

Connie's voice was low, heavy with regret. 'I have my orders, Tom. You know I have to stay.'

'And I have to leave.' I'd never heard my brother sound so sad. The air between them was thick with an untold story. I bit my lip, wishing I could give them some privacy to say goodbye properly. I wanted to beg Connie to come with us, but I knew there was nothing I could say that would persuade her to abandon whatever it was that she was involved in.

'Yes, Tom,' she agreed. 'Go. You're no good to me injured, and every day you're here puts the rest of my mission at risk.' She leaned in and held his hand with both of hers as if she never wanted to let go. 'Go home, fly boy. Get yourself healed.'

'I will. But only so that I can come back with reinforcements. Stay safe, Constance.'

Edward cleared his throat. 'I hate to interrupt, but we ran into an enemy patrol boat not twenty minutes ago.'

'He's right,' I said. 'Come on, Tommy. We need to get out of here.'

Transferring Tommy from one boat to the other was tricky. With his arm out of action and both boats bobbing in protest at the shifting weight, he nearly ended up dunked in the water.

Eventually we managed it. I turned to say goodbye to Connie. 'Good luck, my friend.'

'We'll meet again,' she said.

'We will. Trafalgar Square, remember?' My throat was too thick to say any more.

'I'll see you there. You can count on it.' She pushed off, bobbing away from us, then unshipped her oars and rowed away into the darkness.

Tommy sat in silence for several seconds, staring after her, while Edward and I sprang in to action. We were not out of the woods and there were still plenty of things that could go wrong. 'Father will be wondering where we are,' I muttered, checking the compass.

'Father?' Tommy's tone was incredulous. 'Don't tell me the old man's here?'

'All right, I won't,' I said. 'If it'll make you happy, the gentleman currently moored offshore in *The Lady* is not actually our father. He just looks a lot like him.'

Tommy whistled. 'Was this his plan, then?'

'No,' said Edward. 'This was all Wren's idea. Although your dad helped with some of the logistics.'

'Blimey. That's a turn-up for the books. You and him working together, Wren. I can hardly believe it.'

I rolled my eyes. 'I could hardly row you back to England in this thing, could I?'

'I wouldn't put it past you, sister dear. Let's face it, you've gotten me caught up in sillier situations than this in the past. Usually trying to outwit Father.'

'Not this time,' I said. 'There's no way we'd have made it over here without him.'

'Tell me more. I can't wait to hear this particular story.'

'Another time, perhaps,' said Edward, pulling on the oars. 'It's a tale best told over a glass of brandy next to a roaring fire.'

'True,' I said. 'We're not out of the woods yet.'

Rowing was hard work. The tender sat much lower in the water, thanks to Tommy's additional weight, and it moved with all the grace of a wet sock. Slumped in the bottom of the boat on a mound of tarpaulin, a cocktail of anxiety and exhaustion carving huge furrows into his brow, Tommy stared at the receding land mass. That he was torn about leaving France was clear. My heart broke for him. I had no words of comfort to offer. We all knew Connie's chances of getting out of France alive were slim. For all her bravado about meeting up after the war, the odds were not in her favour. Anger at the enemy burned in my chest alongside pure admiration for Connie's sheer bravery.

'We must be getting close now.' I strained my eyes out into the darkness, searching for Father's signal to guide us. 'We should be able to see the signal by now. Unless we've drifted way off course.'

Edward's expression was grim. He rowed solidly on.

Tommy turned his gaze away from France and out to sea. 'What are we looking for?'

'Three short bursts of torchlight,' I replied.

Minutes ticked by.

'There!' He pointed. 'Is that it?'

I caught a glimmer from the corner of my eye only it was gone before I could really see it. 'I don't know. If it is, he'll repeat it in fifteen minutes. Do you have a watch?' Tommy nodded. 'Good. You keep an eye on the time. We'll head that way anyway while we wait. We don't exactly have any other options.' I shuddered, realising how flimsy my plan really was. I'd focused too much on getting to Tommy, and not enough on escaping afterwards.

'It's all right, Wren,' muttered Edward. 'We're doing fine.'

A tense hush fell over the boat as we rowed, staring into the darkness for another signal.

'There!' said Tommy again.

He was right. Three bursts of light and then no more. I released breath I hadn't realised I was holding. Adjusting our course each time the lights appeared, soon the shape of *The Lady* began to materialise from the darkness.

Father leaned over the side. 'Wren? Did you find him?'

'We did.' I couldn't keep the triumph from my words. The tender bumped gently against the larger boat's fenders. 'And he looks like he's in one piece.'

'Just about,' said Tommy, scrambling aboard. 'Hello, Father.'

'Oh, my dear boy.' Father's voice broke. He coughed, sniffed and blew his nose on his handkerchief. 'Look at you. You're injured.'

'A broken arm, a couple of bullet wounds and a few bashed ribs. Nothing that won't mend,' said Tommy with all the blasé brashness of someone referring to a splinter.

Edward offered me his hand. 'Go on, Wren. You get on board next. You look done in.'

'I'm fine.' A huge yawn belied my words.

'Of course you are.' He followed me onto *The Lady*, and secured the little boat astern with the painter. 'There's nothing more for you to do, other than give the order to head back.'

I yawned again. 'Father, would you mind taking us home, please?'

'Aye-aye, Captain. Let's get back to Blighty.' The sea anchor was hauled aboard, the engine sprang to life and Father set course for home.

Tommy sat in the cockpit, watching the French coast until it disappeared from sight. I nudged him gently. 'What are you thinking?'

'If anything happens to her, I'll never forgive myself,' he said. Pain was chiselled into his features.

'She's strong and talented and highly trained, Tom. If anyone can survive over there, it's her.' I mentally crossed my fingers, hoping I was right.

'Do you think so?'

'I know so. The best thing you can do for her, right now, is get well. That's what she'd want.'

'Wren's right,' said Edward. The glance that passed between us was loaded with concern. Whatever had happened in France had taken a heavy toll on Tommy. He was a shadow of his former self.

'Why don't you go below and rest, Tom? Father and I have everything under control up here. You'll feel stronger if you get some sleep.'

Tommy shook his head. 'I can help.'

I threw him a sardonic grin. 'Take a hint, brother dear. You're in the way. This cockpit isn't built for four.'

'I could do with a bit of shut-eye myself, Tom,' said Edward. 'Why don't you and I make use of a couple of the fancy berths below deck? Then we can come up in a couple of hours and take over.'

Tommy gave in and allowed Edward to help him down the companionway. Five minutes later, Edward poked his head back out. 'He's asleep. Almost before his head hit the pillow. Can I do anything to help up here?'

I glanced at Father for confirmation. He shook his head.

'We're all good here,' I said.

Edward narrowed his eyes at me. 'Wren, you're shattered. Why not get some rest?'

I shook my head. 'I want to see this through up here. Can you keep an eye on Tommy below decks for me?'

'Of course. I'll fire up the stove and see if I can't rustle up some tea.' Edward threw me a blanket. 'Keep yourself warm. We don't want you catching a chill after that little swim of ours.' He ducked back below deck, leaving Father and I alone.

After a few minutes, Father asked, 'Swim?'

'An enemy patrol got a little too close for comfort. We had no choice but to slip over the side and wait for them to pass. We had to tread water for a bit. It was close. But we were fine.'

Silence fell on the little cockpit. Father checked the compass and adjusted course. He took a deep breath as if readying himself to speak.

I waited.

He sighed but otherwise stayed silent.

Time passed. Finally, he spoke. 'Serenity... uh... Wren, I...'

'What is it, Father?'

He stared out to sea. 'After your mother died, I was lost. I didn't know what to do.'

'It must have been very hard,' I murmured, wondering why he was bringing my mother up. 'You loved her so much.'

'Yes, I did. But that's not what I mean.' He scratched his head before continuing. 'I didn't know what to do with *you*.'

The weight of his words tumbled into the silence of the night around us.

'Tommy was fine,' he continued. 'I understood boys and what they need. But, what could I possibly know about raising a girl? I had no sisters, aunts or female cousins to turn to for advice. I wanted to do it right. Raise you in the correct way. Like your mother would have. I wanted to make her proud.'

I bowed my head. 'I'm sorry, I'm not the perfect young lady you want me to be.'

'You misunderstand, Wren. It wasn't really about you. I wanted her to be proud of *me*. For the way I raised you. Only—' his eyes darted back to me and then away again '—I made rather a hash of it, I'm afraid.'

Now it was my turn to struggle with words. 'You did your best.'

'I did. But I tried to make you fit into what society expected of a lady. I suspect I should have allowed you to be the strong, spirited, independent person I can see that you are. I'm sorry for... well, for getting it wrong.'

'Please. Don't.' A lump closed my throat. 'I was difficult.'

'No. You were just you. And, for what it is worth, I think your mother would be proud of you. I—' He leaned over, giving my shoulder a firm nudge with his own. '*I'm* proud of you, Wren. Don't ever forget that.'

There was no doubting the sincerity in his voice. 'Thank you,' I mumbled, through wobbly lips. 'That means the world to me.'

The cockpit hatch slid back and Edward stumbled up with three mugs in hand. 'Here you are. It's hot and wet, but whether it tastes anything like tea is anyone's guess.'

As I reached for my mug, a strange sound alerted me to trouble. 'Hush!' I said. 'What's that?' A low rumble crept across the water towards us. It was getting steadily louder. 'We need to go dark. Now!' I dived to extinguish the cockpit lamp.

Edward disappeared below deck and dowsed the lamp in the cabin.

The rumble became a deep-seated physical thrum that juddered through us, making the boat shake and even the tea in our mugs start to tremble as the sound grew in volume and intensity, swallowing up the sky overhead. Hands over our ears, we sat holding our collective breath, eyes glued to the sky.

'There.' I pointed to a break in the blanket of clouds where the vast undercarriage of a Heinkel bomber passed overhead, with another in its wake. They were so close it felt as if I could reach up and touch them. The outline of each metal panel, solder and rivets holding them together, were visible to the naked eye.

The fleet was huge. We watched until the last plane passed, disappearing into the distance, taking the noise and commotion with it.

Father gave a snort of disgust. 'On their way to batter seven bells out of Southampton again.'

'Yes, probably,' muttered Edward.

I shivered, pulling the blanket closer around my shoulders. 'Poor souls. How do they stand it? Night after night.'

'You were right about what you said.' Father patted my arm. 'The mothers with their babies do need shelter. We should be proud of the role Ashworth is playing in this war. I'm rather ashamed of my earlier reaction.' He turned to Edward. 'And I'm beginning to suspect that there is a lot more going on at Ashworth than I thought.'

Edward grinned. 'I couldn't possibly say, sir.'

'No,' Father snorted. 'I'm sure you couldn't.'

I tried to stifle a yawn and failed.

'For goodness' sake,' Father grunted. 'Go below. Both of you. Get some rest. No doubt there will be plenty more things you can't tell me about that you need to do tomorrow. I'll get us all home in one piece.'

'Thank you, Father.' I kissed his cheek and stumbled down the gangway. Edward pulled me onto a berth with him and we slept soundly, arms wrapped around each other, rocked by the gentle swell of the waves.

44

The next day, in the office, typing and taking messages, everything felt surreal. *The Lady* was back in dry dock. Father was back at the gatehouse. Tommy was with him, having been checked over by one of the doctors visiting patients at the maternity home. I stared at the typewriter keys, a strange sense of disconnect buzzing through my head as I listened to Edward speaking into the telephone. He rang off, his brow creased with concern.

I sprang to my feet and hurried over to him. 'Is everything all right?'

He pulled a face. 'Can you send a note to the gatehouse asking your father and Tommy to come up here, please?'

'Of course. When?'

He glanced at the clock. 'As soon as possible. We're about to have a visit from the War Office. They are sending a team to debrief us.'

'Goodness. That's quick.' I bit my lip. 'I hope we made the right decision telling them.'

'We had no choice other than to tell the truth.' He put his

arms around me, giving me a gentle squeeze. 'There's no other way to explain Tommy's reappearance on English soil. I'm not ashamed of what we did.'

'Neither am I. I'd do it again in a heartbeat.'

'Me too.' He pulled me into a warm embrace. 'You were so brave.'

'No more than you were. In fact, most of the time, I was scared out of my wits.'

A smile curled the corners of his mouth. 'That's what I mean. Being scared but doing it anyway. That's true bravery. Whichever way you look at it.'

I leaned my forehead onto his chest. 'I don't feel brave now. The prospect of being court martialled is pretty scary.'

'You'll be fine.'

'I'm not worried about me.' I broke free from his arms and spun away to stare out of the window, fighting to stop my voice from wobbling. 'I couldn't bear it if you end up getting punished, when the whole thing was my idea.'

'Hey! Hey! Hey!' He steered me back around to face him. 'We saved Tommy together. We'll bear the consequences together. Yes?'

I gazed into his beautiful eyes, thinking I would give anything to stay with him. 'Yes.'

'Good. Let's get that note down to the gatehouse then, shall we?'

* * *

An hour later, I stood on the drive and watched a military car pull up. Major Stapleton emerged followed by Colonel Williams and an RAF group captain. All looked serious. None of them spoke. I ushered them into the office.

Major Stapleton settled herself at Edward's desk with the colonel and group captain either side of her. I stood before her with Father, Tommy and Edward. The major checked her watch, tutted and glanced towards the closed door.

'Are we expecting someone else, ma'am?' I asked.

There was a loud knock and Lexi burst in. Her uniform was rumpled and there was a smudge of oil on her chin. She stood to attention and gave a smart salute. 'Sorry I'm late, Major. My bike broke down; it took a while to fix.' She shot me a covert wink and gestured to my desk. 'Is it all right if I sit here?' Without waiting for a reply, she sat and pulled a notepad and a pencil from her pocket. 'Did I miss anything, ma'am?'

'We're just starting,' said Major Stapleton. 'Flight Officer Thomas Ashworth. It is good to see you looking so well, considering your recent time spent in France.'

Tommy saluted. 'Thank you, ma'am.'

'At ease. Your commanding officer wishes to see you as soon as you are fit to travel. He will debrief you on your time in France. In the meantime, I am here to find out about your miraculous escape. I would like to speak to each of you in turn, and hear in your own words how the events leading to Flight Officer Ashworth's rescue unfolded. After which we will consider what is to be done moving forward.' Her gaze roamed from Edward to me to Father and then Tommy. 'Flight Officer Ashworth, we'll start with you, shall we? Perhaps everyone else can wait outside.'

Before we knew it, Father, Edward and I were banished to pace the corridor and get in the way of hospital staff as they went about their business.

Minutes ticked by like centuries. Eventually, the door opened and Tommy came out, a grim expression on his face. Colonel Williams and the group captain were with him.

Tommy offered Father his hand. 'I've to say goodbye. They're sending me back to base.'

Father grasped his hand, pulling him into an embrace, shock chiselling deep channels into his forehead. 'Now? But... my boy... what about your injuries?'

'Try not to worry,' Colonel Williams said. 'He'll have a full medical assessment. Plus, Group Captain Danvers, here, plans to recommend several weeks of recuperation, preferably here at Ashworth, followed by a program of light duties until Flight Officer Ashworth has recovered sufficiently for redeployment.'

'Thank you,' muttered Father.

Colonel Williams placed a comforting hand on Father's shoulder. 'They want to speak to you, now.'

Father disappeared into the office. Tommy turned to Edward and I. 'Hopefully, I'll see you both very soon.'

Colonel Williams cleared his throat. 'The car's waiting.' Group Captain Danvers gestured for Tommy to precede them down the corridor.

I threw my arms around my brother. 'Stay safe.'

'You too,' he said. 'Thank you, for everything. I'm sorry that I've caused so much trouble.'

'Don't be.' I kissed his cheek and stepped back. 'We stick together, remember? Next time, I fully expect it to be *you* digging *me* out of a hole.'

'I look forward to it.' Tommy grinned, shook Edward's hand and walked away.

I blinked back hot tears, wrapping both arms tight around my waist as if I could hold myself together with sheer force of will.

Edward put an arm around me. 'He'll be all right.'

'Yes.' I blotted my eyes with my handkerchief. 'You're right. At least there's no reason for them to court martial *him*. As for us... who knows?' I glanced at the closed office door. 'Edward, I am sorry I dragged you into this.'

'Hush. Stop that.' He gave me a gentle shake. 'You didn't drag me anywhere. I'd walk through fire for you, Wren. Surely you know that?'

'I... I...'

The sound of Colonel Williams returning forced us to spring apart. If he saw us, he made no comment, merely re-entered the office. Moments later, he escorted Father out, whisking him past us so fast that there was no opportunity to gauge how things had gone. Major Stapleton called Edward in. I was left alone outside. Just as the wait became unbearable, I heard a hiss from along the corridor.

June's sweet face peered through the library door. 'What's with all the senior officers, Wren? Is everything all right?'

I forced a smile. 'I can't tell you. I'm sorry. It's confidential. But, how are you?'

She wrinkled her nose. 'We've been run off our feet since Matron left. She just disappeared. No one seems to know where she went. I've been promoted temporarily until someone else can arrive.'

'That's good, isn't it?'

She grinned. 'I prefer paperwork to chasing naughty toddlers around, that's for sure.'

'Maybe you'll get to keep the post.'

She gave a low chuckle. 'Who knows? Anyway, I'd better get back, but whatever is going on here, I hope it works out for you.'

'Thanks,' I whispered back, grateful for the unconditional support. Just then the door sprang open, making me jump. It was my turn to face the music.

It was a strange feeling, sat in the middle of the office on a spindly wooden chair, facing cross-examination, as if the world had been tilted slightly and everything was a fraction out of line. Major Stapleton, her expression stern, fired question after question at me. Lexi took copious notes. Colonel Williams stood by the window, his hands behind his back, listening intently, his face giving nothing away. I explained what had happened as carefully and calmly as I could, trying to keep mounting frustration in check. Getting emotional wouldn't solve anything.

After I'd finished my tale, Major Stapleton leaned forward, her elbows on the desk. 'You realise that this little adventure of yours was highly unorthodox, don't you?'

'Yes. I do.' I shot a quick glance at Lexi, who couldn't, or wouldn't, meet my eyes. 'I do. I also know that there was no other way to get Tommy back to England because of other operations underway on the French Coast.'

'So, why take it on yourself to interfere?'

'He's my brother. My twin. I was damned if I was going to let him die over there. Not if there was something I could do to save him.'

Major Stapleton glanced at Colonel Williams. 'Please ask Colonel Ashworth and Commander Landers to rejoin us?'

The colonel left the room, closing the door softly behind him.

'Tell me, Wren,' Major Stapleton asked, her voice soft but intent. 'Do you regret your actions?'

'No, I don't.' I looked her in the eye, my heart resolute. 'I'd do it again in a heartbeat.'

'Good.'

I lurched to my feet, frustration powering my actions. 'I don't care what you say, I... you... What did you say?'

She smiled. 'I said, good.'

I sank back onto my seat. 'I don't understand.'

'I'm glad you rescued your brother. It's what I hoped you would do.'

'But... I...' My eyes darted from the major across to Lexi and back again. 'I thought...'

'We couldn't officially authorise a rescue,' said the major. 'There was no way to justify it. Not under current circumstances. It wasn't about being cruel or heartless, merely practical. The greater good. You understand?'

'Yes. I do see that.'

'Adaptability is exactly what this special unit of ours is all about, Wren. I want my operatives thinking on their feet.' She shook her head. 'If the worst happens in this war, and the enemy succeed in overrunning us, heaven knows what conditions you will have to live under or what you will have to do. There's no doubt that adjusting protocol to suit an ever-changing environment will be essential if you're to survive and work towards ultimate victory.' In an abrupt change of tack, she sat back. 'Tell me about Commander Landers.'

'What do you want to know?'

'How much does he know about the unit?'

'You're asking if I've told him, aren't you? About special ops.'

'In a way, yes.' Her face was an impenetrable mask.

'I haven't.'

'Are you sure?'

'Yes.' I crossed my arms, defiance bleeding from every pore. 'I've not said a word. And I won't. That doesn't mean he doesn't suspect, but he hasn't pushed me on it. And I don't think he will.'

'I see. Thank you for your honesty.'

'He's a good man,' I said. 'He's intelligent, brave and honourable, and there's no way yesterday's mission would have succeeded without him.'

'I appreciate that—'

I leaned forward, full of dread at where this might be going. 'Please, don't punish him. I talked him into my crazy plan. He advised caution. If anyone should be court martialled, it's me.'

There was a knock at the door.

'Come in,' said Major Stapleton.

Father and Edward filed in behind Colonel Williams and stood to attention. I got to my feet and stood next to Edward, determined to face whatever was coming by his side.

Major Stapleton stood too and fixed us all with an unyielding stare. 'Yesterday, you all took a huge gamble. A gamble that shouldn't have paid off. And yet it did.' She paused. 'The question I have for you now is this: can it be done again?'

Silence as thick as butter filled the room.

Father was the first to respond. 'Yes, ma'am. It can.'

'Good.' The major smiled.

'What are you saying?' I asked, unable to believe what I was hearing as a small bubble of hope began to swell in my middle.

'Flight Officer Ashworth was able to give us important intelligence on the situation in the Landemer region. It's a section of France in which we have had little to no communication with the Resistance prior to now. He was also able to inform us of the potential whereabouts of several other missing British citizens.'

My thoughts flew to Connie. 'And that changes things?'

'It does. There may be more personnel who need to be brought home.'

'And you'd like us to go and get them?' asked Edward.

Major Stapleton raised an eyebrow. 'Exactly.'

'With enough fuel, I can take *The Lady* across to France and back as many times as you need me to, ma'am,' said Father. 'I didn't get a chance to be part of Dunkirk; I'll be damned if I miss this.'

'Thank you, Colonel. Your enthusiasm is noted.' She turned to Edward and I. 'And what about you two?'

I exchanged a look with Edward. He wiggled his eyebrows at me, his eyes dancing with excitement. 'I'm in, if you are,' he said. 'I hear the swimming conditions off the coast of France at this time of year are excellent.'

I could hardly believe we were having this conversation but my heart leapt at the thought of saving more trapped personnel. And who knew, one day it might be Connie I was bringing back. I smiled. 'Fine, we'll do it. But only—'

Edward interrupted me. 'Only if you're in charge. Yes. That goes without saying. We wouldn't have it any other way.' He glanced across at Father. 'Would we, sir?'

Father laughed. 'No, indeed not.'

'Excellent.' Major Stapleton turned to Colonel Williams. 'In which case, would you please go with Major Ashworth to discuss basic organisational procedures for any potential future cross-Channel trips.'

The two officers saluted and left.

The major turned to address me. 'Private Ashworth. You have permission to brief Commander Landers on your mission here in full.'

I blinked. 'You mean...?'

'I do.'

The curt nod that accompanied her words left no doubt, but I had to ask. 'But what about the whole "the fewer people who know makes it safer for everyone" thing...'

'There are exceptions to every rule,' she replied. 'And the situation here at Ashworth is unique.' She fixed Edward with a serious stare. 'You have already signed the Official Secrets Act, Commander Landers. Anything you learn from Private Ashworth must go no further.'

'I understand,' he said.

'And while she is technically your secretary when working in this office,' she continued, 'for any matters relating to her mission, *Private Ashworth* is the superior officer, regardless of superficial rank. Is that clear?'

'It is.' There was absolute conviction in his voice as he said those two small words.

It was more than I could have dared hope for.

'I have a feeling the two of you will make a formidable team,' said Major Stapleton. 'It is good to know that this section of coast is in safe hands. Good luck to you both.' She stood and glanced across at Lexi. 'Come along, Private, we must be on our way.'

'Yes, ma'am.' Lexi bounced to her feet, threw me a wink, and whispered, 'I'll be in touch,' before following Major Stapleton from the room and closing the door behind her.

'Does that mean a court martial is off the table?' I wondered aloud.

Edward pulled me into his arms. 'I think it does. Plus, it looks like you and I are going to be working more closely together than ever.'

'Oh dear,' I teased, pressing a kiss to his lips. 'How on earth will you cope as my junior officer?'

He dropped his arms and backed away.

A flare of alarm exploded in my chest. 'What is it? What did I say?' I'd thought he understood that this was the deal, or had that merely been for Major Stapleton's benefit?

He frowned as if searching for the right words, before locking his eyes to mine. 'I think you are the most amazing person I have ever met, Wren. It is an honour to work with you in *any* capacity. I don't care about rank. Senior or junior, it doesn't matter. It's important to me that you know that. I mean, really know that.'

I returned his serious gaze with one of my own. 'I see.'

'Do you? I'm falling in love with you, Wren.'

A wave of happiness threatened to consume me whole. 'I'm falling in love with you, too.'

His strong arms swept around me again, drawing me close once more. His chest rumbled with relieved laughter. 'Thank goodness for that, otherwise, working together for the rest of the war might be a little awkward.'

I laughed. His lips met mine in a long, slow, intense kiss that I never wanted to end. Being able to share everything with him, at last, was a dream come true. I'd found a brave, sexy, talented man who valued me for me. And now, with no secrets between us, we could move forward in life as equals. Convinced that there was nothing more I could ever want, I sank into the warmth of his embrace.

Eventually, noises from out in the corridor brought us back to reality. Edward pulled back with an evident show of reluctance. 'So, what do we do now?'

I grinned. 'Lock the door.' I walked over to the panelling behind my desk and reached for the hidden mechanism. 'There's something I need to show you.'

A NOTE FROM THE AUTHOR

Dear Reader,

Thank you for coming on Wren's journey with me.

Please note that while *The Resistance Girls* is a work of fiction, there really was a secret army of women who operated undercover in Britain during World War Two.

Enemy troops advanced across Europe with shocking ease in 1940. When they reached the English Channel, it was clear that a Nazi invasion of Britain was a genuine possibility. Spies and enemy agents were infiltrating British coastal communities looking for a way in. The government put a number of clandestine operations in place in case the worst happened. One of the most important of these secret operations was an underground army: troops specifically trained to carry out acts of sabotage behind enemy lines if Britain was overrun. These hidden troops were called auxiliary units. The security surrounding them was so intense that, even now, so many years on, there is very little evidence of their existence. Even less is known about the Special Duties Section, a vital sub-branch of the operation.

In 1941, Commander Beatrice Temple (the inspiration for my

character Major Belinda Stapleton) was commissioned to run part of the Special Duties Branch on behalf of the Auxiliary Territorial Service (i.e. the women's division of the British army). Her orders were to find suitable women to staff a system of secret underground bunkers. These women were to be highly trained in a wide range of useful skills.

Potential candidates were chosen by Commander Temple. Each received a letter out of the blue inviting them to meet her at Harrods. Over tea, the commander could assess their suitability for the proposed role. A voice test followed in a remote location in Suffolk. Successful candidates were then sent to Highworth.

On arrival at Highworth, candidates were ordered to report to the village post mistress, Mabel Anne Stranks. Mabel Stranks is the inspiration for my character, Mrs Margaret Street. According to reports, Mabel Stranks was part of a carefully crafted final security check on the arrivals prior to permitting them to travel on to Colehill and then to Hannington Hall for training. If they didn't pass the security check they were misdirected.

There is very little information available on what specific training took place at Highworth, so I have allowed my imagination free rein with regard to my description of both Highworth itself and what happened there.

Those women who completed the training became part of a 300-strong army of women assigned a dangerous mission. They were placed in local communities, working in plain sight, doing relatively menial tasks whilst also watching out for spies. In addition, should a successful Nazi invasion take place, these women were instructed to hold their position and spy on the invading force. If they were compromised, they were to retreat to specially equipped bunkers hidden underground. There they were to stay, for as long as possible, operating as part of a co-ordinated British Resistance.

I read one report that estimated that the life expectancy of an underground operative in occupied territory was only two to three weeks, which made me realise how brave these women were.

The organisation was so secret that after the war, none of the women received recognition for their service. They had all signed the Official Secrets Act and stayed silent. Most died without ever speaking about the risks they took to keep British shores safe.

Some of the few reports that are available about their exploits refer to them as Churchill's Secret Sweeties, which is a term that doesn't sit well in modern parlance. Hence, I have avoid using it in my novel in favour of the name; the women's secret army.

As no comprehensive reports exist about the women's secret army – i.e. who was in it and what they did – I have taken the few facts that are available and allowed my imagination to fill in the rest. Any factual mistakes in this book are my own and I hope they will be forgiven.

Ashworth Manor and Ashworth Bay are fictional too, although heavily influenced by the local area on the edge of the New Forest where I live.

The result of all that, both fact and fiction, is this novel, *The Resistance Girls*.

It is the first in a series. I hope you enjoyed reading it as much as I enjoyed writing it.

Love

Alice

PS. Watch this space for Felicity's story, which is coming soon.

ACKNOWLEDGEMENTS

Writing this book has been a team effort from the word go, and I wouldn't have survived the process if it weren't for a number of amazing people.

First and foremost, a massive thank you to my husband Steve, for holding me together every time I faltered and making me believe that I could do it.

I am grateful to everyone who has supported my dream to become a writer over the last few years. Specifically, my family, who have been on the front line of the creative process, encouraging me to keep going. They have also put up with far too many burned dinners because I scurried away at the last minute to make 'just one quick note' or because I disappeared down yet another historical research rabbit hole. And a special thank you to my lovely dad, for all the World War 2 DVDs and books he has lent me recently.

Heartfelt thanks to Hannah Kingsley (the awesomely talented author of Soul Hate) for making me realise that if I really wanted to be a writer then I should jolly well get on with it.

Thank you to all the writing friends I have met along the way, including those at The Writing Sphere who put up with many different versions of the first few chapters and gave positive and constructive comments. Thank you to Jenny Kane (who also writes as Jennifer Ash) for reading an early draft, sharing wisdom on its potential and insisting that I should keep going.

And massive thanks to Natalie Gregory for the many encouraging telephone calls.

Credit must also go to the awesome Elane Retford and Sarah Snook of www.iaminprint.co.uk for running their fabulous Historical Novel Competition. Placing fifth with the first three chapters of *The Resistance Girls* motivated me to finish the whole manuscript.

Thank you to the Romantic Novelist Association and all their friendly, supportive members. The RNA New Writers' Scheme is an incredible resource for writers learning their craft and the RNA conferences are a great opportunity to meet other writers, learn new skills, meet industry professionals and have fun with like-minded people.

Finally, huge thanks to Emily Ruston (Publishing Director for Boldwood Books) for believing in my manuscript and offering it a home with Boldwood Books. Thanks also to the rest of the Boldwood team for helping to polish *The Resistance Girls* to make it the best that it can be. I am delighted to join the Boldwood family and am grateful to everyone at Boldwood Books for making me feel so welcome.

ABOUT THE AUTHOR

Alice G. May is an artist and the author of several fiction and non-fiction books. Born in Sheffield and brought up in South Wales, she went to Southampton University and then moved to the New Forest. She spent twenty years running a GP surgery, and now teaches art and creative writing as a casual tutor for the Hampshire Learning in Libraries program.

Sign up to Alice G. May's mailing list for news, competitions and updates on future books.

Visit Alice's website: www.alicegmay.com

Follow Alice on social media here:

- instagram.com/alicegmay
- x.com/AliceMay_Author
- facebook.com/100013404690385
- tiktok.com/@alicegmayartandbooks
- bsky.app/profile/alicegmay.bsky.social

Sixpence Stories

Introducing Sixpence Stories!

Discover page-turning historical novels from your favourite authors, meet new friends and be transported back in time.

Join our book club
Facebook group

https://bit.ly/SixpenceGroup

Sign up to our
newsletter

https://bit.ly/SixpenceNews

Boldwood

Boldwood Books is an award-winning fiction publishing company seeking out the best stories from around the world.

Find out more at www.boldwoodbooks.com

Join our reader community for brilliant books, competitions and offers!

Follow us
@BoldwoodBooks
@TheBoldBookClub

Sign up to our weekly deals newsletter

https://bit.ly/BoldwoodBNewsletter

Printed in Dunstable, United Kingdom